VENGEANCE SERIES

KAYLEA CROSS

BEAUTIFUL VENGEANCE

Copyright © 2020 Kaylea Cross

* * * * *

Cover Art: Sweet 'N Spicy Designs
Developmental edits: Deborah Nemeth
Line Edits: Joan Nichols
Digital Formatting: LK Campbell
Print Formatting: Sweet 'N Spicy Designs

* * * * *

ISBN: 9798617379701

DEDICATION

For Pamela Clare, a dear friend and one hell of a talented writer. Love you!

And for Hazel, for helping me make Marcus sound like a proper bloody Yorkshireman.

Author's Note

Saying goodbye to a cast of characters I've fallen in love with is always bittersweet, and it's no different with the Vengeance crew and my kickass Valkyries. It's been my sincere pleasure in bringing them all happy endings, but especially Marcus and Kiyomi! I can't think of two more deserving characters after all they've been through.

Happy reading,
Kaylea

Prologue

*H**e's coming.*

At the sound of the footsteps moving overhead, Kiyomi struggled to open her eyes. The lids were so swollen her field of vision was reduced to a single tiny strip on the left side. Fear crawled through her, foreign and terrifying.

Chains rattled as she gingerly turned onto her belly, the manacles around her wrists and ankles biting into her skin as she faced the front of her iron cage. A shadowed staircase stood mere feet away in the dim room. In moments he would appear in the doorway at the top and advance down those stairs.

Her entire body ached from the deep bruises he'd already inflicted all over her. The shimmering gold lamé dress she'd worn to the private party a few nights ago was now torn and filthy.

She shivered, pushed up a bit on her right arm, struggling to overcome the weakness that hung over her like a fog. Through the gloom she was able to make out the shape of the woman lying in the cage next to hers. She was still curled into a ball, appearing not to have changed position since Kiyomi had passed out.

"Hannah," she whispered, blood trickling over her tongue as the cut in her lip broke open. The other Valkyrie didn't move or respond in any way. She was probably dead by now.

The unexpected pang of empathy caught Kiyomi off guard. She had come here to kill Hannah because the traitor had killed Kiyomi's best friend, and had wound up Rahman's personal captive instead. Now he and his men appeared to have taken care of Hannah for her.

The other Valkyrie's suffering was over, while Kiyomi's was only just beginning. She'd betrayed Rahman, made him fall in love with her, and he would make her hurt for it.

The footsteps upstairs drew closer to the door.

Kiyomi's flesh crawled at the knowledge of what was coming. He wanted to break her. Not just physically. Mentally and emotionally too. He wanted to watch her break, hear her beg him for mercy.

She'd die before she gave him the satisfaction of either.

The door opened. She stayed completely still, gathering her remaining strength to endure what was coming.

His silhouette appeared in the doorway. She squinted when he switched on the lights, the sudden brightness piercing her sore eyes. The door shut and he started down the stairs in slow, measured steps as her eyes adjusted.

He was dressed as he always was. Immaculate in his custom-made suit, his white dress shirt open at the neck and startlingly bright against his bronze skin. He was clean-shaven, his dark hair perfect, swept off his forehead and without a trace of gray in it yet, though he was in his mid-thirties.

"You're awake. Good." Satisfaction and anticipation dripped from every word.

He had something in his hand.

She stared at it as he drew nearer, stepping out of the shadows and into the light. Something round.

Then he reached the bottom of the stairs and turned toward her. Rage and helplessness exploded inside her when she saw what he held.

A coiled bullwhip.

He glanced briefly at Hannah, dismissed her a heartbeat later and turned to stare down at Kiyomi, a half-smile on his handsome face. Shrugging out of his jacket with slow deliberation, he let her see the whip.

"I know what you are," he said as he came to stand in front of her cage.

Cold rippled through her. He'd seen the brand on her hip. Did he now know what it meant? Or did he just think he did?

He stood there staring down at her for a long moment, his chilling gaze filled with rage and lust as he let the silence drag out. Underscoring the lopsided power dynamic between them. His control pitted against her helplessness.

Revulsion slid through her as she recalled what had passed between them. Him touching her intimately, her pleasuring him all those times, taking him inside, acting the ecstatic lover while she made her mind go elsewhere.

Lying next to him in his bed night after night, waiting for him to reach for her. Playing the role of worshipful sycophant she'd chosen to gain entry into his world in order to get within striking distance of Hannah. All the while, waiting. Waiting.

He'd fallen for it completely, believing she revered him and his body, that she couldn't get enough of him. That she was falling in love with him.

Then everything had gone horribly, irrevocably wrong.

The terrible memories of her capture four nights ago flashed through her mind as he unlocked the cage door and swung it open.

She forced herself to lie still and not react as he came to stand above her, filled with hatred as she stared up at him through her slitted eye. Only a pathetic coward would chain a woman down so he could beat her.

And that's exactly what Fayez Rahman was, even if he wasn't stupid. Because he knew if she hadn't been chained, she would kill him.

He was even more afraid of her than he was obsessed with her. And his fear was the only comfort she had in this terrible, desolate moment.

"I'm going to send you back to your maker." An evil smirk split his face, the outline of an erection pressing against the front of his pants. "The one who created you."

She braced for the pain and stared defiantly up into those dark, cruel eyes, refusing to cower or let him think he'd won. His taunting words were an empty threat. He wouldn't kill her. He was too afraid of the wealthy buyer he had lined up for her to do that, the one he'd taunted her with for the past three days. The Architect.

Anything short of death, she could handle. She had no other choice.

Her training kicked in. The only thing stopping her from cowering now.

You're a Valkyrie. You can take this. Separate your mind and body. Don't give him the satisfaction of reacting, no matter what he does.

Rahman relaxed his fist, allowing the long tail of the bullwhip to touch the concrete floor. He gave a deliberate flick of his wrist, making the leather slither back and forth over the concrete like a snake ready to strike. Then he raised his arm, lifting the braided handle high.

Kiyomi clenched her teeth to keep from crying out as it snapped across the skin between her shoulder blades. Fire raced along her nerve endings.

She sucked in a breath and tensed, clenching her

teeth and fists as she awaited the next blow. She fought to stay above the pain, to let her mind float free. But as she did, she made a vow to herself.

You will not break me. But one day, I'll kill you for this.

Someday, she would stare down into those evil, dark eyes. She would watch his triumph turn to shock and then abject terror just before she snuffed the life from him.

Chapter One
Bitchilantes Ride Or Die

November fifth—Bonfire Night. His least favorite night of the year.

Marcus leaned forward in his tufted leather desk chair to pull up last night's security feeds, focusing on the cameras posted on the gatehouse and along a section of fence that ran parallel to the road in front of his property. For the past three nights the annual ritual of teenage boys setting off firecrackers had started up soon after darkness fell, and continued until nearly midnight.

As a combat veteran who had survived captivity and torture, fireworks and other explosives going off always set him on edge, not to mention they also spooked his dog and horses. This year, it was far more than that.

The teenagers didn't know it, but he had a house full of lethal operatives staying here at Laidlaw Hall, and given the current threat against them all, everyone was on edge.

Despite all the team's efforts in searching for a lead on their number one suspect, no one yet knew who the

Architect was—the person thought to be behind the massive operation to kill all remaining Valkyrie operatives. After the clandestine CIA program was exposed and disbanded due to the media attention after one of its former trainers had been sent to trial for his crimes, all surviving Valkyries had become targets.

The Architect had power, resources, and remained a lethal threat to them all. With the search ongoing, security here had been tightened. The team was now taking two-person shifts to watch for threats anywhere near the property.

Given all of that, Bonfire Night couldn't have come at a worse time for them. With every banger those teens set off, they were unknowingly playing with fire.

On screen he watched a trio of boys ranging in age from about fourteen to seventeen or so cruise up the gravel road running in front of the property on their bikes. They paused near the front gate, lit a handful of fireworks and threw them toward the gatehouse, just as Megan and Ty had reported at the time.

A part of Marcus was still convinced that the faceless enemy stalking his guests might try to attack tonight, using the fireworks to camouflage their initial attack. At the same time he told himself he was just being a paranoid bastard.

There was no indication whatsoever that anyone had discovered Laidlaw Hall was now Valkyrie headquarters. On the off chance he was wrong, everyone here was on alert and doing patrols, making sure the premises remained secure, him most of all. This was his home. He considered it his responsibility to keep everyone here safe.

After watching the video and checking the other feeds from around the property, he grabbed his cane and stood, the familiar stiffness and pain in his left hip and thigh making him pause for a moment. "Karas."

His rescue Anatolian Shepherd rolled from her side onto her belly and looked up at him expectantly from her cozy bed in front of the fireplace.

"Come." He started for the study door, Karas right behind him. "We've got work to do."

The house was quiet, all nine team members currently staying here each working on their assigned tasks. Everything was as he'd left it in the kitchen hours before, the smell of the roast already permeating the air.

He strode out the back door into the formal garden and up the gravel path, past the stables to where he kept his ATV. Karas hopped into the front seat beside him, ears perked, and they started off over the pasture where he and a couple of the lads had piled some lumber last night.

After constructing the big bonfire for tonight, he did a perimeter check of the entire several-hundred-acre property. Debris littered the grass near the northwest corner, evidence of more fireworks, but nothing else appeared touched, and none of the sentries had reported other disturbances.

He made a mental list of repairs to be done around the property and stopped at the stables to let the horses out into the field before going back into the house to get the rest of the meal going. With the recent time change it would already be dark in another few hours.

"Roast beef?" an eager voice said from the kitchen doorway.

Marcus looked up from the meat he was tenting on a cutting board and smiled at Megan. "Aye." His life had never been the same after meeting her, and it had all led to this.

With an appreciative sound she walked over to peek under the foil. "Been a long time since we had one of those. What's the occasion?"

"It's Bonfire Night and Mrs. Biddington has the day off, so I thought I'd make us a proper Sunday roast for tea."

"Tea?" She glanced at her watch. "You mean dinner."

He shook his head, smiling. Dinner to him was at midday. "Supper, then."

"Yum. I'll help." She reached into a drawer and pulled out an apron, quickly tying it around her waist. "What can I do?"

The roast and potatoes he'd basted with the drippings were already done. "You can peel and prep the rest of the veg."

She made a face. "Fine." She took the peeler and stood at the sink to begin peeling the pile of carrots. "You watched the security feeds yet?"

"Aye. They've been setting off more in the northwest corner as well."

She grunted, dropping long, orange peelings into the sink as she worked. "They'll stop in a couple days, but we're all on edge enough already. What do you want me to do with these when I'm done?"

"Slice them into chunks and drop them in that pot of salted water on the stove."

She reached for a paring knife from the butcher block on the counter. "When's the last time we cooked together?"

"A while ago." Too long. Though they hadn't spent much time together lately, they shared a special bond.

The day they'd met, she'd pulled him from the jaws of certain death—against his wishes—and forced him to live. The least he could do when she'd needed protection after the Valkyrie Program was disbanded and she'd become a target was let her stay with him, but when she'd come here all those months ago, he'd never imagined how attached he'd become to her.

They'd gone riding together often and he'd set up archery targets for her along the trails. Most evenings they'd sit in his study enjoying a hot brew and reading. But now that she'd married Ty and moved into the gatehouse, they didn't spend a lot of time together anymore. He missed it.

"Man, that roast smells good. Are you gonna make Yorkshire puddings too?" Her voice held a hopeful note.

A smile tugged at the corners of his mouth. "Of course." It wasn't a proper roast beef supper without Yorkshire puds.

"Awesome. You'd better make extra, or we'll all end up fighting over them. Where did you learn to make this, anyway?"

"My Aunt Lucy."

Megan stopped and raised her eyebrows at him. "You never told me you had an aunt."

He shrugged. "Not a real one. Me mum's best mate. She taught me to make a proper roast with all the trimmings when I was around twelve or so." He wasn't a fancy cook and didn't cook all that often, but this was one meal he had down pat.

Just as he finished tossing the potatoes and tenting the meat, a quivering black nose appeared over the edge of the granite countertop beside the roasting pan. Karas never strayed too far from him, especially in the kitchen in case something got dropped on the floor.

"Away wi' you, spoiled brat," he said with a grin, tossing Karas a small chunk of carrot. She sniffed it, walked away in disdain and lay down with a groan on the mat in front of the sink, watching him with reproachful brown eyes. How dare he try and sneak a vegetable into her.

"Oh, Karas, knock it off," Megan said with a laugh. "You'll get plenty of meat later and you know it. Such a diva." She put the carrots on to boil. "Do you remember much else about Aunt Lucy?"

"Aye. She was nice to me. Would read to me and let

me help decorate biscuits and make mince pies at Christmas."

"That sounds nice." Megan's voice was wistful. She didn't often talk about her past.

"Do you remember anything about your aunt?" The only other relative she'd ever mentioned to him other than her parents, who had died in a car accident when she was young.

"Not really. Just her being at our house for Christmas dinner once or twice. I don't think she and my mom got along. Although I do remember her taking us for ice cream after our parents died. But then she decided she didn't want to be our guardian. That was the last time we saw her, in the lawyer's office."

We meaning her and her older sister, Amber, their resident technical wizard and hacker. They'd been separated not long after they were put into foster care, then shunted into the Valkyrie Program in facilities on opposite sides of the country.

It still horrified him. They'd only found each other again last summer, when Megan and Ty had literally hunted Amber down. "Do you think she ever tried to find you both again later?"

"Don't know, and don't care." She tossed her long brown hair over her shoulder. "But Amber's hell-bent on finding her and getting answers about why she ditched us."

"And what are you two up to in here?"

Marcus's head snapped up at the sound of that soft voice coming from the kitchen doorway. The sight of Kiyomi standing there made his entire body tighten.

She'd filled out during the time she'd been here, and it looked damn good on her. She wore snug jeans that clung to her hips and thighs, and a cherry-red sweater that hugged her small breasts. Her shiny black hair was pulled up in a clip, and the smoky eye makeup made her dark brown eyes look dramatic and mysterious. He couldn't take his eyes off her.

"Marcus is making us Sunday dinner," Megan replied.

"Supper," he corrected.

"Is he?" Kiyomi watched him with a little smile that made his pulse skip.

She'd transformed before his eyes in the few months she'd been here at Laidlaw Hall. From the beaten, half-starved captive that Amber and her boyfriend Jesse had pulled out of that dungeon in Damascus, to this vibrant, stunning woman standing in front of him. All the Valkyries were in danger, but there was a multi-million-dollar bounty on Kiyomi's head that put her most at risk.

"Aye," he said, doing everything he could to hide his reaction to her while reminding himself why she was off-limits.

She'd healed physically, but he wasn't so sure about the mental or emotional wounds, and after what she'd endured there was no way she was ready to be with a man yet. Not only that, he couldn't make a move because he was essentially her landlord and didn't want her to feel like she owed him anything simply because she was staying in his house.

"Can I help?" she asked, coming toward him.

"Yes, come help me with these carrots," Megan said, waving her over.

Marcus caught himself drawing in a deep breath as Kiyomi passed by, pulling in her light floral scent. He didn't know if it was her shampoo or lotion or what, but it drove him crazy and he wanted to bury his face in her hair, the side of her neck to inhale more of it.

Banishing those thoughts, he spooned some of the drippings into the bottom of each muffin tin for the Yorkshire puds, then slid the roasting pan onto the stove and lit the burner to start the gravy while the women chatted.

"Did the fireworks keep you up last night?" Kiyomi asked him a minute later.

"No, I was still awake." He didn't sleep well or much. He added the flour and started whisking. "You?"

"Same. Here, let me do that and you can make these Yorkshire puddings I've heard so much about. What are they, anyway?"

He glanced at her in surprise. "You've never had them?"

"Never."

"They're a savory batter baked with hot beef drippings and served with roast meat."

"Like crispy little pillows of deliciousness to pour gravy into," Megan added. "You'll love 'em."

The three of them worked in comfortable silence to get the rest of the meal ready, and Kiyomi watched closely as he made his aunt's Yorkshire puddings. When everything was done, Marcus wiped his hands on the tea towel and stepped back from the cooling puds. "Right, I think we're ready. Call in the troops."

"Roger." Megan dropped her apron on the counter and sauntered out of the kitchen as Marcus reached for the platter of sliced beef.

"I've got it." Kiyomi took it from him, standing so close that her hip brushed his groin as she turned away.

Marcus froze, biting back a hiss at the contact. He was in trouble. One unintentional touch and it lit his whole body up. She tempted him like no other woman ever had, and his body was on edge around her.

Once he had himself back under control he carried everything to the table in the dining room, and soon everyone arrived. Six Valkyries and four significant others, every one of them a skilled operative in their own right. They rarely got a chance to eat as a group. Marcus enjoyed it.

When everyone was seated, he stood at the head of

the table and raised his glass as Karas laid down beside his chair. "To friends, who have become family."

He caught Megan's eye, and gave her a private smile. After he'd made it through SAS selection, The Regiment had become his family. Since the mission in Syria he'd been alone, missing that sense of purpose and belonging. Megan and the rest of the people around this table had given that back to him.

"Hear, hear," everyone chorused. They tapped their glasses together, then tucked into their meal.

Though he would never admit it aloud, he was chuffed to bits that everyone enjoyed the meal so much, especially his Yorkshire puds and gravy. While he ate, he snuck a piece of roast under the table to Karas, who took it gently from his fingers and stared up at him with alert, hopeful eyes.

"What's for dessert?" Chloe asked as she finished off her last Yorkshire. The woman ate as much as he did, though usually she stuffed her gob with junk food.

"Nothing, unless you made it," Megan told her dryly.

"Dessert's outside in just a bit," Marcus said, and Chloe shot Megan a smug look across the table. Things had been tense for them all lately. Marcus figured they could do with a bit of fun.

While everyone cleaned up the supper dishes, he went out back with Karas to light the bonfire. He'd chosen the location with care, in a spot where no one but them would be able to see the fire. The sky was already growing dark and a crisp, cold wind blew across the hills. Once the fire was really roaring, he texted the others to come outside.

"Oh, wow," Chloe said as she marched toward the fire with an unholy grin on her face. "How'd you start it?" Her down vest was open, revealing a shirt that read: *I love a good bang.*

"Without explosives," he answered, earning a

snicker from everyone else. If he didn't know that Chloe was an explosives and demolition expert, he would have sworn she was a pyromaniac.

She looked disappointed. "Man, I wish we could risk setting off some fireworks. Just imagine the display I could put on for us."

Her boyfriend Heath wound an arm around her shoulders. "There are already plenty of fireworks whenever you're around, firecracker, trust me."

Drawing attention to themselves, even with fireworks, was dangerous to them all. The whole point of them staying here was to keep a low profile and stay off the radar of whoever was hunting them.

Marcus passed out sticks he'd sharpened to points at one end earlier and then passed around bags of marshmallows. "I also brought this, to keep the chill away." He handed Ty an open bottle of whisky.

"Now you're talkin'," Ty said, taking a sip before passing it to Megan.

While everyone talked, drank and roasted marshmallows, Marcus stood close to the fire next to Karas, leaning on his cane as he enjoyed the heat of it on the right side of his face, where no scars dulled the sensation. He joined in the conversation a few times but mostly listened, watching Kiyomi when her attention was elsewhere.

She was so utterly beautiful, and it did his heart good to see her so relaxed here. Happy, even.

A small explosion in the distance made him jolt. Conversation ceased, all heads whipping toward the source of the noise past the front of the house. Karas raced off toward it in the darkness, barking.

"The assholes are back," Megan muttered, setting her roasting stick aside. "We'll run them off and hopefully they won't be back." She took Ty's hand and they left the fire to head to their gatehouse near the road that ran past the front of the property.

Minutes later more sharp explosions thudded in the night. A few seconds after that, his mobile buzzed in his pocket. A text from Megan.

Karas is hurt.

His heart dropped. He gripped his cane and started off across the field as fast as his gimpy leg would allow.

"What's wrong?" Kiyomi was at his side in an instant, watching him in concern.

"Karas is hurt." He pushed himself to go faster, ignoring the sharp pain in his hip and thigh.

"What happened?"

"I don't know." He hurried on, cursing his damned limp. Kiyomi stayed beside him, and by the time they reached the front of the house, Megan and Ty were coming up the driveway. Ty was carrying Karas.

Marcus's stomach lurched. "How bad?"

"I think she's mostly just shaken up," Megan answered, rushing to keep up with Ty's long strides.

"It's her right foreleg," Ty said, stopping in front of Marcus.

Marcus bent to take her sweet face in his hands. Her eyes were fixed on him. She was panting and trembling, clearly in distress but he didn't see any blood. "Bring her inside."

Ty carried her into the study and placed her down on her bed in front of the fire.

Marcus knelt in front of her and took her chin in his hand. "What happened, lass?" Her pupils were even, but she trembled so much her collar jangled. The fur on her right shoulder was singed, and when he picked up her right front paw, she licked her lips and flattened her ears against her head.

"It's all right, lass," he murmured, stroking her head with his free hand as he bent closer to examine her foreleg. The side and back of it were burned, all the fur missing. But the bone seemed sound. His jaw tightened. "Did those bloody bastards throw one of those things at her?"

"I'm checking that right now," Megan muttered. Kiyomi was beside her at his desk, pulling up the security feeds on the computer screen.

"Yeah," Kiyomi said a moment later, her dark gaze swinging to his. "That's exactly what they did."

She turned the screen around so Marcus could see. The three teens from the last few nights arrived on their bikes, dropped them near the front gate and began lighting off bangers. When Karas appeared in view a minute later, racing toward them up the driveway, they started lobbing them at her.

The first two missed. She cowered, tucking her tail beneath her as she darted away, but the shortest of the three boys threw another at her. It detonated right below her leg.

She dropped to the ground when it exploded and the boys took off, laughing and high-fiving each other. Marcus clenched his jaw, anger pumping through him.

The silence was broken by the sound of a can being cracked open behind him. Chloe stood in the doorway next to Heath, a can of her favorite energy drink in her hand.

Staring hard at the computer screen, she narrowed her eyes. "Those little shits need to be taught a lesson."

Aye, they bloody did.

Chapter Two

Kiyomi wanted to stay and help with Karas, but it was obvious that Marcus wanted to be alone. Heath brought him a med kit and offered to dress Karas's wound, but Marcus dismissed him with a curt "I'll do it."

In silence everyone filed out of the study, the easy, carefree mood from earlier destroyed. Kiyomi was pissed. Those kids were cruel idiots. And the fireworks were grating on her nerves. The major bounty on her head was never far from her mind, or the two people currently hunting her.

"Can you believe those assholes? Unreal," Megan muttered as she and Kiyomi followed Chloe down the hall to the kitchen, where a small mountain of dishes was waiting to be cleaned up.

"Oh, it was definitely real," Chloe said, a savage edge in her voice.

Megan eyed her sharply. "Don't do anything stupid, Twitch. Let Marcus handle this."

Chloe shot Megan an annoyed scowl over her shoulder. "I won't, *Itch*."

The two of them called each other by the nicknames they'd adopted as trainees in the Program when they'd roomed together. "They won't come back tonight," Kiyomi said, certain of it. Poor Karas. Those little bastards were a menace.

"If they're smart, they won't come back at all," Megan said darkly.

"They're teenage boys," Chloe muttered. "They'll come back."

The others were already working in the kitchen when they walked in. "How's Karas?" Trinity asked, a dishtowel in one hand.

"Burned and traumatized," Megan answered. "Poor thing. She had such a rough start in life, those firecrackers probably reminded her of the bombs. I can't believe she'd be hurt here of all places."

Trinity nodded. "How's Marcus?"

"Pissed as hell," Chloe answered. "And rightly so."

Kiyomi stayed quiet, helping where needed as they finished the clean up. She'd never seen Marcus angry before. It made him even quieter and more intense.

After everyone pitched in, Kiyomi waited until it was just her and Megan left in the kitchen before approaching her. Megan was putting up the last of the dishes while Kiyomi wiped the countertops down. "What will Marcus do?" Kiyomi asked.

"Meaning, will he go after them?"

She frowned. "I don't think he'd—"

"No, he wouldn't, because he's too honorable to do something like that. He'll probably just file a complaint with the police at most, though maybe not because he doesn't want to draw any attention to him or this place."

Because of them.

Karas's tormentors might go unpunished because Marcus wanted to protect the team. Kiyomi felt badly. "I hate that Karas was hurt, and also that it spoiled the night.

Marcus went to a lot of trouble for all of us."

He was a hard worker, rising early every day to check things and fix things around the property, and staying up late to work on all the finance and accounting needed to keep a huge place like this going. He also put a lot of effort into staying strong and in shape. His leg bothered him but he never complained, never let on. She admired him for all of it.

"Yeah. I knew we'd all grow on him after a while, even though he's pretty much a recluse." Megan's smile was fond as she placed a deep blue platter in the cupboard next to the chef-quality gas range.

Kiyomi wanted to do something for him. Even something little, to show she cared. "Should I bring him something? A brandy maybe?" She didn't even know if he drank it.

"Take him a cup of tea. He'd like that."

"All right." She went to the cupboard where the tea and coffee were kept. "What kind?" Though she already knew exactly what kind, because she made a point of noticing every little detail about Marcus, but didn't want to tip her hand and let Megan know just how interested in him she was.

"Yorkshire Gold. What else would you expect from a proper Yorkshireman? Just a bit of milk, nothing else. And here, this is his favorite mug." Megan reached into the upper cabinet next to her and took out a battered mug with the SAS symbol on it.

Yes, Kiyomi knew that too. The one with the winged dagger and a stylized scroll beneath it that read *Who Dares Wins*. "Thanks." She filled the kettle and put it on the stove to boil, then finished wiping the countertops while it heated.

When it began to whistle she turned off the burner and poured water over the teabag in the mug. She didn't often get to talk with Megan alone, and there were so many questions burning inside her. "Has there been anyone else in Marcus's life in the time you've known him?" she asked, trying to sound casual.

"No, no one."

Kiyomi glanced at her, surprised. "Really? No girlfriends? Not even any dates?"

"Nope. He pretty much shut himself away here after he came back from Syria. Would probably have never left the property if I hadn't come along and forced him out of his funk."

Kiyomi frowned. That couldn't be right. "He hasn't dated or anything since he came back from Syria? Wasn't that over two years ago now?"

"Nope, and yep."

Wow. Why did he shut himself away from the world here? To punish himself? It couldn't possibly be because he was embarrassed about his scars. Only the ones on the left side of his face and neck were visible, and they did nothing to detract from his looks.

She couldn't understand it. Marcus was a handsome, powerfully built man who carried himself with an air of quiet confidence that was downright mesmerizing. "What was he like before he was wounded, do you know?"

Megan turned to face her and leaned back against the counter, crossing her arms and ankles. "Still serious, I think. But not like he is now. And for sure he used to be more social. He cut contact with most of his military buddies, but he's told me some stories about wild parties and other stuff he and some fellow NCOs used to get up to. While he's never come right out and said it, I get the impression he was pretty popular with the ladies, too."

"I'll bet he was." She set the kettle aside. "How strong does he like it?"

"Strong." Kiyomi looked up, something in Megan's tone and gaze telling her she meant more than tea. Plainly letting her know that Marcus admired strong women, too.

"What about you?" Megan countered. "Are you ready for this?"

Kiyomi blinked. "For bringing him tea?"

Megan gave her an insulted look, and Kiyomi realized Megan had seen right through her. "You know what I mean." Megan's hazel eyes were serious as they assessed her. "Have you ever had a relationship? A…"

"A consensual one? No. Can you hand me the milk, please?"

Megan frowned but didn't say anything as she turned to take the milk out of the fridge.

"Thanks," Kiyomi murmured, adding some to the mug. "Do we have any cookies or something to go with it?"

"These. And they're biscuits, not cookies," she said with a teasing tilt of her lips, handing Kiyomi a package of dark chocolate-dipped digestive biscuits.

"Perfect." She eyed the sleeve of cookies with interest. Before her capture, she wouldn't have looked twice at them. Wouldn't have been the least bit tempted by them. Now all sorts of new things tempted her, especially the owner of this incredible house.

Most of her life had been about deprivation. From food, friendship, affection. Sex.

She didn't consider what she'd done during her career real sex. Every time she'd slept with someone, it had been part of a mission. She'd been merely acting the part, using her body to get what she needed. Sometimes that meant intel. Other times, waiting until her target was at his most vulnerable before killing him.

For the past few months she'd been trying to learn how to put all that behind her. It hadn't been easy, or linear. She'd spent many years being part flawless actress, part robot. Able to shut all emotion and feeling off, shove it all down into a box deep inside her where she never had to look at it.

That wasn't possible anymore. The nightmares weren't as frequent now as they'd been when she'd first arrived here, but they were powerful and terrifying.

The work she'd done with Trinity and her therapist over the past month-and-a-half was painful because it involved prying the lid off that box and exposing every dark, terrible thing she'd ever done or endured. Getting in touch with her body was proving the hardest part.

She'd been trained not to feel. Allowing herself to feel now was hard. The infrequent number of times she'd experimentally given herself pleasure lately, it had taken total concentration and fantasies of Marcus to send her over the edge. That was probably unhealthy in the extreme, but harmless enough.

She aimed a smile at Megan and held up the biscuits. "Want some?"

Megan's mouth twitched. "No, and you're good. That shift in conversation to deflect attention away from the topic at hand was almost flawless."

It better be, because she was an expert at it. In her world it meant the difference between survival and death.

Megan straightened up and grabbed the dishtowel from the counter. "I know you're really close with Trinity, but I just want you to know, you can talk to me anytime too. About anything."

The offer warmed Kiyomi's heart and made her smile. It was true, she was closest to Trin, but only because they had similar backgrounds. They had both been "intimate assassins", whereas the others had different areas of expertise. "Thank you. And I know that."

"Good." She rubbed a hand over Kiyomi's upper arm, then started from the kitchen. "Give Karas a pat from me."

"I will." It seemed stupid, but nerves danced in the pit of her stomach as she carried the tea and biscuits down the hall. Megan's rapid footsteps went up the stairs to the left as Kiyomi paused at the study door and knocked.

"Come," came the deep reply.

She eased the door open and stepped inside with the sense she was entering Marcus's most private, intimate domain as the smell of old leather and wood smoke wrapped around her. Marcus was sitting on the floor in front of the fire next to Karas's bed. The dog perked her ears at Kiyomi's entrance but didn't raise her head, her bandaged right paw dangling over the side of the bed.

"I brought you some tea."

His half-smile changed him from brooding and hot to heart-stoppingly sexy in his cream, cable knit sweater. If he ever gave her a full smile, she didn't know if her heart could take it. "Cheers," he said as he took the mug and plate from her. "You don't want any?"

"No, I'm still full from that incredible dinner you made. I mostly drink green tea, anyway."

He made a face. "That stuff's bitter as hell."

She laughed softly. "Yeah, but it reminds me of my mom. I don't have many memories of her, but one clear one is us drinking green tea in little ceramic cups with a traditional Japanese tea set."

He nodded, watching her. "What happened to her?"

Her smile faded. "She drowned. I didn't know what to call it at the time, but now I know she suffered from manic depression. I think she went into the ocean that day intending to end her suffering."

"How old were you?"

"Seven. How old were you when you lost your parents?" All she knew was that they'd been killed in a car crash while he was in high school.

"Fifteen. Were you alone when she died?"

"No, she'd left me with family friends, or maybe with an aunt and uncle, I can't remember. But whoever it was, I was taken away right after her funeral." Soon after that, she'd been put into the secret CIA program that had changed the course of her life forever.

Not wanting to talk about any of that, she sank to the floor on the other side of Karas. "How's our patient doing?" She stroked a hand over the dog's head and neck. Karas stared up at her with sad eyes, looked decidedly sorry for herself.

"She's sore. I put ointment on the burn before I dressed it, but I'll be taking her to the vet first thing tomorrow to get antibiotics."

Kiyomi nodded, unsurprised. The way Marcus took care of his dog and horses told her so much about the kind of man he was. "How did you first find her? I've never heard the story."

"We were out on patrol one night. A large area of the sector we were in had been completely destroyed by an artillery strike. We were hiding in the rubble doing a recce and one of my troopers heard these tiny little whimpers coming from somewhere close by. She'd crawled into a hole between some cinder blocks in a wall that had collapsed."

He stroked Karas's head as he spoke, his long, lean fingers caressing her white-and-brown fur. "She was like a little gray ghost, covered in concrete dust, no bigger than me hand. She was shivering and half-starved, so I put her in my jacket, fed her some of my rations, and took her back to base with us after the mission was over."

"Your CO must have loved that."

"Eh, he didn't mind. The lads all loved her. She was a morale booster on base, but Anatolians generally only bond to one person."

She smiled. "She certainly *is* bonded to you."

The right side of his mouth lifted, stretching the scars around his left eye. "Aye. She slept on my bunk every night. When I was out on a patrol or a mission the lads told me she would curl up on my pillow and wait there, aloof as you please with everyone else. There was never any question that she was my dog, and that she would come home wi' me one day."

Karas groaned and rolled to her left side, laying her head in Kiyomi's lap. Kiyomi couldn't help but smile. "Look who's decided to warm up to me."

"Aye, she likes you," Marcus said, his deep voice like a caress.

"I'm glad. When did you bring her back here to the UK?"

His smile faded. "The lads brought her into the hospital after I'd… After Megan got me out of the prison I was held at. The staff set up a little bed for her on the floor and took turns taking care of her while I was laid up. They flew us back to the UK together, and the rest is history."

Kiyomi had so many questions about what had happened to him. About how Megan had managed to rescue him. But she couldn't ask him about something so private. "And now she lives like a princess in this beautiful manor," she murmured, stroking one of Karas's velvety brown ears.

"Aye, she does that." He took a sip of the tea, the low sound of appreciation he made setting off a curl of heat in her lower belly.

"How is it?"

Those dark-chocolate eyes warmed as he looked at her. "Perfect. Thank you."

"My pleasure." And speaking of pleasure, she was pretty sure she wanted the chance to experience some with him.

She stood, giving her the chance to conceal her attraction to him. "Mind if I borrow a book?"

"Help yourself. I've got some accounting to do anyway." He planted his palms on the floor and pushed up onto his left knee, a slight grimace of pain pulling at his features as he stood. She had to stem the urge to help him, not wanting to bruise his pride or make him think she saw him as weak.

She went to the bookcase nearest his desk to consider her options, and her gaze immediately fell on the leather-bound copy of The Secret Garden.

A little over a week ago he'd shown her how it could open the bookcase to reveal the secret passage beyond it, and the old priest hole dating back centuries that he and Megan had turned into an impressively equipped loadout room. Precautions were smart, but Kiyomi hoped they wouldn't need it before the time came for all of them to leave this place.

Breaking from her thoughts, she turned slightly to let him pass her on the way to his desk. Their eyes met. Held.

Breathless seconds stretched out while her heart began to race with excitement and tingles spread through her lower belly. Her gaze dipped to his mouth, tracing the shape of his lips, already imagining the moment when they touched hers.

Don't. You'll taint him.

The whisper in the back of her mind took her off guard, stabbed the most vulnerable spot in her battered heart. All the self-loathing, all the shame rose up, coalescing into a single face.

Fayez Rahman.

The memory stopped her cold, instantly killing all anticipation and building arousal.

All the therapy she'd done thus far hadn't yet reached the ugliness inside her, but everything she'd buried had risen to the surface. She felt unworthy, contaminated because of what she'd done and what had been done to her by other men.

Rahman had changed everything. He'd broken the seal on that box inside her, and there was no fixing it now. Not when he had a bounty on her sizeable enough to attract all sorts of hitters. Not when he'd been planning to sell her to earn it back.

Breaking eye contact, she grabbed a random book from the shelf. "Thanks. I'll see you in the morning." She spun around and headed for the door, imagining the feel of Marcus's arms around her and his mouth on hers, even as her skin crawled with shame.

It only hardened her resolve to end this, and Rahman with it.

Her fellow Valkyries had flat-out refused to entertain the idea of her posing as bait to draw Rahman out. But no matter what, they would get him. And when they did, Kiyomi would end him personally.

He had to die by her hand. It was the only way she could move forward.

Chapter Three

Fayez tugged at the hem of his tailored sport jacket as he stepped out of the armored vehicle in front of the three-story, cream stucco mansion in Latakia, on the Syrian coast.

Two of his bodyguards accompanied him up the walkway to the front door while the salty breeze blew around them. His head of security remained in the vehicle, having already cleared him to enter the house.

A servant opened the front door and bowed slightly. "Good evening, sir. She's outside on the balcony."

He nodded and continued into the house. The smell of something delicious hung in the air, spiced with the faint fragrance of cinnamon and cardamom as he walked through the entry and past the kitchen, where a chef and his assistant were busy preparing the evening meal.

Everything was immaculate, each room furnished to exacting standards. He hated the place. It reminded him too much of his childhood house, which had been more a prison than a home.

He opened the French-style doors and stepped out onto the wide balcony, the soft breeze washing over him and the sea rolling against the beach a few hundred yards away.

"You're here," an impatient voice said from the corner. "Good."

He faced her and put on a smile. "Hello, Mother."

She struggled up from her seat and maneuvered into her walker. "Come. We'll eat."

"You're looking well," he said when she got close.

She scoffed. "My body's falling apart. I wish I was dead."

He wished that too. Though he would never say it to her face.

She shuffled past him without another glance. And as much as he should be used to the rebuffs by now, dammit, it still hurt. Just once he wanted her to see him. See him and care.

Feeling like a prisoner serving out a sentence, he followed her back inside and to the dining room. If the house bothered him, this room was ten times worse.

On the antique sideboard at the end of the long table was a collection of framed photos. Of the two-dozen or so on display, only one included him—a family shot taken six years ago. The rest were of his dead father and brother.

His mother kept them on display because she was still grieving their losses…but also to remind him that the best parts of her life were gone forever. That no matter what he did or how successful he was, he would never be enough for her.

"How long are you staying for?" she asked as Fayez pushed her chair in for her.

"I'm leaving in a few hours."

Her shrewd brown eyes cut to him. "Ah. Urgent business in Damascus, I suppose."

"Yes." She didn't know what he did exactly. Because she didn't care.

She didn't give a shit about anything he did because he would never measure up to his sainted father and brother who'd been killed in the war. Didn't give a shit about him at all apart from him supporting her in the life-style she'd become accustomed to.

When his father and brother had been alive, things had been different. He'd mattered. Now…all that was gone. And he resented her for every breath she took.

"I saw a picture of you with a woman awhile ago," she said as she spooned up a mouthful of the soup served for the starter course.

He grunted. "Where did you see that?"

She waved a hand. "Someone sent it to me. You were at a charity gala or something, all dressed up."

He stiffened in his seat. The last charity event he'd attended had been… "What did she look like?"

"Young. Asian. Attractive girl wearing a gold dress. Are you still seeing her?"

His stomach clenched into a hard ball. He wasn't even sure why his mother was asking, since she never cared about anything he did. "No."

His leaden tone gave him away because she paused to look down the table at him. "Was it serious?"

He'd thought it was. At first. "No," he bit out.

"That's not what I heard." There was a distinctly smug edge to her voice as she spooned up another mouth-ful of soup.

"Well, you heard wrong." They ate in silence for a minute, while acid churned in his gut. "Who sent it to you?" he finally asked, because he couldn't let it go.

"An acquaintance at the gala. Why?"

Because I'll do anything to get her back. As the sub-stantial bounty he'd offered proved.

His mother set her spoon down to study him. "What happened?"

"Nothing."

"Then where is she?"

I don't know. And it ate him alive every single day.

"She left the country," he said in a flat voice that warned her to drop the subject.

"So you let her go." She shook her head, sighed in disappointment and picked up her spoon.

His fingers clenched around his spoon, the spike in his temper getting harder and harder to control. *Just get through the meal, then you can leave.*

There was no point in continuing this conversation. He would just sound defensive and confirm what she already thought of him—that he was weak. He wouldn't see her at all anymore except that she was his mother, and his last surviving relative. And there was a tiny part of him that kept hoping one day he would gain her approval.

"Why did you let her go?" his mother pressed, the pitch of her voice raking down his spine like the edge of chalk down a blackboard.

I would never *have let her go*, his mind hissed.

Kiyomi had changed his entire world. From the moment she walked into the hotel lobby that day wearing a red satin dress that hugged her sleek curves, she'd captivated him.

His mother laughed. A nasty laugh that made him want to slap her across the face. "She left you because you couldn't keep her." She laughed again, shaking her head. "All that money and power you love, and you couldn't keep her."

Fayez shoved to his feet. Nailing his mother with a long, fulminating glare, he threw his linen napkin on the table and stalked from the room. He didn't stop in the next one.

He kept going to the foyer, where his bodyguards were waiting. "We're leaving," he said curtly.

They escorted him outside and to his car. He hoped his mother fucking choked on the dinner he'd paid for.

Alone in the back of the vehicle, his bitter thoughts turned back to Kiyomi. He'd never met a woman like her.

Confident. Incredibly intelligent. Quiet. Calm. The sexiest thing he'd ever laid eyes on.

And when she'd looked at him, she'd seen him. The real him, hidden beneath the money and the power and empire he'd built.

He'd fallen fast and hard. So hard, he was willing to give her anything. Including his heart.

But then he'd found out everything between them was a lie. That she was a lie, just like every other woman who'd ever been in his life. Worse, she'd *used* him, was actually some American government assassin.

The betrayal had sliced deep, opening wounds he'd carried with him from childhood. She'd fooled him. Made a fool *out* of him.

Then he'd found out what the brand on her left hip had meant. Before that he hadn't even known the Valkyries existed.

Once he'd learned the truth he'd had no choice but to punish her. No one betrayed him and lived, and he couldn't risk appearing weak. But he couldn't kill her, because an interested buyer had come along at the right moment, offering a fitting punishment for her.

Her mark was how he'd been introduced to the Architect. The Architect had been hunting Valkyries and was willing to pay three million to have Kiyomi, and in addition promised to deliver her a lifetime of servitude and suffering. Kiyomi would have lived the rest of her days praying for death while remembering that he was the reason she had been captured in the first place.

And then…she'd disappeared. Someone had broken her out of her cell one night and he hadn't been able to find a single trace of her since. Only rumors. Never a concrete lead. It tore him up inside.

She was still out there, and he couldn't bear or allow that. He would never stop searching for her, no matter how long it took or how much it cost. He would use every last resource at his disposal to make sure he brought her back to pay for her betrayal.

No matter what he had to do, what he had to pay and who he had to kill, Kiyomi would be his again one day. And this time, he would succeed in breaking her before he sold her to the Architect.

Chapter Four

Marcus was out checking the perimeter fence lines early the next morning in the steady drizzle when Megan called him on his mobile. It was just past oh-six-hundred, and she didn't usually call this early unless she wanted to go riding. "Morning."

"Hey. The police are at the gate wanting to talk to you."

Ah, shite. He'd been hoping they would just call him rather than show up. "I filed a complaint about Karas last night," he said, walking back to his ATV. He'd gone back and forth about it for several hours, then decided he couldn't let it go. Filing a complaint should have no consequences whatsoever on the situation with his houseguests.

"Well, that's part of what they want to see you about."

He frowned as he started the engine. "Why, what else is there?"

"They won't say. I've stalled them here at the gatehouse and alerted everyone at the main house to give them time to get out of sight."

"All right. Tell them I'll be there in ten minutes."

"Got it."

Karas being injured aside, what was so important that the police were here at daybreak to see him? He drove the ATV back to the shed and arrived at the main house in eight minutes. The house was quiet and still, everyone having scattered after Megan's warning. He was waiting out on the front steps when the police car parked at the top of the driveway. He recognized both constables.

"Good morning," he said, shaking hands with them, then stepped back. "Please come in."

He brought them into his study and shut the door. Karas lifted her head when they entered but otherwise didn't budge from her bed in front of the fire. Marcus had stoked it three times overnight to make sure it stayed lit for her, because even with the heat on, this time of year the house was chilly. He'd slept on the sofa beside it rather than in his room, not wanting to move Karas.

"I assume you're here about my complaint about what happened to my dog last night," Marcus began.

"Yes." The first constable, a man in his early thirties or thereabouts crouched down to let Karas sniff at his hand. "Hey, sweet girl. I'm sorry this happened to you."

"We're also here about an incident that occurred late last night near your property," the older constable said.

"What incident?" Marcus asked, setting his cane aside as he lowered himself into the chair behind his desk.

The older cop remained standing as he spoke. "It seems three teenage boys were attacked not far from your front gate."

He already didn't like where this was going. "Attacked how?"

"They claim someone jumped out of a tree and ambushed them, cuffed them with plastic zip ties, then stripped them down to their undershorts and left them tied to the trunk of the tree where they were found later."

Marcus's eyebrows drew together. "What?"

The younger cop pushed to his feet. "Someone called in about it just after midnight and we were sent to pick them up."

"Were they harmed?" Marcus asked.

"Just their egos," the younger said.

"One of them had a sign taped to his chest that read *I'm an animal abuser*. And, ah… *Because I'm a coward with a small dick*." The older cop cleared his throat, his gaze never wavering from Marcus. "They're claiming it was you who attacked them."

Anger punched through him, but he kept his expression and tone neutral. Dammit. One of the Valkyries had done this. And he had a fair idea of which one. "They claim I jumped out of a tree and attacked them," he repeated.

"Uh, yes," the younger cop said, his eyes darting to Marcus's cane.

Marcus leaned back in his chair, stretching his left leg out onto the ottoman. He didn't want pity or to draw attention to his disability, but there was no help for it here. "Does it look like I'm capable of climbing a tree, let alone jumping out of one to ambush three lads?"

"You're former military," the older one said. "Possibly former special forces, from what I've heard."

One of the few things Marcus disliked about living in a rural area like this was that the locals all knew each other and they talked too damn much. "I haven't been able to climb a tree in over two years now," Marcus replied, a cold edge to his voice. And being selected for The Regiment meant he had better control and discipline than most people walking this earth. "So it wasn't me."

The man acknowledged his statement with a nod. "Then who?"

"I have no idea."

"Someone who knew about what happened to your

dog."

"The lads might have hurt another animal last night too. They've been setting off bangers three nights in a row now, and deliberately throwing them onto people's property to spook the animals. It could have been someone else's dog, or even a sheep the person who left the note was talking about."

The two constables shared a look, then the older one turned his attention back to Marcus. "I understand you have security cameras set up near the front gate. Mind if we look over the footage from last night?"

"Not at all." Though he already knew what they'd find. He would bet this house that as soon as Megan had informed Amber of what was going on, Amber had wiped the video feed clean.

Wanting the cops out of his house and this entire situation done with so they could all move forward and he and his houseguests could go back to staying off the radar, Marcus turned his computer screen around for the constables and pulled up the video feed from last night.

He showed them the clip of the boys arriving during the bonfire, and one of them throwing the device at Karas. It still made his blood boil. "What time did the boys say they were attacked?" he asked when it finished.

"Just after twenty-three-hundred hours."

Marcus fast-forwarded through the feed, stopping short of the mark before he played it for them. As expected, nothing showed up on video. No sign of the boys coming anywhere near the range of the cameras.

He fast-forwarded again, looking for any sign of them at all, but of course there was nothing right through oh-one-hundred-hours this morning. Amber's edit was seamless. Not that he would expect anything less.

When the video feed in question was done, he eased back in his chair to regard the men and raised an eyebrow. "Satisfied?"

They both nodded, looking slightly uncomfortable. "Thank you for your cooperation. We'll keep looking into the matter," the older one said.

"As for the matter concerning my dog," Marcus added, "how long will it take for the lads to be charged and reported to the Crown Prosecution Service? I keep to myself and prefer to live a quiet life. I don't want this matter dragged out or publicized in any way, and I don't want my name showing up in the local paper. This is a small town. People will talk. I want to avoid that at all cost."

The older cop regarded him for a moment, then nodded. "Understood. The process will likely take months."

Kiyomi and the others would be long gone by then, perhaps not even in the UK anymore. The tension in his shoulders eased. "Thank you. Now if you'll excuse me, I need to get my dog in to see the vet first thing."

"Of course."

He walked them out, anxious for them to leave. He waited on the front step until their car turned out of the gate at the end of the driveway, then shut the door and stood there a moment and expelled a long breath. Crisis averted.

Seconds later came the sound of voices as the others came in through the back door, no doubt alerted by Megan the moment the police had driven away from the house. She and Ty were absent, as were Jesse and Amber.

Marcus spun around and started down the hallway, heading for the breakfast room. All conversation ceased the moment he entered, everyone gathered around the table.

Five sets of eyes fastened on him, including Kiyomi's, but his gaze paused on her only for a moment before cutting to Chloe. "Had an eventful night, did you?"

She blinked her big brown eyes at him, wearing a T-shirt that read: *Explosives expert. If you see me running, try to catch up.* "What do you mean?"

She wasn't fooling anyone with the innocent routine. "Three teenage boys matching the same description as the ones who hurt Karas last night were found tied up just after midnight. You wouldn't know anything about that, would you?"

Across the table, Heath cut his girlfriend a wary look. "Chloe," he said in a warning tone. "What did you do?"

Marcus glanced over his shoulder as someone came up behind him in the hallway. It was Trinity, holding a newspaper. "She in there?" she asked.

There was no doubt about who she meant, or that they'd come to the same conclusion. Nodding, he stepped aside to let her pass.

"Well, there you go, Chlo. You finally made the local paper." She tossed the paper onto Chloe's plate, front page up, and folded her arms.

"Me?" Chloe said, feigning offense.

The others craned their necks to see the paper as Chloe read the headline aloud. "Local teens terrorized on Bonfire Night." She snorted. "Terrorized, my ass. They don't have a clue what terrorized even looks like."

Eden snatched the paper up to continue reading, a slight frown pulling at her forehead. "'A bloody ninja jumped out of this tree and attacked us,' one of the boys reported. 'We didn't get a good look at him, but the guy had stun grenades and everything.' After a tip to police from a concerned local, the boys were found…" Her eyes widened as she trailed off to stare at Chloe. "Stripped to their underwear and tied to a tree in a field just off the A436."

Trinity made a strangled sound and covered it with a cough, her blue eyes wide. Snickers broke out around the table, then laughter, and even Marcus couldn't help but grin.

Heath wasn't laughing. He was shaking his head at Chloe in alarm. "There's something very wrong with you.

You know that, right?"

When Chloe gave a careless shrug, Heath narrowed his eyes in accusation. "You said you were going downstairs to make hot chocolate because you couldn't sleep."

"I did, and I couldn't," she said with a defensive scowl. "Then I waited for those little bastards to come back, because I knew they would. And when they did, I taught them a lesson they won't soon forget."

When Heath just kept scowling at her, Chloe huffed out an annoyed breath and slathered a piece of toast with a sickening amount of Mrs. Biddington's homemade raspberry jam. "Relax, they were only out there for half an hour before I called in the tip."

Kiyomi smothered a laugh, and Eden and Zack were both smiling.

Trinity shook her head at Chloe, her expression fond. "You're still as much trouble as ever. Good thing we're already getting ready to leave here soon anyway, so I guess there's no harm done."

At the reminder, Marcus's gaze strayed to Kiyomi, a shock of awareness ripping through him when he found her watching him. Time was running out in Laidlaw Hall's tenure as Valkyrie headquarters.

The team leaving here and spreading everyone out was the smart choice at this point, but part of him didn't want to see it end. Seemed strange now, but he'd gotten used to having everyone around, and having the old house full of life instead of just him and Karas knocking around this great pile of stone. He would miss them all when it was over, especially Kiyomi and Megan.

"Amber managed to wipe the security feed clean?" Trinity said to him.

"Aye, it was flawless."

"Good. If those idiots know we've got them on video attacking Karas, let's hope they figure out their only option is to admit what they did and take the punishment."

"They never saw my face. They even assumed I was a man." Chloe's expression was full of annoyance. "Little misogynist pricks have no idea. I should have left them out there for an hour-and-a-half."

"It's *November*, Chloe," Trinity reminded her. "Half an hour in their underwear when it's just above freezing was more than enough to drive your point home."

"How is Karas, anyway?" Chloe asked Marcus.

The woman was diabolical, but adorable, and he had a soft spot for animal lovers, especially when someone had gone to the trouble of avenging his beloved dog. He didn't have the heart to be annoyed with Chloe anymore. "Sore. I'll be taking her in to see the vet. But if she could understand what you did, I think she'd approve."

Chloe beamed. "I think so too."

"Well, I'd best shove off. I want to have Karas at the vet office the moment it opens." His gaze strayed over to Kiyomi as she stood.

"I'll come with you."

Her announcement surprised him. He'd thought that she and the others would want to hole up here and keep a low profile now, getting everything packed and organized for the upcoming move. "Under the circumstances, are you sure it's a good idea—"

"Yes. I need a break from our investigation and I've been wanting to look around the area for ages. Maybe you can even show me around Stow for a bit later, if Karas is up to it."

He'd love to spend hours taking her around town and showing her the places he loved most, but a short visit was all he would allow, for safety's sake. "All right," he said with a nod, and she followed him out into the hallway.

He felt her presence with every step, the rush of awareness and desire growing stronger every passing hour. He wanted to touch her. Hold her.

Take her to his bed. Protect her. Make her smile.

Maker her laugh.

Make her *his*.

That would never happen now, and it was for the best that she was leaving here soon. Safer for her.

And for you.

Aye. A woman like her would never want a cripple like him. Even if she did, the ever-present ghosts he carried with him were always there as a reminder that after what had happened that fateful night in Syria, he was the last person on earth who deserved happiness.

Chapter Five

Kiyomi got out of Marcus's old Land Rover at the vet clinic just outside of town, sorry that the trip was necessary but glad to get away from the manor for awhile. The investigation to find Rahman and the Architect was wearing on her, and she had an intensive online therapy session coming up tomorrow that she'd been dreading for a while now.

In spite of all their efforts, no one had a clue yet who the Architect might be. It had to be someone connected to the Valkyrie Program or the CIA who knew or had known Kiyomi, but no one stood out in her memory.

They still didn't know whether the Architect was responsible for all of this, and who the women with the stylized tats on their hips were, killed by Kiyomi's team on a recent mission in Virginia. The design of the tattoo was different from the brand Kiyomi and the others had, but the similarities were disturbing.

It was almost like they were dealing with another group similar to the Valkyries, which should have been impossible since everything had been shut down after the shit storm following the Balducci trial. So yeah, she desperately needed this quick break, even if it only lasted less than an hour.

"I'll text you when we're done, then come find you," Marcus said to her as he lifted Karas out of the back.

"Sure." She stroked Karas's head, then watched as he carried the dog inside the old stone building. What would it be like, to be with a man who treated her with such care?

The increase of traffic was immediate as soon as she reached The Bell, a centuries-old pub Marcus sometimes went to at the bottom of the town. Her insides tightened at the sudden, sharp rise in anxiety caused by a sense of exposure, even with a hat and sunglasses helping to disguise her. Instinctively she was still on alert, watching for threats.

As soon as she realized what she'd done, she berated herself. She was in the middle of the freaking Cotswolds, not Syria, and she could damn well walk around this countryside market town like a normal person without seeing a threat in every shadow.

It was only a few minutes' walk along the hill up Sheep Street to reach the heart of Stow-on-the-Wold, the highest village in all the Cotswolds. Once a bustling wool market town, it remained a collection of narrow, winding streets filled with charming, old, honey-gold stone buildings housing vacation rentals, shops, tea rooms and restaurants.

A light carpet of orange and gold leaves dotted the sidewalks and grassy areas. Brilliant splashes of scarlet Virginia Creeper clambered up the front of an antique shop, while glossy green ivy and colorful lemon and plum-colored mums spilled out of window boxes along the buildings lining the street.

Her senses remained on high alert, but it gave her the chance to sharpen her awareness after months of being isolated from the outside world. The sun was out, and Stow's main square was packed with cars and busloads of tourists. A lot of them were Asian, so at least she didn't feel like she stood out too much, or that anyone was staring at her as she walked past the old stone shops and businesses.

Kiyomi counted the number of people she saw. Assessed them for threat level, watching for any sign of a weapon, or heightened interest in her.

Just off the main square she spotted the fabled Huffkins bakery and teahouse she'd heard so much about from the others, and popped in to order treats for everyone. With fifteen minutes to kill before her order was ready, she decided to satisfy her curiosity and take a look around the rest of the town.

Walking around here in broad daylight was a self-imposed test she needed to pass in order to feel hopeful about any sort of a future after their mission was over. Since her arrival at Laidlaw Hall she'd kept strictly to the manor and its ground. She'd wanted to come alone on her first visit to town, so she could get her bearings on her own and prove to herself she wasn't so damaged that she couldn't be out in a public place anymore without having a panic attack.

Crowds would always bother her now. Rahman had taken her captive at a party with more than a hundred people watching. None of them had lifted a finger to help her. Given her training and experience, she'd thought she was invincible. That she was the one controlling the situation. He'd shown her just how wrong she'd been, and a lesson like that was never forgotten.

The ring of nearby church bells pulled her from her thoughts, the magical sound beckoning her closer. She walked up the sidewalk and took a sharp turn into a narrow alley that led toward the churchyard. St. Edward's Church stood proud in the center of it, a famous Norman church dating back to the eleventh Century, built of the same honey-toned Cotswold limestone as the rest of the town.

She paused on the leaf-strewn pathway to stop where a group of Mandarin-speaking tourists were posing for pictures. On either side of the arched, wooden door, ancient yew trees flanked the north entrance. She continued on the path that led around the west side of the church, pausing to read the gravestones. Near the end of the path, she stopped in front of a headstone when her eye caught on the names.

William Laidlaw and his wife, Elizabeth. Born in the early 1700s, and buried here before the turn of the century. Two of Marcus's ancestors. And there was also a stone memorial to the final battle of the English Civil War fought at Stow.

Venturing off the path, she examined some of the other headstones. There were quite a few Laidlaws buried here, but many more stones were illegible, the names and dates chiseled into the slabs long since worn away by the elements over the centuries.

How incredible, for him to own Laidlaw Hall and live where his ancestors had for hundreds of years before him. She'd never had roots of any kind, never been able to stay in one place long enough to form a connection. But here…she felt a bone-deep connection somehow. To this place, and especially Laidlaw Hall and its enigmatic owner.

It was the nearest thing to a home she'd ever known. Knowing she had to leave soon dimmed her mood considerably.

When it was time to pick up her order at Huffkins she chose a quieter path out of the churchyard and back along the alley toward the square. The smell of the baked goods reached her from the sidewalk.

She'd never been one to eat sweets, since they were all fat and sugar and she'd always been calorie conscious to maintain a certain look with her figure because her body was her lure as well as her weapon.

But now that she was trying to move forward, she could eat whatever she damn well pleased. Since arriving at Laidlaw Hall she'd put on a good ten pounds, and for the first time ever, she wasn't stressing about her weight or body.

The counseling and conversations with Trinity were a godsend. Over the past few months she'd come a long way in terms of body image and self-worth, but it hadn't been easy and she still had a long way to go because Rahman had robbed her of something she was determined to reclaim.

She was more than her face and body. She had value as a person, outside of her looks and skillset.

Getting to know the real Kiyomi Tanaka was both exciting and terrifying. Every day she discovered something new about herself, and it made her even more resolved never to give her hard-won autonomy up.

The nightmares kept coming, however, all borne from the terrible sense of helplessness she'd experienced as a captive. She fantasized about killing Rahman, about the look on his face when he realized he was about to die. It was cathartic.

At this point he was still their best link to finding out the Architect's identity. As soon as Amber had a solid lock on his location, they could plan an op to capture him.

Although capturing him wasn't enough for Kiyomi. He had to die, and she had to be the one to kill him.

Raised voices caught her attention as she stepped out of Huffkins and faced the main square. She stopped when she spotted Marcus standing in front of his Land Rover a stone's throw away…being confronted by two men.

An instant surge of protectiveness shot through her. She set her bags down and moved slowly toward them, watching the men's hands. One of them held a cricket bat.

"I did *not* attack your sons last night," she heard Marcus say in a low voice. He was calm, but standing his ground.

"It had to be you," the shorter man with the bat said. "It was right off your property, and everyone knows you're a nutter, holing up in your mansion with your PTSD or whatever the fuck is wrong with you."

Kiyomi wanted to garrote the bastard for speaking to Marcus that way but she held herself back, staying far enough away not to distract Marcus but close enough to intervene if necessary. People were watching in the square now, having figured out something was wrong.

Marcus's jaw flexed, his eyes boring a hole into the shorter man's face. "I never touched your sons. I could never have done what they claim I did." He shifted the base of his handcrafted wooden cane on the ground, driving his point home.

"If it wasn't you, then you had someone do it for you," the taller one snapped.

"I had nothing to do with it," Marcus said coldly. "I came into town to take my dog to the vet. Would you like t'see the burns on her leg that your sons gave her? Because I can undo the bandages if you want. Or better yet, I can show you the video footage of them throwing the banger at her in the first place."

The shorter man bristled and stepped forward, raising the bat.

Kiyomi took a lunging step forward, but she'd barely moved before Marcus swiveled and brought his cane up to block it. A loud clack of wood on wood sounded.

With a single, expert twist of his cane, in the blink of an eye Marcus disarmed the bastard and shoved him to the ground on his ass, using just enough force necessary and then stopping, when he could easily have killed or maimed the man with a single blow if he'd wanted to.

The taller man backed up with his palms out, eyes

wide as he gaped at Marcus. "Whoa, pal. Whoa."

Marcus turned his gaze on the one he'd just put on the ground, his bearing intimidating but not threatening as he towered over the piece of shit. "I give you my word that I had nothing to do with what happened to your sons. Now get outta here and leave me alone." He turned away, giving them his back as he reached for the door of his vehicle.

Kiyomi grabbed her bags and hurried up the sidewalk just as the taller man bent to help his friend up. She stuck her foot out as she walked past, knocking them both off balance. She pretended to stumble as they hit the ground, whirling to face them as she babbled an apology to them in Japanese.

The men scowled, dismissed her and hurried away, muttering to each other and casting dark looks at Marcus. Assholes.

When she looked up, Marcus was staring at her through the windshield. She smiled at him, lowered her sunglasses to give him a wink, then pushed them back up the bridge of her nose and sauntered past his vehicle in case the men were still watching.

She continued down the sidewalk with all her bags. In the shop windows she followed Marcus's progress as he drove toward her. When they were a block away from the main square, he pulled up to the curb and she angled across to meet him.

He leaned over to open her door for her, took the bags and set them on the seat. "Sorry about that," he muttered, his expression tight.

"Nothing to apologize for. I know you couldn't in public, but man, I'd have loved to see you lay that guy out instead of just bruising his ego."

The side of his mouth pulled upward as he drove down the cobbled street. The town was so damn quaint, like something from a postcard. "So bloodthirsty."

"Only when it comes to assholes."

He was quiet a moment as they stopped in traffic to let some pedestrians cross the street. The narrow streets caused a lot of congestion with all the tourists flooding the town. "Sorry I didn't get to show you around."

"It's fine. Maybe another time."

He glanced over at her, the impact of his dark gaze like a touch. "After all this, it's not safe here for all of you anymore."

"I know." It made her heart heavy. She'd become attached to Marcus and the others, and didn't want to leave without forging certain memories for her to carry with her through whatever came next.

"So what did the vet say?" she asked to change the subject, swiveling in her seat to pet Karas, who had her snoot shoved between the front seats.

"She'll be all right. Just needs a few days to heal up, and take her antibiotics."

"You're a good dog dad, Marcus."

He aimed a grin at her that almost stopped her heart. "It's my pleasure. She's a good lass."

The urge to lean across the seat and kiss him was so overwhelming she had to look away.

Pleasure.

That word, spoken in his deep voice, caused another frisson of warmth low in her belly. He was a reserved, disciplined man with high expectations of himself. But there was fire in him, hidden away beneath that calm exterior.

What was he like in bed? From what she'd seen he liked control, and she bet that extended into sex as well.

That gave her pause. She'd never let herself go and enjoyed sex with anyone before—only doing it as an act, always remaining physically and emotionally detached, her mind clear—yet the idea of doing it with Marcus was more and more tantalizing. He would never hurt or degrade her. And she got the sense that he would be an attentive, maybe even generous lover.

Combining all that with his quiet intensity, her mind had conjured up several fantasies about it lately. Her pulse beat faster, a flush of heat sweeping through her body as images of them together swirled in her head.

They drove back to the manor without speaking again. A large, intricate wrought iron gate bearing the Laidlaw coat of arms marked the entrance to the estate, the stone gatehouse sat at the end of the long, crushed gravel driveway.

At the other end of it, Laidlaw Hall stood perched on a rise in the middle of a small valley nestled between the surrounding rolling hills, a three-story mansion built of Cotswold limestone that glowed in the sun. Lush green lawn sloped away from it, the front of the house bordered by neatly trimmed boxwood and yew hedges, and the trees clustered around the house and on the deep green hillsides were afire with a gorgeous flush of scarlet, orange and gold.

While Kiyomi's heart sang at the sight of it, she wound tighter and tighter inside. She didn't want to leave Marcus yet. She wanted more time with him, time to explore what was between them. But it would hurt more when she left.

What's a little more pain after what you've been through?

Marcus carried Karas back into the study and placed her on her bed in front of the fire, then took the bags from Kiyomi in the entry hall and continued on to the kitchen. The voices coming from there grew louder as they neared it.

"Is there a party going on in here, or what?" she asked, coming in behind Marcus.

Everyone was gathered around the island in the center of the room, drinking out of champagne glasses. "Here, have a mimosa," Megan said, thrusting a flute at her and Marcus.

"What are we celebrating?" she asked, looking around. The atmosphere was downright festive.

With a slow grin, Jesse wrapped an arm around Amber's shoulders and tugged her into his side. "We just got hitched."

Kiyomi's eyes widened. "What?"

Amber flushed a little as she smiled. "Yep. He wore me down, but neither of us wanted the hassle of a wedding, so we eloped instead."

"*That's* why you guys weren't here this morning," she said, looking to Megan.

"Yep. Ty and I were their witnesses. And so now that we're all here… To my sister and Jesse." She smiled at the newlyweds. "May you have a long, happy life together." She raised her glass. "Cheers."

"Cheers," everyone chorused.

Hugs and handshakes were doled out. Kiyomi embraced Amber, then Chloe engulfed them both in a hug and shouted, "Group hug!"

Eden and Trinity joined in too. Chloe bounced up and down a little, always a ball of restless energy about to explode, and crowed, "Bitchilantes ride or die!"

Everyone laughed and once they all let go, Kiyomi stepped back to smile at Amber. "I'm so happy for you."

Amber smiled back, looking happier and more relaxed than Kiyomi had ever seen her. "Thanks."

Kiyomi moved out of the way as Trinity came to hug the bride, her gaze moving to Marcus. He stood on the other side of the island next to Heath, nodding at something the other man was saying. He met her gaze, and there was something weary and almost sad in his eyes as he put on a smile for her.

A bittersweet pain lanced her chest. Surrounded by this group of people she'd come to love like family and celebrating a new marriage, she'd never been so keenly aware of how alone she was. Of how emotionally broken she was.

When she left Laidlaw Hall soon, she would lose any chance of being with Marcus. And once this mission was over, all her Valkyrie sisters would move on with their partners. But she and Marcus would both be alone once more.

****

"Where was this taken?" Fayez demanded as he strode to his office with his head of security. He'd just been alerted that they might have a sighting on Kiyomi.

"Barcelona. This morning."

Fayez hurried to his desk and typed in his password to his computer, heart thudding as he clicked on the video in question and waited for it to load. The scene showed a busy street in the heart of the old town center, the camera mounted on the exterior of a bank.

"Where is she?" he demanded, impatience eating at him. Months without even so much as a single sighting of her.

"In about five seconds she'll walk out of this building." The man pointed to another bank across the street. "There. Watch."

Fayez held his breath, pulse drumming in his ears as a woman exited the bank. Definitely Asian. Right build and height, a large hat shading her face and dark sunglasses covering her eyes.

"Her face is obscured, but the recognition software said it's an eighty-five-percent—" He stopped abruptly when Fayez raised a hand to silence him.

On screen the woman crossed the street, walking directly toward the camera. In three seconds he had his answer.

"It's not her," he growled, disappointment and frustration punching him hard in the chest.

"Are you sure?" His head bodyguard leaned closer, peering at the woman.

"Of course I'm sure," he snapped, growing irritated. "She doesn't move like Kiyomi moves."

"What? How can you know that? She might have changed her posture or gait, or—"

"No. It's not her." This woman might resemble Kiyomi in some ways, but to him the difference was obvious. This woman didn't have half the grace or poise that Kiyomi did. *No* one did.

He shoved back his chair and stood, abruptly turning for the door. "Keep searching. And don't ask me to look at anything else unless it's a near-perfect match."

Because he couldn't take any more disappointments where she was concerned.

Chapter Six

She'd been dreading this moment for a long time now.

Confronting the empty chair before her the next morning, Kiyomi tamped down the urge to fidget or shift in her seat. Of all the things she'd done in therapy so far, this empty chair exercise was the hardest by far.

She'd done it twice already using different scenarios, and each time the emotional toll was greater. Though she'd been dreading this particular session for weeks, it was necessary if she ever wanted a chance at healing the wounds inside her so she could have a somewhat "normal" life after this was all over.

Today's session was going to either make her or break her.

She was conscious of Trinity sitting off to the side of the room situated above the stables, watching silently. Kiyomi had asked her to be here for this. No one else could understand what was about to happen better than Trin, and if Kiyomi's fears came true and she lost it, at least Trin would be there to cushion the fall.

"Are you comfortable?" the female therapist asked on screen via the secure video chat they used for these sessions. She had worked with Trinity for the past few years, her credentials were impeccable and she was a retired Air Force colonel. Trinity had sworn by her and her discretion, so Kiyomi had agreed to give it a try.

"Yes." She might seem composed on the outside, but inside she was a giant freaking knot of nerves, afraid of what would happen when she cracked open the vault she'd sealed all of this shit inside years ago and subsequently just kept stuffing more into it.

"All right. You know what this involves. Last time we talked about what eight-year-old Kiyomi was feeling after her mother died and she was placed into foster care and then into the Program. Today we're moving forward in time."

Kiyomi took a deep breath, keeping her expression impassive. It felt like she was under a spotlight. Even here in the safety of this private room, with only the therapist and Trinity as an audience, she was still programmed not to show discomfort or fear.

"In the chair in front of you, I want you to imagine a teenage Kiyomi. She's sixteen, maybe seventeen. Can you picture her?"

"Yes." She was a hardened version of her younger self by then, though not nearly as hard as she would become in a few short years after that.

"What does she look like?"

She described her image of teenage Kiyomi. The teenager was dressed in form-hugging clothes, her long hair styled perfectly straight as it fell around her breasts. Her posture was stiff, her eyes watchful. Mistrustful.

"What's happened to her in the past few months?"

Her stomach muscles grabbed, the painful things she'd shoved into her emotional vault pounding against the inside of the lid with angry fists. She forced her body to relax and took a calming breath. This was so hard. "Training."

"What sort of training?"

"CQB. Weapons. Recon. Infiltration." Plus a million other things, mostly to do with honing her powers of seduction and manipulation.

"Anything else significant?"

Yes. The thing that had put that hard edge into teenage Kiyomi's gaze. "Sex."

The therapist made a soft sound of acknowledgment. "Tell me more about that."

The therapist already knew most of this because they'd talked about it beforehand. But the whole point of this exercise was to allow Kiyomi to feel empathy for the girl in the empty chair. To grieve for all she'd been through, and everything she'd been deprived of.

Her fingers twitched in her lap before she could control them, her heart rate increasing already. This was going to hurt so bad... "It was her first time."

"I see. Was it consensual?"

She hesitated. "Yes. Or at least, she thought so at the time."

"Who was it with?"

"A trainer." She forced herself to keep going, just wanting to be done with this. "The cadre knew she had a crush on one of her instructors, so they allowed him to do the honors of taking her virginity."

"I see. And what was that like for her?"

"She was nervous. Glad to get the first time over with."

The therapist nodded. "Was it enjoyable at all for her?"

She withheld a snort. "No. It was a means to an end, and they both knew it. She wasn't allowed to feel anything. They'd trained her not to. The most important part was, she had to keep up the act, make him think she was enjoying it, even when it hurt."

The woman was quiet a moment, allowing Kiyomi

to process that before continuing. "What happened after?"

"He left her room and went to report to the cadre."

"Did it happen again?"

"Not with him. With others. They wanted her—me, to become desensitized to the vulnerability of it." She'd hated that phase, the sense of violation she hadn't yet been able to totally shut off.

"How many others were there?"

Kiyomi swallowed, her fingers knotting into fists on her thighs. "I don't know." At least ten while she was still a trainee. After that? She'd stopped keeping count, for her own sanity.

"What else happened during that phase?"

"She...had an operation."

"A hysterectomy?"

"Yes." The muscles in her belly knotted tighter.

"Was that voluntary?"

"They made it seem like it was. That it was my decision, that it was the best decision to prevent problems once I graduated and went into the field."

"Teenage Kiyomi is in the chair across from you right now. What did she feel about the hysterectomy?"

"Scared," she whispered, the word scraping against her throat. The lid of the vault was loose now. Ready to burst open. And when it did...

"Yes, I'll bet she was." Another pause. "What else?"

"She was angry." She shifted in her seat, unable to stay still any longer. Her heart was thudding hard against her ribs, little tremors shaking her belly. Her breathing was uneven, her palms growing damp.

"Yes. Anything else?"

"Resentful. She's been programmed by the cadre and she just wants to break free of everyone at the facility. Leave this part of her life behind, get out into the world to start using her skills. Start taking out targets, making a difference in the world, as they'd trained her to do."

"And did she?"

"Yes."

"How old was she when she killed her first target?"

"Twenty-one. And it…"

"It what?"

"It was easier than she thought it would be." She'd been turned into a weapon. That first kill hadn't even registered against the mental firewall they'd implanted in her mind.

The therapist made another soft sound. "Was she good at it?"

"Yes." Her voice was barely above a whisper now. She didn't feel regret or guilt about any of the men she'd killed. Every last one of them had been evil and in need of killing. But now the feeling of being used and discarded by the government that had created her…that was the hardest to take after all she'd done.

"What about the rest of what you said about her a minute ago. Did she ever manage to break free?"

Her jaw muscles started to tremble, her breath hitching. Mentally she shoved the lid on the vault shut again, knowing it was only buying her seconds, maybe minutes, but so afraid to unleash everything that was hidden in there. "N-no."

"Kiyomi." She blinked at the screen, the therapist's face coming into focus again as the woman continued. "I think we should stop now—"

"*No.*" She had to do this. It was like an infected boil inside her, it needed to be lanced, drained and then cauterized. Emptied and sealed shut forever, so she never had to go through this again. "I want to keep going." Trinity was here. It would be okay.

"Are you sure?"

"Yes." She had to do this, no matter what the consequences were.

The woman studied her for a long moment, then relented with a nod. "All right. Then I want you to look at teenage Kiyomi. I want you to look right into her eyes and feel everything she's feeling after graduation. Her pain. Her anger. Her sense of loneliness and isolation. Her betrayal."

The picture that formed was intense. Kiyomi sucked in a breath, her mind screaming at her to stop, her body quivering like a bowstring drawn taut.

"She's hurting and has no one to turn to. No one who cares about her."

It was true. There had been no one, only a distant handler who would check in periodically and hand her new assignments. Unlike some of the other Valkyries, her handler had never become a friend.

"What would you say to her if you could go back in time and be her friend?"

So many things. Everything she'd so desperately wanted to hear from someone—anyone—who gave a shit about her. But there had been no one.

"Look at her and tell her what you want to say," the woman said softly.

Kiyomi knotted her hands together to keep them from shaking, the tension inside her rising, rising. Pushing her toward her breaking point, her insides trembling with dread.

The image of her teenage self in the chair before her was so clear. Horribly, painfully clear.

"It's not your fault," she blurted out. "You did nothing wrong. *They* did this to you. They *used* you. They raped you. Hurt you. They stole your life from you."

Tears scalded the backs of her eyes. She blinked them back, forced more painful words out through chattering teeth while she began to unravel inside.

The lid flew off and all the suppressed emotions exploded out. All the humiliation and shame she'd buried her entire adult life. All the fear and uncertainty. The constant, exhausting roller coaster of adrenaline rushes to counteract her natural fear response, and the artificial numbness afterward to bury it all. The terrible loneliness and exhaustion.

"You're not tainted." Her voice cracked, grief clawing at her.

It wasn't fair. Wasn't fair what had been taken from her, what had been done to her. What she'd been turned into and what she'd been forced to endure because of it.

"Or broken. You have nothing to be ashamed of. Because there's still a piece of you deep inside that they can never touch—that no one can ever touch unless you let them. But you won't, until…"

Marcus.

Against her better judgment, she'd allowed Marcus to touch that secret part of her, even if he wasn't aware of it. And she was terrified that he would see all the ugliness inside her, all the terrible shame she carried from being a government whore for so many years, and reject her.

The tears spilled over, fat and hot as they rolled down her cheeks. More shame welled up, threatening to drown her. Her mind screamed at her to stop, her automatic programming trying to take over.

She wasn't supposed to feel. Wasn't allowed to be weak. But that kept her a slave. She wanted to be free.

"Kiyomi," the therapist said softly, her voice filled with empathy.

She shook her head sharply, refusing to stop. She couldn't stop now. "You're n-not dead inside. You still matter. You're s-still worthy." She sucked in a choppy breath, the vision of her teenage self so clear, the pain in those dark eyes slicing her deep inside.

God, she wanted to hold that girl. Hold her close and tell her she was loved. That the grown-up Kiyomi would protect her no matter what, be there for her through everything.

But she couldn't. That girl was long dead, and only the shattered woman in this chair remained.

"You're worthy," she said in a louder voice, a sharp punch of anger burning through the pain. A deep rage she'd kept bottled up for far too long. "And if I could, I'd go back and k-kill those bastards for what they did to you. I'd kill them all, to stop what's coming. Things you c-can't even imagine—"

She sucked in a breath, dizzy as the rage intensified, a scream building in her throat her mind fast-forwarded through her most memorable ops, ending with Rahman. Of what it had been like to be at his mercy—though he had none. "Because you matter. B-because *I* matter, god d-dammit, and it wasn't fair. It wasn't *fair*!"

Her chair toppled over as she shot to her feet. She was vaguely aware of the therapist's soothing voice in the background, of Trinity rising in the far corner, but she was lost in the storm of memories bombarding her. Of unwanted hands on her body. The sense of continual violation she'd never been able to acknowledge.

She closed her eyes and let it all engulf her. Her mouth opened, a feral scream of rage bursting free. Her entire body corded with it, the sound of all her repressed pain finally given a voice.

Comforting arms enveloped her and drew her into a tight embrace. A familiar scent penetrated the fog of agony.

Trinity.

Like a bullet shattering a pane of glass, the rage splintered, leaving nothing but grief and exhaustion in its wake. She sagged forward, her face pressed to Trinity's chest as she crumpled. Jagged, painful sobs ripped through her, all her pent-up grief flooding out in a river of scalding tears.

She cried until her chest and throat burned. Until her eyes were swollen and sore and she was limp in Trinity's embrace. Somehow they had wound up on the floor. Trinity was on her back, cradling Kiyomi to her, stroking her hair.

"You are worthy and deserving of love," Trinity whispered fiercely, her voice rough. "You're not stained, or broken. You're a survivor. You survived everything they put you through and you're still here. And now you're *free*."

Free. She'd longed for it for so long, but had never let herself hope for it. "Not until Rahman and the others are dead," she managed in a hoarse whisper. The people responsible had to be punished. Only then would it truly be over.

"We'll get them," Trinity vowed, then sniffed and lifted a hand to wipe her face. "We'll get them all."

Kiyomi sighed and laid her head on Trinity's shoulder. She was completely drained, too tired to move. "You're so comfy," she said after a few minutes, grateful for her friend's presence. Trin got her in a way no one else ever could.

A soft chuckle shook Trinity. "Glad I make a good pillow."

Kiyomi wiped at her wet face, a little embarrassed but not morbidly so. The room was still intact. She hadn't freaked out and trashed everything. "So I'm guessing the therapy session's over?"

"Yep. I shut the computer in the therapist's face." She patted Kiyomi's back. "You need a nap and a bottle of wine."

"A nap sounds awesome. Don't move."

Trinity chuckled again and rubbed a hand slowly up and down Kiyomi's back. "You were so damn brave. God, I'm so proud of you. How do you feel right now?"

She thought about it for a moment. "Bruised." Inside

and out.

"Yeah."

Kiyomi's gaze caught on the flash of Trinity's engagement ring. "Did you do this kind of therapy before you met Brody?" Brody Colebrook was sniper team leader with the FBI's Hostage Rescue Team back in the States.

"No, after. And it was not fun. At all."

No, it really wasn't. But damned if she didn't feel a bit lighter inside now.

She toyed with Trinity's ring. A symbol of commitment and faith. Brody knew all about Trinity's past, and he loved her unconditionally. What an incredible thought. "How did you know he was the one?"

"Because I trust him completely. And when I'm with him, it's like the rest of the world ceases to exist."

Yes. She felt like that around Marcus sometimes. "Why haven't you set the date yet?"

Trinity expelled a long breath, pulled her hand out of reach and resumed playing with Kiyomi's hair. It was relaxing. Soothing. "Because I still struggle with feeling unworthy. And that he's better off without me and my stupid baggage."

Surprised, Kiyomi lifted her head to look at her friend that was more like a sister and mother-figure combined. "Do you really feel that way?"

"Sometimes. Deep down, when my insecurities get the better of me." She gave Kiyomi a brave smile. "But I'm working on that."

"Good. You deserve to be happy."

Trinity kissed the top of her head. "We *all* do, sweetheart."

Yes. They did.

Kiyomi frowned, thinking. "Orphans are too vulnerable. Especially young girls. More needs to be done to protect them."

"That's for damn sure."

There must be something Kiyomi could do to make a difference. Help protect them from exploitation. Maybe when this was all over…

She blew out a breath, setting the thought aside. There was so much shit left to be dealt with before she could think about anything else.

They lay there for another few minutes, then Kiyomi gathered the remainder of her waning energy and sat up. "Okay. I'm ready to get outta here now." She stood, righted the chair she'd knocked over and paused to look at the empty one, imagining teenage Kiyomi sitting there watching her.

We're going to be okay, Kiyomi told her silently. *I'll make sure of it.*

She grabbed her journal and pen before leaving the room. At the bottom of the stairs she and Trinity stepped into the stables, the sweet, dusty scent of hay and horses greeting them. Trinity looped an arm across her shoulders. "You did good, kid."

"Thanks. It wasn't pretty, but it was worth it. Thank you for being there."

"Good. And you're welcome. I'll always be there for you."

The vow squeezed her heart.

Together they stepped out into the bright fall sunshine. Kiyomi froze when she saw Marcus coming up the path with Karas limping after him. Their gazes met from about thirty yards apart, and her muscles tensed.

Oh, shit, why *now*?

His dark brows crashed together as he stared at her, concern filling his expression. "What is it? What's wrong?"

"Oh, no," she whispered. All she'd wanted was to get back into the house unseen, and here she'd had to run right into the object of all her fantasies.

"Nothing's wrong," Trinity said, her hand solid on Kiyomi's shoulder.

Kiyomi eased out from under Trinity's arm. "It's okay," she murmured to her friend. "You can go."

Trin eyed her. "You sure?"

"Yes."

"Okay. I'll be around if you need me."

Kiyomi nodded, her eyes on Marcus as Trinity walked off toward the house. She slid her hands into the back pockets of her jeans, knowing she looked a mess but there was no help for it.

Marcus walked up and stopped in front of her, his eyes searching hers, that worried frown still in place. "What happened?"

"I had a really intense therapy session I'd been dreading for a while, that's all." She shrugged, gave him a wry smile. "But I survived."

He lifted a hand toward her, paused for a moment as if he thought better of it, then warmth burst through her when his palm cradled the side of her cheek. His gaze swept over her face, taking in her blotchy skin and swollen eyes. With a low sound he dropped his cane and wrapped his arms around her, drawing her to his broad, hard chest.

She sucked in a sharp breath as all her senses came to life. She leaned into him, closed her sore eyes and rested her cheek in the hollow of his shoulder, feeling like she was dreaming. Floating. Because this couldn't be real. Marcus couldn't really be holding her the way she'd been imagining.

"Brave lass," he murmured in his deep, Yorkshire accent. His tone and words warmed her like a fire on a cold winter's night.

God he felt incredible, the raw strength of his arms making her feel protected and cherished. Safe in a way she never had before. Because she knew that this man would stand between her and any threat if she'd let him.

The thought gave her pause.

She'd been trained to be a man's fantasy, whatever that may be. It was easy for her to figure out what they wanted, and in order to get what she wanted, she gave it to them. While she was being intimate with someone, she shut down inside, disassociated from the physical part.

It wouldn't be like that with Marcus. It would be totally different, because his attraction to her made her *want* to engage rather than shut down. But what was his fantasy? She could do it all: demure and submissive, sex kitten, bold and confident, dominatrix, innocent, and everything in between. What did he prefer?

Sighing, she cuddled closer, allowing her mind to drift even as her body remained vividly awake, an almost humming sensation traveling over her skin.

One big hand began gently stroking her hair. She squeezed her eyes shut, every lonely part of her soaking up the affection like a parched sponge. She wanted to turn her head and kiss him. Lose herself in the comfort and pleasure he might offer, but she sensed he wasn't ready for it yet, and right at this moment she was too raw and fragile inside anyway.

She thought he brushed a kiss to the crown of her head, then he released her and leaned back to look down into her face. "Do you need anything?"

You.

She wrestled the word back before it could come out. "Just a little rest, maybe." With him. God, how amazing would it feel to have him wrapped around her as she drifted off?

He nodded once. "I'll take you back inside."

She was about to tell him she didn't need an escort, but shut her mouth because she wanted to spend as much time with him as possible, even the minute it would take them to get into the house.

Marcus bent, picked up his cane, then gave her a gentle smile that warmed her insides before setting his free hand at the small of her back. They walked side by side while Karas limped ahead of them, the heat of his palm sinking through her sweater.

His touch was protective rather than proprietary. Silently telling her he had her back. And that meant more than anything he could possibly have said.

"Poor Karas," she said, watching the dog hobble up the gravel path.

"She'll be all right." He shot her a sideways glance. "She's strong, like you. And some rest will do both of you good."

Inside the house she expected him to drop his hand and leave. Instead he paused inside the back door and looked down at her. "Fancy a nap on the couch by the fire while I get some work done?"

She smiled, her heart fluttering. He wanted more time with her too, or maybe he sensed she'd feel safer with him there to keep watch. "I'd like that."

He nodded once. "Go on then, get settled. I'll make you a hot brew."

Too tired to protest, she made her way to the study. Karas went with her, flopping down on her bed in front of the fire with a loud groan and immediately shut her eyes, as if the short walk to the stable and back had exhausted her.

Kiyomi sat on the tufted leather sofa and opened her journal. She sometimes jotted down things after a session, but right now she was too drained.

Marcus came in a few minutes later with a mug. "It's green tea and honey," he said, handing it to her.

"Thank you."

He nodded and knelt beside the dog to stroke her head a few times before stacking kindling and logs in the grate. "This'll keep you both warm as toast," he said, striking a long match and lighting the kindling.

Warm, golden-orange light flickered over her, the heat already spilling out into the room. "Here," he told her, laying one of the throw pillows on the end of the sofa flat. "Stretch out."

Feeling a little silly but also like a pampered princess, Kiyomi laid down and curled up on her side, her notebook beside her and pen still in her hand. Maybe she'd rest for a bit and then do some writing in here where it was quiet.

Marcus took a woven tartan blanket from the wide ottoman that served as a coffee table, shook it out and spread it over her. Her heart squeezed when he gently tucked it around her, then straightened, his deep brown gaze sweeping her face as he passed a gentle hand over her hair.

"Sleep for a while," he murmured, that low, accented voice wrapping around her.

The emotional purge earlier had exhausted her. Being tucked all cozy and warm beneath the blanket that smelled of Marcus while he watched over her from his desk allowed her mind to relax completely. She was safe, cared about, and the sound of the fire crackling in the hearth soon had her eyes drifting shut.

One last thought drifted through her mind before she faded into sleep, bringing a spurt of anxiety. Marcus was here, watching her.

She prayed her subconscious would keep her nightmares at bay.

Chapter Seven

Marcus glanced up from his computer screen a while later when Kiyomi's breathing suddenly turned choppy. The fire was burning low in the grate. He couldn't see her from his vantage point behind his desk, but he could see the edge of the pillow move as she shifted.

She made a distressed sound and moved restlessly, still asleep. On her bed next to the fire, Karas lifted her head, her gaze trained on Kiyomi.

Marcus reached for his cane and quietly pushed to his feet, then waited. He could see her now, lying on her side. Her brows were drawn together in a deep frown and she seemed agitated. His heart went out to her. Nightmares and night terrors were horrifically raw and real for anyone experiencing them.

For someone who had undergone capture and torture like they had, it was hell.

When she made another low sound and her legs twitched as if she was kicking someone in her dream, he couldn't stand by and watch her suffer a moment more. He quickly rounded his desk and went down on one knee in front of the sofa. Her notebook lay on the floor. She still had the pen clutched in her hand.

He set his cane down and reached a hand toward her shoulder. "Kiyomi."

Her eyes flew open, blind with panic and terror. Her fist drove upward, the end of the pen aimed at his face. Marcus reared his head back and caught her wrist in his hand just in time, stopping it inches from his eye.

Realizing what she'd done, Kiyomi heaved upright with a wrenching gasp and tore her hand free, dropping the pen as she shrank back into the corner of the sofa. "Sorry," she whispered hoarsely, her face pale. "Sorry."

"It's all right."

She shook her head and scooted farther away from him, dragging a trembling hand through her hair.

He couldn't bear to watch her berate herself for something she had no control over. "It's all right," he repeated in a low voice. "No harm done. And I know what that kind of nightmare is like."

She dragged a hand over her pale face and exhaled a shaky breath, still avoiding his gaze. "Yeah, I bet you do."

They had that in common, something none of the others could relate to. "Here." He offered her the mug of unfinished tea. "It's cold now, but the honey will help."

Kiyomi accepted it and took a sip, still not looking at him. "Thank you."

He didn't answer, trying to think of something to say to ease her embarrassment. To his surprise she set the mug down, leaned forward and wrapped her arms around his neck.

Recovering fast, he drew her close, pushing up onto the sofa to draw her into his lap. Kiyomi nestled in closer, and the way she pressed her face into the side of his neck squeezed his heart like a fist. This woman was as strong as they came. For her to reach for him like this and admit she wanted him to hold her told him just how shaken she was, and how much she trusted him.

"You're safe," he murmured against her hair. It smelled like strawberries and she felt like heaven, soft and warm in his arms. "You're safe now."

She inhaled deeply and let the breath out slowly, her arms tight around his neck.

Marcus held her like that for a few minutes. Slowly her grip on him relaxed, but she didn't let go. Didn't try to pull away, still wanting to be close. Unable to help himself, he nuzzled her hair with his cheek, eased one hand up and down her back in a soothing motion.

She sighed and seemed to melt into his hold. "I keep dreaming the same thing over and over," she whispered finally.

His hand paused on her back. "About what?" he asked, and resumed the motion.

She was silent a long moment. "Rahman."

He made a low sound that told her he was listening, but didn't say anything, waiting for her to decide whether she wanted to say more.

"I'm chained to the floor in my cell," she continued and Marcus's whole body went taut, outrage and protectiveness roaring through him. "He's got the whip in his hand. And I can't move. I know what's coming, but I can't get away no matter what I do."

His own ghosts stirred, sending a ripple of cold over his skin.

Cold. Hungry. Tired. Pain.

Hands and feet tied to the chair they'd shoved him into the day before.

The man in the mask standing in front of him with the metal pipe in his hands. Waiting to slam it into Marcus's pulverized thigh again.

He banished the horrific memory, focused on the scent and feel of Kiyomi instead. "Helplessness." He knew it all too well.

Kiyomi lifted her head, their faces inches apart as she

stared into his eyes. Hers were like mirrors, a deep, liquid brown so dark he could see his own reflection in them. "Did the men who hurt you die?"

"Eventually, yes." Unfortunately he hadn't been given the satisfaction of killing them himself. He curved his palm around the back of her head, gently ran it down the cool, silky fall of her straight hair to where it stopped between her shoulder blades.

"One day I'm going to kill Rahman for what he did to me."

The conviction and steely edge to her words sent a streak of foreboding through him. He believed her. Without a doubt, she would find a way to make it happen. Though it likely wouldn't make her feel much better.

She searched his eyes a moment. "Does that change the way you see me?"

"No." He understood her need to kill the man who had terrorized her, left her scarred inside and out. But if she thought taking Rahman's life would make everything okay, she was in for a huge disappointment.

Lifting a hand, she grazed her fingertips over the beard on the right side of his jaw. Marcus stilled as sensation sparked across his nerve endings, a surge of heat rushing through him. With superhuman effort he kept his hands on her back, instead of plunging them into her hair to bring his mouth down on hers.

He stayed perfectly still while his heart tried to pound out of his chest, the light brush of her fingers trailing over his chin to the other, scarred side of his face, and finally to the corner of his mouth.

His fingers flexed against her back as need slammed into him. He'd never wanted to kiss a woman this badly, but he wanted to mean something more than comfort to her, and he was a selfish bastard for wanting her when she'd been through so much.

She drew the tip of her index finger across his lower

lip, her expression absorbed as she studied it. He stared at her mouth, just inches away, his muscles rigid with the need to kiss her, taste her.

Catching her wrist, he held her gently and pressed a slow, tender kiss to the pad of her finger. He glanced up in time to see her pupils dilate, those gorgeous lips part as she leaned forward a fraction.

It was like trying to fight gravity. He was falling toward her and there was no stopping it, no matter if he shouldn't touch her, no matter that he wasn't worthy.

Biting back a groan, he surrendered to the inexorable pull between them and angled his head to cover her mouth with his.

Kiyomi slid her hands into his hair and returned the kiss. He held her still, forcing her to take it slow as he learned the shape and feel of her lips. Soft, pliant, he sank into them, exploring first the top and then the bottom as he caressed and nibbled. It was tender. Reverent.

He wanted to give, not take. Give her as much or as little of him as she wanted. She'd been forced to do things that would have broken most people. He wanted her to feel safe with him, to know that he held complete control over himself and wouldn't rush her.

Her tiny moan went straight to his groin, making him rock hard in his jeans beneath the weight of her backside.

Kiyomi's fingers dug harder into his scalp, her mouth opening in invitation beneath his. Needing more, he cradled her face in his hands and touched his tongue to her lower lip before gently easing it along the inner seam.

She made a soft sound and touched her tongue to his, the motion so erotic it made the blood pound in his ears. He caressed her softly, the restraint intensifying the heat pulsing through him. Kiyomi wiggled closer, her rear shifting against his erect cock and her breasts flattening to his chest.

Marcus couldn't hold back the rough groan at the

back of his throat. She felt so bloody perfect, better than anything he'd imagined. He wanted to touch and taste her all over, strip off everything she wore so he could drown her in the pleasure she deserved, the best antidote he could think of to erase the pain and terror she'd suffered.

Something cold and wet poked into the side of his face.

Startled, Marcus drew back to find Karas's face inches from their own. She stared into his eyes, ears perked, tail wagging in a hesitant swish.

Kiyomi laughed as she slid off his lap. "Is she jealous?"

Marcus scowled at his dog and gently swept her aside with one arm. "Away wi' ye, green-eyed monster."

Instead of obeying, Karas plopped her back end down on the rug and stared at him with accusing eyes.

Kiyomi laughed again, the bright sound making him smile. "I see I've got a rival."

"No." No one could ever rival Kiyomi. He ruffled the top of Karas's head and pointed at her bed by the fire. "Bed. Now."

Karas almost glared back at him, then sulkily turned and limped over to her bed, flopping down with a theatrical sigh and gazing up at him with wounded eyes.

"She should be on stage," Kiyomi said.

Marcus grinned. "Aye. Drama queen." Damn, he loved her though. Karas was as loyal as they came, and she'd got him through some dark times with her unconditional acceptance and love.

He faced Kiyomi, sorry she'd moved away from him. "Sorry about that," he muttered.

"It's okay." Her lips curved, a soft look in her eyes. "Thank you."

He frowned. "For what?"

"My first real kiss." She rose before he could say anything, notebook in hand, and walked out of the room.

Marcus stared after her, feeling like she'd just knocked the breath out of him. It took every bit of willpower he possessed not to go after her, drag her back inside and press her up against the door so he could kiss her again, this time with full body contact.

He expelled a hard breath. As much as he wanted her, it was probably never going to happen. His job was to protect her, not get her into his bed.

There were faceless, lethal enemies out there wanting to see her and the others dead. Marcus was prepared to do whatever was necessary to keep Kiyomi safe.

Even if it meant letting her go.

****

The whir of saws and screwdrivers echoed in the vast space of the warehouse as Janelle walked through the building site. Everything was finally coming together, after dumping more funds into the project and motivating the project manager to get it moving. In another few weeks, this place would be ready.

Shortly after that, the first test subjects would arrive. And if everything went according to plan, the woman who had inspired this entire project would be back where she belonged at last.

"Janelle. I didn't realize you were coming in."

She put on a smile for the project manager as he approached. "I like to keep on top of things."

His eyes gleamed with unmistakable interest, hoping for the repeat performance he wasn't going to get. Even though she was in her late-fifties, she still had it, and looked far younger than her age. "Yes, you do."

Fucking him hadn't been a complete chore, but it had done the job in motivating him to get things with the facility back on schedule. And he was so clueless about what was going on here, she didn't even have to kill him when this was done. "Everything's going smoothly, I trust?"

"Perfect."

"That's what I like to hear." Her cell rang. The caller was in the UK, where she'd had a team combing through newspapers and other data, trying to locate any of the missing Valkyries. "Excuse me." Moving a discreet distance away so the PM couldn't overhear, she answered.

"I think we might have found something," the female voice said. One of her operatives.

"Oh?" Up on the second floor they were installing the sound-proofing material inside the test rooms. None of the crew had any idea what they were for. Everyone thought this was going to be a medical research lab, looking for cures for cancer, MS and ALS.

That wasn't even close to the truth, but it suited her purpose.

"We've been following up dozens of new leads. None of them have panned out yet, but this one caught our interest. A story out of a town here in the Cotswolds."

Janelle's attention sharpened. Every potential lead they'd followed had resulted in a dead end. "I'm listening."

"I've sent you the link, but basically three teenagers were caught doing stupid shit on Bonfire Night. That's—"

"I know what it is. And?"

"It involves a disabled veteran. There are no names mentioned, but the description of the event was interesting. The boys claim someone jumped out of a tree and attacked them, using flashbangs to stun them, then took them all down singlehandedly, stripped them and left them tied to a tree for an hour or two. One of them specifically used the word 'ninja.' Other reports from locals say it couldn't be the veteran, and two of the boys said the person who attacked them was slightly built."

"So it could have been a woman." Perhaps even a Valkyrie.

"Yes."

Janelle smiled. Men always underestimated them. Teenage boys would be no different. "Anything else?"

"A police report was filed by a guy named Marcus Laidlaw, a disabled vet. I checked a map of the area and there's a large property called Laidlaw Hall. Matches the address listed. Locals say he's sort of a hermit, keeps to himself mostly, but there've been cars coming and going from there recently. He's got no family, no close friends that anyone knows of."

"It could be their base," she finished, intrigued by the idea. "What's the name of the town?"

"Stow-on-the-Wold. Heart of the Cotswolds, thirty minute drive from Cheltenham."

Where members of the missing Valkyrie team had last been spotted nine days earlier. Her pulse picked up. The timing and location fit. This could be it. "Start doing some recon."

"Already working on it. Got a team ready to pose as city workers fixing a water line in the area."

"Good. Keep me informed." She ended the call and read the article, the scientific part of her fascinated by the prospect of Valkyries teaming up and living in a secluded location.

Looked like she would be flying across the pond any day now to put the final phase into action. Right after she laid the groundwork for the invitation she would be sending.

Glancing around her facility one last time, Janelle took in every delicious detail and envisioning what would happen here soon. Seeing her design brought to life was almost as thrilling as what she was on the verge of accomplishing.

After more than two decades, she was closer than

ever to finding her remaining targets, who were now all in their early to late thirties. How convenient for her if they'd decided to stay together in one place.

Once she found them, it was just a matter of separating the wheat from the chaff.

The blueprints were in place. Her soldiers were ready to be deployed. Planning and design were her specialties—she just used them in non-traditional applications.

She smiled to herself as she walked to her vehicle, the physical form of her dream nearing completion behind her.

And to think her parents had said she wouldn't amount to anything as an architect.

Chapter Eight

Kiyomi mentally prepared herself before entering Amber's room the next morning after breakfast. As usual Marcus had been up and gone by the time she'd arrived in the breakfast room.

Things had finally shifted between them last night. She wanted him more than ever, and time was running out. She was torn between wanting to leave to spare him more pain and danger, and wanting to stay.

Trinity was peering over Amber's shoulder as Kiyomi approached them. Three computer screens were set up on the wide desk beneath the picture window overlooking the west lawn. Kiyomi pretended her heart and head weren't at war. "Well, roomie? What do you think of my final contenders?"

She had been in charge of finding places for everyone to rent in the Coventry area once they moved out of Laidlaw Hall. While everyone else moved in with their significant other, she and Trinity would be roommates.

"I'm leaning toward the cottage," Trinity replied, her eyes on screen as she draped an arm across Kiyomi's shoulders. "Only because it's more private."

"Works for me. Moving date still set for the end of the week?"

Trinity nodded, studying the map on screen where

Amber had put a series of red dots to mark everyone's rental accommodations. They were grouped within a few miles of each other, making logistics easier. "Maybe sooner, depending on how this shakes out."

A wave of sadness hit her. She loved it here and wanted more time with Marcus. Though it was for the best if they left soon. He'd done more than enough for them, and he'd put himself at risk by having them here in the first place. Sure he was former SAS and could handle himself, but she didn't want to endanger him any further. They all had targets on their backs. The bounty made her a high-risk houseguest. "Anything new on Rahman from those possible sightings I sent you?"

"Yep." Amber switched keyboards and began typing something. "Last sighting of him was when he left Latakia the other night."

A coastal town almost a four-hour drive from Damascus, the capital city being his usual base of operations. "Visiting his mother, I presume." He went there so infrequently it was impossible to target him there. It was also hard to believe a monster like that even had a mother, but for some reason he doted on her. That made his cruel treatment of women all the worse.

"Must have been. The last security cam footage I have of his vehicle is leaving the city at twenty-one-hundred-hours two nights ago. I couldn't find it entering Damascus after that."

"He'd have changed vehicles again. Probably won't go back to Damascus for a few days now anyway." That was his pattern, never going straight back to the capital after he'd been away. Always trying to throw off anyone who might be trying to track him.

She straightened, didn't resist when Trinity pulled her closer and gave her a squeeze. "A lot of smart people are looking for him. Only a matter of time before he makes a mistake, and then we've got him," Trin said.

Kiyomi nodded, tamping down her frustration. Finding Rahman couldn't happen fast enough for her liking. She needed *them* to be the ones to get a bead on him, not leave his capture up to another organization or government.

Amber turned slightly to aim a smile at her, green eyes sparkling. "In happier news, I found your DNA results listed in your old Program files."

"Oh." She hadn't even known Amber was looking for that. "Anything in there about who my father was?"

"Nope. But I did find something else you might find interesting." A few keystrokes later, another map popped up on screen. "You've still got relatives living in Japan."

Kiyomi held her breath as she studied the dots on the map and names on screen. "Who are they?"

"Most are distant, from what I can tell. But there's one lady who I'm pretty sure was your mom's half-sibling living in Kiyoto."

Kiyomi had never known her mother had any siblings. A smile spread across her face, awe and excitement temporarily banishing all thoughts of Rahman. "My aunt."

"Yes." Amber smiled at her. "You've definitely got family out there."

But none of them wanted me. Kiyomi blocked the thought and wrapped her arm around Trinity and set her other hand on Amber's shoulder to squeeze it. "I've already found my family." They might come from completely different backgrounds and had only known each other for a short time, but these women were like blood to her.

"If we're having a group hug, I want in," a voice said from behind them.

Chloe sauntered in wearing a long-sleeve T-shirt that read *I love a good bang*, her blond hair plaited in a long braid. Kiyomi lifted an arm to invite her in and they all chuckled as they did a group hug. "What did we find to-day?" Chloe asked, the scent of her mint gum wafting in the air.

"Some of Kiyomi's relatives in Japan. I've been looking into everyone's families, trying to find anyone who might be a surviving relative."

"Yeah? Cool." She chewed her gum as she studied the screens in front of them. "What about you and Me-gan?" she asked Amber. "Any luck finding your rela-tives?"

"Still trying to track down our long lost aunt. I'm down to eleven possible leads. It's tricky to ask the women on my list what I need to know without giving away anything sensitive about our backgrounds."

"If anyone can do it, it's you," Chloe said.

"In theory, yes." Amber swiveled in her chair to face them, an annoyed expression on her face. "A second cousin I'd contacted took it upon herself to reach out to one of the women on my shortlist of suspects."

"Why?" Kiyomi asked, immediately suspicious. "Just being nosy?"

"Not sure, but I'm keeping close tabs on her. She doesn't even know me, has no way of verifying anything I say, yet she drops everything to help track a possible distant relative down?"

"Maybe she's a busybody with nothing else to do," Chloe said, jaw working as she chewed her gum. "Or maybe she's just really nice and actually wants to help."

Amber's expression said she didn't believe that last part one iota. "I'm watching her, just in case."

Chloe nodded. "What are you gonna do if you find your aunt?"

"Get closure."

Kiyomi didn't blame her. The rest of them hadn't had any immediate family to take them in after their parent or parents had died. For Amber and Megan's aunt to give them up to avoid inconvenience to her own life was beyond shitty, even if she hadn't realized what would become of them.

"And what about Rahman and the Architect. Anything new there?" Chloe asked.

"Rahman's in the wind again," Kiyomi said, unable to stem a surge of frustration. "Still no solid leads on the connection between him and the Architect. I've racked my brain and I can't think of anyone who it could be."

Chloe nodded, then her expression brightened as she turned her attention to the first screen. "Now this is more like it." Her eyes gleamed as she studied the figures. "How much money've we got now?"

Amber laughed. She'd been secretly funneling funds away from human traffickers, terrorists and other criminals they'd tangled with, hiding it all away in various accounts in the Caymans, Bahamas and Switzerland. "More than enough for each of us to walk away from this and live in luxury for the rest of our lives."

Since Kiyomi was good with numbers, she and Trinity had been helping Amber manage the finances. While she didn't know the exact total at the moment, it broke down to over twenty million US per Valkyrie so far—and counting.

The catch was, when this was finally all over, for security reasons they would all likely have to split up and go their separate ways under new identities.

An ache started up beneath Kiyomi's sternum at the thought of never seeing her fellow Valkyries again. But if the only way to ensure their safety was to go ahead with the WITSEC-style program they'd been working on, then that was just how it had to be.

And there was someone else who deserved a share of the pot too. "What about Marcus?" Kiyomi asked.

Trinity blinked at her. "What about him?"

"We're going to compensate him for everything, for

having us all here, right?"

He deserved at least that. She'd seen him poring over his spreadsheets, juggling his finances and paying endless bills for repairs and the staff required to keep Laidlaw Hall from falling apart. Running a place like this cost a fortune and he'd already had to sell off over half the property when he'd first inherited it in order to pay off debts accrued against it.

"Yeah, of course," Amber answered. "The six of us will talk about that when the time comes and come up with a number we can all agree on."

Kiyomi nodded, satisfied. She would give him a share of her cut if she didn't think the number was high enough. He was a private man, but she knew he'd come to like having them all here. She hated to think of him holing up here all by himself, shutting out the rest of the world and just going through the motions of living once they all left. After what he'd endured, he deserved to truly live again and find happiness.

Even if it wasn't with her.

They all turned at a knock on the door. Kiyomi's heart leapt when she saw Marcus in the doorway, cane in hand and Karas beside him. His gaze locked with hers, and her welcoming smile faded at the seriousness of his expression. "Something wrong?" she asked.

"We've been called to MI6 HQ in London," he said, looking between her and Trinity.

"Why?"

The sharp chime of a ringtone went off. Trinity removed her arm from Kiyomi's waist and fished her cell out of her pocket. "That'll be Rycroft," Marcus said.

Alex Rycroft, former NSA legend. Trinity had done contract work for him over the past few years, and he was close with another Valkyrie named Briar.

As soon as Rycroft had heard about the threat against them all, he'd stepped up and offered to help spearhead their mission. He had enough contacts and pull with intelligence agencies all over the world that he continued to be a valuable asset for them, acting as their liaison without compromising their location or identities.

Trinity answered the phone, watching Marcus. "Hey, good timing. I hear some of us are going to London?" She paused, listening, then nodded. "Understood. We'll meet you there."

"What's going on?" Kiyomi said to Marcus as Trinity ended the call.

His eyes were grave. "The SAS is conducting an op to raid a militant camp in the Syrian Desert tonight. Rahman's suspected to be there."

She stopped breathing, her heart beating faster. "Capture or kill order?"

"Capture. It's my former squadron. One of my former troopers is the assault team leader. They want us in the ops room when it happens so you can help ID Rahman and his inner circle. And also because they feel you could offer real-time insights on what he might do."

Because of her...intimate association with him.

A protest rushed into her throat but she swallowed it down. Wanting to bring Rahman down personally was secondary to nailing his oily ass to the wall. If the SAS captured him, then she could come up with a plan to kill him once he was in custody.

Kiyomi straightened. "When are we leaving?"

****

It had been more than two years since Marcus had stepped foot in this place, and yet it felt like yesterday as they cleared initial security and drove beneath the SIS building at Vauxhall Cross on the south bank of the Thames.

Alex Rycroft was waiting for them next to the secure

elevator in the underground car park beneath the building. A tall, fit man in his mid-fifties, he'd been a vital part of the current Valkyrie mission from its inception.

Upstairs, Marcus's former commander was waiting outside the ops room. "Laidlaw. Good to see you."

"Ken." Marcus shook his hand.

Ken turned to Kiyomi, an intrigued smile on his face. "And you must be Ms. Tanaka."

She shook his hand. "Hello."

After exchanging pleasantries with Rycroft and Trinity, Ken gestured for Kiyomi and Marcus to follow him into the secure ops room. "We've got a headset for you," he told Kiyomi, gesturing for her to approach the bank of monitors mounted on the far wall, and the team of analysts monitoring them from desks below.

Marcus followed and hung back with Ken as another aide spoke to Kiyomi and explained what was going on. The first two screens showed views of the target camp; one via satellite and the other via thermal-imaging drone. "What are the odds that Rahman's there?" he asked Ken.

"Upwards of ninety-percent."

Marcus watched Kiyomi as she stood in front of the monitor showing the drone footage. Her posture was relaxed, her expression calm, but he knew what this op meant to her.

She would have mixed feelings about not being there, but at least if they captured Rahman tonight, they would be able to interrogate and pump him for intel. He wished he could be leading the op and capture Rahman for her. Kill him even, once they had what they needed.

Someone handed Ken a sat phone. He answered, spoke to whoever it was for a moment, then passed it to Marcus. "It's Rory."

A sudden, suffocating pressure closed around his lungs as a picture of his mate's face flashed in his mind, bringing with it other images he wished he could forget.

He forced in a deep breath and took the phone, blocking the rush of memories. "Rory."

"So you are still alive. I wasn't convinced until just now," Rory said dryly in his Geordie accent. "How are you, mate?"

"Fair t' middlin'. How are things there? The lads ready?"

"Always. I hear you'll be watching it live?"

"Looks that way."

"Well, take notes. I'm gonna show you how it's supposed to be done."

Marcus cracked a grin. "That's some bloody cheek."

"Learned it from the best. Anyway, just wanted to say hello before the curtain goes up on this thing. And next time I'm back in the UK, we're meeting for a pint."

Marcus could do better than that. "You can come stay with me for a while."

"An invitation to your fancy big house? I'm flattered."

"Don't let it go to your head."

"Too late." Someone said something in the background. "Gotta go, we're wheels up in five minutes. Enjoy the show."

Marcus handed the sat phone back to Ken. "Can't believe how much I've missed that tosser."

"He grows on you over time, though, doesn't he?" Ken said with a fond smile.

Marcus stood a ways back from Kiyomi as the four teams took off from their base, loaded onto two helos. The room went silent and the audio feed began on the headsets.

Marcus recognized Rory's voice as he issued commands. The third screen on the wall switched to a view from Rory's helmet cam, the landscape lit up in green by the night vision optics.

Minutes later the lead helo touched down. Rory's

team jumped out, breaking into two assault elements as they rushed up the back side of the hill toward the camp perimeter. An overhead view from the drones showed the heat signatures of the troopers as they got into position.

Marcus's muscles tightened, his pulse picking up as he waited for the order. Watching from this side of the camera was difficult, highlighting just how useless he'd become.

A few minutes later, Rory's voice came through the headset. "Execute."

The men burst from behind cover and converged on the camp. Taken by surprise, the sentries scrambled to fire but were cut down. Seconds later Rory's team was at the main structure door. The screen went neon with the bursts of light as they breached the doors and rushed in.

An echo of adrenaline coursed through Marcus. Part of him felt like he was there making the assault. If he hadn't been wounded and medically retired, it would have been him leading the op and giving orders. He knew their every move, anticipated every action and reaction as the team cleared the building.

I should be there.

It killed him to be out of the action, to stand here holding his fucking cane and be forced to watch his former teammates carry out the op without him. Unable to go after the man who had hurt Kiyomi so badly. Although if he hadn't been wounded, he never would have met her.

The enemy body count piled up both inside and outside the main building. In a matter of minutes, it was all over.

"Main building's clear," Rory reported. "Starting ID process."

Marcus shifted his focus back to Kiyomi. She hadn't moved, was still standing before the screen showing Rory's helmet cam, watching intently.

As the faces of the prisoners and casualties began to

flood in, analysts ran them through their software. Kiyomi stopped them three times to verify an ID, giving them her insider info about the men she'd flagged.

Ten minutes later, the team was finished searching the camp.

Kiyomi turned to look at him, a frown creasing her forehead as she said what Marcus had already begun to dread. "He's not there."

Chapter Nine

Conflicting emotions clashed inside Kiyomi as she stared at Marcus. Anger because Rahman had managed yet again to escape justice. Relief because now she might still have a chance to bring him down personally.

MI6 had been so sure Rahman would be at the camp. Either they'd received bad intel, or he'd been warned in time to escape. She was betting on the latter.

Frowning, the MI6 agent who'd been speaking with Marcus strode forward, scanning the monitor in front of the analyst she had just been working with to identify the enemy prisoners and casualties. "Are you sure?" he asked her.

She shot him a hard look. "Positive." She removed her headset and tossed it onto the desk beside her. "Someone tipped him off." She walked straight to Marcus, drawn to him by an invisible force she couldn't resist. His strength, calm and protectiveness were irresistible.

He stayed at her side as they passed through the inner security doors to the next room, where Rycroft and Trinity were waiting. "He wasn't there," Kiyomi told them.

Rycroft gave a nod, spoke briefly to the military official who had granted them all access, then motioned for Kiyomi and the others to follow him out of the room. He waited until they all were down in the underground lot before speaking.

"What do you want to do about Rahman?" he asked, looking between her and Trinity.

"Fly to Damascus as soon as possible," Kiyomi answered, drawing sharp looks from Marcus and Trinity. *So I can nail his ass personally.*

Trinity watched her for a moment, then nodded. "You two go ahead and drive back to the manor," she said to Kiyomi and Marcus. "Alex and I will talk everything over, and I'll let everyone know what our next step will be as soon as I know."

Kiyomi wanted to stay and fight for the Damascus option, but she didn't know Rycroft well and Trinity was team leader. Kiyomi trusted her implicitly. If there was a way to get a green light for an op in Damascus targeting Rahman, Trinity would make it happen.

She turned to Marcus. If she couldn't stay and fight for what she wanted, then she wanted to leave and selfishly eat up all the time she could get alone with him instead. Because if she went after Rahman, there was a good chance she might not come back from it. "Shall we go?"

With a nod he crossed to where they'd parked their rental vehicle, a new Range Rover with tinted windows. He unlocked it and opened her door for her, earning a smile from her. She loved how old fashioned he was in his manners. And it gave her butterflies just thinking of the way he'd kissed her last night. "Thanks."

He glanced at her as he started the engine a few moments later. "Are you all right?"

"Fine." Rahman was still free but he wouldn't be that way forever, and at least this way her plan might still happen.

Outside the building, the London traffic was insane as usual. It took them almost thirty minutes just to get across the Thames via the Vauxhall Bridge Road, and forty more to reach the M40. Not that she was complaining. Being alone with him helped settle her chaotic emotions.

"I'm starving," she announced when they finally merged onto the motorway. "Can we stop somewhere on the way and grab something to eat?" Yeah, she was using stall tactics, not wanting the few hours they had alone to pass too quickly.

"Aye, I could do with some scran too." He changed lanes and they finally picked up a bit of speed as the traffic thinned out a little.

Neither of them spoke for the next several minutes. Then he asked, "If you go to Damascus, how will you find him?"

"Amber. She'll have to come too."

"And if you find him, then what? You'll all capture him together?"

"For a start." Unless they got a break about the Architect before then. The only reason they would need to capture Rahman rather than kill him outright was to extract that intel. If he was no longer needed for that purpose, she could move on to the more satisfying phase of her plan.

"Are you so sure that's where he's gone?"

"Sure as I can be. It's what he usually does, moves around in between visits to his power base in the capital." She should know, she'd spent weeks studying and following him before entering his circle. He was a disgusting pig disguised in a pretty package.

"How large a team would you take?"

She shrugged. "Five people maybe, I dunno. That'll be up to Trinity, since she's team leader."

"If you go, I'm coming with you."

She jerked her head around to stare at him, caught off guard. "Why would you do that?"

His jaw flexed, his eyes fixed on the road ahead of them. "Because I want to be there and help get that bastard."

Warmth flooded her at the steely edge to his voice. "That's really kind of you, but—"

He cut her off with a hard look. "I'm well qualified and still capable of holding my own on an op, even with my physical…limitations."

"I know you are," she said quietly, sorry she'd wounded his already bruised pride.

Watching his former teammates conduct the op without him tonight must have been hard, and she'd just jabbed the equivalent of a sharp stick in that newly opened wound. "I'd have you on my team any day, because I know how skilled you are, and because I trust that you'd have my back."

That seemed to appease him because the tension in his shoulders eased. "I would."

"I know." But hearing it from him made her heart turn over. As incredible as it seemed, this amazing man who had suffered so much wanted to protect and avenge her. *Her*. Not some fantasy version of herself that she'd played for so many others throughout her life. Just her, baggage and all.

"What made you want to join the SAS?" she asked, curious.

"The challenge of it. The brotherhood. Being in the thick of the action."

She understood what that was like. Shitty as the Valkyrie Program had been in some aspects, she had loved the feeling of being a part of something so elite. "Did you love it?"

His expression turned fond, a faraway look in his eyes. "Aye. Most of the time."

"What part of selection did you find the hardest?"

"Jungle training. Six weeks working in upwards of ninety-degree heat and the same in humidity, being bitten by every insect that came across me in the Brunei jungle. You're constantly wet, itching and bleeding. Then there are the infections and fever."

"Sounds lovely," she said dryly.

He lifted a shoulder. "In those conditions, a man finds out in short order whether he has what it takes or not. But I was either going to pass the training or leave in a body bag."

That made her smile. In the sorts of training they'd endured, mental toughness was key. More important than skill or physical condition, and often was the deciding factor between success and failure. "And that's exactly why you made it."

He smiled back, his eyes shining with admiration. "Aye. And you."

Sometimes she forgot how much he knew about the Program, from Megan. The temptation to lean across the seat and kiss him was overwhelming. She didn't want him to be in danger again, especially not because of her.

Last night had made her want him even more. He'd kissed her with so much tenderness and care, all the restrained heat she could sense in him tightly leashed, maybe because he'd been worried about scaring her if he let it out. He'd even stopped things when she'd been trying to push him for more. Refusing to rush her or let her rush him.

That had never happened to her before. Every other man she'd been with had wanted to get her into bed as fast as possible. None of them had ever elicited any emotion or sensations in her.

Only Marcus. He made her feel beautiful instead of damaged or broken. Strong instead of weak. Safe. Cherished, even. Around him all she felt was a sense of antic-ipation and yearning…and arousal for the first time in a man's presence.

She glanced at his hands, wrapped around the steer-ing wheel as he drove them through slower moving traf-fic. Strong, clean, long-fingered. A shiver of excitement passed through her as she imagined them moving over her bare skin.

"There's a pub about thirty miles from here that does good pies," he said, tearing her from her wayward thoughts. "That okay?"

"Sounds great." She enjoyed the comfortable quiet between them for the remainder of the drive. The inn was an old, two-story beam and plaster building from the 1700s just off the motorway.

Marcus got them a cozy table for two by the fire. The ceiling was held up by dark, hand-hewn timbers and the interior walls were bare stone. Bathed in warm firelight, they each ate a chicken and mushroom pie and washed it down with a glass of dark beer. He even talked her into sticky toffee pudding for dessert.

"I can't believe you've never had it," he said as he finished off his beer.

"I never ate dessert until I met you," she answered, scooping up another mouthful. It was warm and sweet and gooey, and the cold vanilla ice cream made it extra heav-enly. "Had to maintain a certain weight and size all the time." She flashed him a smug smile. "But not anymore."

He chuckled, a low rumble that warmed her as much as the fire at her back. "I'll be sure to feed you pudding every night, then."

She adored his voice, accent, and the quintessentially British terms he used. "Please do." He was such a beauti-ful man, inside and out. She'd never known it was possi-ble to want someone like this.

Was this how it was for everyone else, people who

chose partners of their own free will? Her body felt alive, almost effervescent with tingles as her mind conjured up all kinds of erotic images of them naked together.

He refused to let her pay for her part of the meal. He settled a guiding hand on the small of her back as they left, and that simple touch had her insides humming. Because unlike other men, his touch wasn't proprietary or controlling. Rather it was supportive, protective and comforting.

It also taught her something new about herself. That she was capable of getting turned on by a nonsexual touch from the right man.

At their vehicle he once again opened her door for her. She was about to reach for him but he shut the door and rounded the hood to get behind the wheel.

Her insides heated at being alone with him in the enclosed, suddenly intimate space, a delicious throb pulsing between her thighs. His woodsy, masculine scent filled her nose, and all she could think about was kissing that sexy mouth.

As if reading her mind, he turned his head to look at her in the dimness of the streetlight on the corner. She could read the desire in his eyes, was ready to scramble over the console and into his lap to kiss the hell out of him when he finally set one big hand on the side of her face and leaned forward to settle his mouth over hers.

Her lower belly flipped, tiny tingles racing across her lips and spreading down her neck and limbs. She reached up to grab his shoulder, squeezing slightly, testing the strength there as his muscles flexed beneath her fingers.

"You're so beautiful," he whispered to her, bringing his other hand up to cradle the back of her head.

She'd heard that a million times before. The difference this time was, she *felt* beautiful. Marcus made her feel beautiful and desirable and free all at the same time. She was dizzy with it, her heart racing at the thought of what else he might make her feel.

He deepened the kiss, bringing her closer with those powerful hands, one on her back while he grazed his fingers down the side of her neck.

Her breath hitched and for just a moment she allowed herself to close her eyes and let go of the constant need to be vigilant, to shut off all sensation in her body and stay mentally alert at all times.

She kissed him back harder, showing him without words how much she wanted him. The need to be in control was still there, scraping against the edges of her consciousness even as she struggled to shut it off.

Marcus shifted the hand on her back to her ribs, coasted it up and down, the heel of his hand grazing the side of her breast. Her nipple beaded tight, aching for attention. She shifted and leaned into his touch, pressing her breast into his hand. He made a low sound and cupped the side of her breast, his thumb stroking gently, moving ever closer to the straining center.

When he finally touched her there she couldn't hold back the tremulous moan that escaped as he sucked on her lower lip. The sound startled her, brought an instant rush of reproach and shame that shattered the spell she'd been under like a bullet through a pane of glass.

She pulled back, her body at war with her mind. Marcus held her gaze, unmoving, his face only inches away but his hands now on his thighs. "Too fast?" he murmured.

She shook her head, cringing inside. "No. No, it's…" Jesus, she felt like an idiot. It was like a breaker had suddenly been tripped in her head. Instinctive and pure reflex, something she had no control over.

"You don't have to explain," he said, leaning back to straighten in his seat.

Her body and heart cried out at the increased distance between them. She grabbed his closest hand and curled her fingers around it, trying to think of a way to explain it so he would understand. It was important that he understand. "I've never been allowed to…"

"To what?" he said quietly after a moment.

"Feel. With anyone," she added, her face heating at the admission.

This was so embarrassing. She'd ruined the moment. Killed it stone dead. Now she felt exposed, more vulnerable than if she'd been sitting here naked.

"You make me *feel*," she explained. "And part of my mind still doesn't want to let me, because it's not safe."

He watched her for a long moment, then exhaled and reached for her. Without a word he pulled her into a tight hug, one hand curved around the back of her head, holding her face to his shoulder. "I would never hurt you or push you for anything you weren't ready to give."

She nodded, breathing in his scent and savoring the strength and security of his embrace. It wasn't just her mind that was in danger with him, but her heart as well. "I know." Until Marcus, she hadn't believed men like this existed. Sometimes she still caught her mind telling her he couldn't be real.

"Good." He kissed her hair, released her and started the engine.

Frustration burned in her gut as he got them back on the road and headed for Stow. She couldn't shake the feeling that she'd just ruined her only chance at something beautiful with him.

Her cell phone rang a few minutes later, a welcome reprieve from her dismal thoughts. "Hey, Trin. What's up?"

"Damascus is a go."

A burst of elation hit her. Marcus glanced over and she gave him a thumbs up to alert him what was going on. "When?"

"Tomorrow. We'll work out the details later tonight

once I get back to the manor. So, this is your baby. Who do you want with you?"

"You." Because she was closest to Trin and wanted her experience on this one. "Amber and Jesse." For logistics, and because they'd both recently been in Damascus. "Megan and Ty. Maybe one more." For recon, backup and in case they had to steal anything. "And Marcus."

A surprised pause filled the line. "Marcus?"

He glanced over again as she awaited Trinity's reply. "Yes." She wanted him with her when she went back to face her demons in Damascus.

He was the only person who could help keep her demons at bay.

Chapter Ten

Marcus stood in the shower of his en suite letting the hot water pound down on his head and shoulders, his mind a chaotic mess. They'd finished the meeting with the entire team ten minutes ago, outlining what would happen tomorrow, and the purpose of the mission.

Capture Fayez Rahman, and pump him for intel on the Architect. Then, while he was in captivity, Rahman would meet a mysterious demise, the details of which only a handful of them would be privy to—not including Marcus.

He'd never been so conflicted about a decision before. Returning to Syria weighed heavy on his mind, even though he'd volunteered to be part of the team. He was going because he needed to be there to ensure Kiyomi was safe. But now that the flight to Damascus loomed on the coming horizon, his demons were out in full force.

Didn't matter. He'd face his demons and any other threat put in front of him to protect Kiyomi.

It was just after midnight. Everyone was headed for bed, and he'd retreated up here to his room because he didn't trust himself to be alone with Kiyomi right now.

The more time he spent with her, the harder it was to keep his hands off her. And her admission outside that pub earlier tonight had rocked him hard.

It was unfathomable that someone so beautiful and full of life had been condemned to an existence of such harsh deprivation. From things as simple as friendship, food, and pleasure.

As usual, thinking of her and pleasure in the same sentence had predictable results on his body. He opened his eyes, glanced down at the erection standing straight up against his belly, and lower to the melted, twisted flesh of his left hip and thigh.

Kiyomi wasn't squeamish and wouldn't be put off by his scars, but the sight of the wreckage was just another reminder that he would never again be the warrior he'd once been. Another reminder that even though he'd kept his shooting and CQB skills sharp, his physical disability could have dangerous consequences for the team if shite went sideways.

His erection deflated. He got out of the shower, got ready for bed and strode naked from the en suite into the bedroom.

He'd lit the fire when he'd first come in. It warmed up the room, which could be cold and drafty this time of year, and he liked the ambiance of it while he fell asleep. Karas was curled up in front of it on her bed, her foreleg sporting the fresh bandage he'd put on before coming upstairs.

He slid between the cozy flannel sheets and pulled the covers up to his waist, letting the hush of the room settle around him as he tried to clear his mind. But the moment he closed his eyes, the ghosts appeared.

Alone in the shadowy room that served as his prison, he shook from cold and pain. They'd stripped him naked to increase the sense of vulnerability and humiliation. His training had prepared him to withstand this, but the reality of his ordeal had pushed him to his breaking point.

Every breath was agony. His left thigh was busted, the flesh lying open so deep that the bone showed in the center of the wound. All around it his skin was blackened and melted, the same on his neck and face. As bad as the physical pain was, it didn't touch the level of suffering on the inside.

Seven of his troopers were dead, on his watch.

He didn't remember how they'd taken him. The only thing he could recall was being out on patrol with his men, and the blinding flash of the IED going off. Then fire. Searing pain. Men screaming in agony all around him.

He'd lost consciousness, only awakening when someone threw icy water in his face and found himself tied to this chair, his hands and feet bound. Two of his soldiers were already dead, lying in the corner off to the right.

Knowing they were there was the worst kind of psychological torture he could have been subjected to. His captors had left them there as a reminder of what would happen to him once they were finished torturing him.

He didn't know how long he'd been like this. Days, maybe. Sometimes he got lucky and the pain pulled him under. But when he woke, there was always more, and always someone there to add to his suffering.

I won't break. I won't let them break me. *He'd die with his dignity intact, would never surrender, fueled by the memory of his men.*

Oh, Jesus, his men…

They were his responsibility. He'd failed them. That agony was far worse than the physical pain.

He opened his eyes and thought he must be hallucinating. Instead of one of his captors, a young woman was bending over him. She was cutting the bindings on his wrists, speaking rapid, hushed English. "I'm getting you out of here, soldier."

Confusion clouded his pain-hazed brain. He didn't know who she was or how she'd got in here, but her accent was American. And she wasn't wearing a uniform.

When she cut his wrists free, his arms fell limply to his sides. Pain stabbed through them like knives.

He couldn't go with her. He was too weak to make it, and couldn't walk. He was a liability to her. She had to leave right now. She'd never make it out of here if she tried to help him. And he didn't deserve to live anyway.

"Go," he croaked out. He was reserving all his remaining strength to take out one of his captors before they killed him. It would be his last act of defiance, of vengeance for his men.

She ignored him, quickly kneeling to slice through the bindings on his feet. He sucked back a scream as it jostled his broken thigh. "I know, I'm sorry, but we don't have time to do this any other way," she muttered, sawing through the plastic zip ties.

He struggled to bring his head up and focus on her through eyes almost swollen shut. He tasted fresh blood in his mouth. "No. Go," he insisted. He would stay, and kill at least one of the sadistic bastards who'd done this to him.

She ignored him, sheathed her knife and put her hands on his aching shoulders to stare into his face. "I'm not leaving here without you. If you stay, we both stay, and then we'll both die."

He opened his mouth to argue but she was already leaning forward and grabbing him to hoist him out of the chair. He swallowed a bellow of agony, would have crumpled to the floor from the unbearable pain, but somehow she had him.

He struggled weakly, trying to pull free. He was already responsible for too many deaths. He didn't want hers added to his conscience. "Just leave me. Leave me, for Christ's sake!"

"No. And we only have six minutes to make it out of the compound before the guards come. Now help me get you out of here, or we're both going to die."

Yanking himself out of the past, Marcus rolled to his back and let out a slow breath to stare at the ceiling where the firelight flickered over the centuries-old plaster and beams. To this day he wasn't sure how they'd made it out of there. Megan had mostly dragged him, ignoring his protests and pleas to let him die.

He hadn't wanted to live, but she hadn't listened, had refused to let him wallow in self-loathing and pity. He'd managed to shoot two guards dead on their way out, but she'd done the rest. Somehow she'd got them out through the gates and made contact with a nearby British army unit to extract them.

On the helicopter, he'd raged and cursed and hated her for saving him. Now he was grateful for what she'd done, the extreme risks she'd taken to help him. If not for her he would have died in that hellhole. He would never have had this time with her here at Laidlaw Hall, or met any of the others.

Including Kiyomi, the woman who had snuck past all his defenses and left him tied in knots.

What the hell was he supposed to do about her? Like Megan, she'd always treated him as a whole man, as an equal. She didn't look at him like he was a cripple or a victim. She looked at him with admiration and desire.

Arousal stirred again, even as he tried to suppress it. Before his injuries he'd never been short of female company if he'd wanted it, but he'd never wanted anyone as badly as Kiyomi. Except with her he couldn't follow the instincts that had never led him wrong before.

All the men before him had used and traumatized her. He couldn't take the lead like he was accustomed to doing, he had to take things slow, and she would be leaving soon, probably after they returned from Damascus.

While he and the others went on the coming op, the remaining team members were already dispersing to rented properties around Coventry, about an hour away.

Time was running out for them. In a few short hours they would be on a plane to Damascus, and once they finished with Rahman, Kiyomi and the others would be gone. He'd be left alone here with only his dog, Mrs. Biddington, the stableman and gardener for company.

He couldn't ask Kiyomi to stay, it would be selfish and unsafe. She and the other Valkyries had been here a while now, and after the Bonfire Night incident there might be more interest about him and his property from curious locals. It was for the best that she and the others leave. But he couldn't stop hoping that she would come back to him when this was all over.

He turned his head toward the door when the old wood floors creaked down the hall outside his room. Eden and Zack, heading into their room.

Letting out a deep breath, he glanced around, listening to the crackle of the flames in the hearth while the wind gusted against the windowpanes. This old place had seemed like a millstone around his neck when he'd first inherited it, but he'd become attached to it over the years.

Whenever he'd stayed here as a lad growing up, he'd dreamed about owning something so grand one day, never knowing his great-uncle would bequeath it to him upon his death.

Turned out the reality of owning an estate like this was far less romantic than what he'd imagined. It was a mountain of never-ending bills and work to keep it in good repair.

And yet…it was part of him now, in his bones and blood. He couldn't imagine selling it. It had belonged to his family for ten generations. He had a duty to his forebears to be Laidlaw Hall's custodian. This was his home. He had to stay.

Just as Kiyomi had no choice but to leave.

Giving up on sleep, he sat up against the headboard and reached for the half-finished paperback on his nightstand. The fire gave him plenty of light to read, and maybe it would keep his mind off losing Kiyomi.

You never had her to begin with.

Aye. Hard enough to let her go as it was. If they crossed the line they'd been flirting with, losing her might break him.

He struggled to focus on the words on the page, his mind stubbornly refusing to get into the story he'd found so absorbing just last night. The floor creaked in the hall. He stopped, listening. Another creak, softer this time. Closer.

The door handle began to turn slowly.

Marcus tossed the book aside and yanked the covers up to make sure he was decent. Who the hell would barge into his room in the middle of the night?

The breath stuck in his lungs when Kiyomi stepped inside and shut the door, her legs bare to mid-thigh beneath the hem of a kimono-style, satin robe.

Chapter Eleven

K iyomi straightened as she released the doorknob, then faced Marcus. Her pulse skipped, then quickened. What a view.

He was sitting up in bed, naked from the waist up, his dark eyes searing her where she stood. The raw power of his body was finally revealed to her in the flickering firelight.

His chest, arms and shoulders were sculpted with muscle, the swirling burn marks scattered down the left side of his neck and chest stopping part way down his ribs. He was beautiful, even more so because of the scars.

A mix of anticipation and nerves danced in her belly as she met his gaze once more. She could read most men easily. Could figure out within a matter of minutes what role she needed to play in order to get their attention and keep it. How to be their fantasy.

Except with Marcus. She still wasn't sure what he liked sexually, but she was guessing someone strong. Confident. Bold. That was why she was standing here in his room in her robe in the middle of the night.

Her time with him was running out fast. She couldn't leave without fully exploring what was between them. No matter what happened after tonight, no matter what fate threw at her next, she would always have this one beautiful memory of him to hold close.

She wanted to feel. Just once, she wanted to feel with a man who wasn't using her. A man she felt safe with and was attracted to. She might never get another chance. There was no way she would let this opportunity pass her by.

Marcus hadn't moved, watching her with a closed expression.

"Can't sleep?" she asked softly, and started toward the bed. Karas watched her from the doggy bed in front of the fire, ears perked.

Marcus shook his head, his eyes now glowing with an unmistakable heat that made her heart pound. "You?"

"Not alone." Stopping two feet from the edge of his bed, she reached for the sash of her robe. One tug and the floral-print, plum satin slid away, parting the two halves of the robe to reveal a strip of naked skin from her throat to the smooth mound between her thighs.

A surge of power and arousal shot through her at the way Marcus's eyes darkened as they slowly dragged down the length of bare skin she'd revealed, stopping between her legs. She felt his gaze like a caress, increasing the throb of desire there.

Encouraged, combatting the nerves that had her pulse hammering in her throat, she closed the remaining distance between them and perched a hip on the edge of his bed, inches from where the sheets ended at his waist.

She could see the outline of his erection pressed against the covers, and the thought of pleasuring this man sent another wave of heat through her. Lifting a hand, she reached out to stroke her fingertips down his bearded cheek.

Marcus caught her wrist and held it, his eyes searching hers. "Why?" he asked quietly. "Tell me why."

So honorable. Most men would have seized the opportunity she'd given him and pounced. Not Marcus.

She drew a steadying breath, then whispered the words that made her tremble inside. "I want to feel with you."

A leap of emotion flashed in his eyes, quickly replaced by a mixture of heat and tenderness that made her heart trip. He kissed the backs of her fingers, then leaned forward to curl a thick arm around her waist and slide her toward him. One big hand slid into the back of her hair as he pulled her in for a kiss.

The moment their lips met, the nervousness fell away. Everything disappeared except for Marcus. She splayed her hands on his sculpted chest, exploring and mapping the muscular terrain with her fingers and palms as they kissed. Touching a man intimately because she wanted to was heady. Addictive.

But then he stopped. She blinked, coming out of her trance to find him cupping her face in his hands, his eyes earnest. "Are you sure?"

She'd never been surer of anything in her life. "Yes."

He didn't let go. "No acting. I don't want some pretend version you think you need to be. I just want you."

He didn't want her to pretend. Didn't want her to fake anything. He wanted the real her, or nothing at all.

Nerves fluttered back to life in the pit of her belly. She'd never done this—been herself in an intimate situation. Didn't know if it was even possible. But she wanted to try, for both of them. So she nodded and leaned in to kiss him again, eager to get out of her head and lose herself in the magic Marcus wielded.

He didn't disappoint. He took his time as he kissed her again, skimming the fingertips of his free hand down the side of her neck, over the front of her throat to the notch between her collarbones.

It was such a revelation. She was always the one who

seduced. Now Marcus had reversed the roles. He was taking the lead, awakening her entire body inch by inch.

His mouth was warm on her neck, nibbling and kissing, the caress of his tongue and slight abrasion of his beard sending a rush of heat straight between her legs. It was so incredibly freeing to not have to do anything but hold on to his broad shoulders and enjoy.

She closed her eyes and let her head fall back. His deft fingers stroked along the valley between her breasts, turning her nipples into tight points that throbbed for his touch. Then down the centerline of her stomach to her navel, and lower to pause on her smooth mound.

Her heart drummed against her ribs, her body suffused with heat and need. By the time he finally reversed course with his fingers, his mouth was at her collarbone.

She sighed as he eased the satin halves of her robe apart slowly, allowing the fabric to caress her sensitized skin. It slid off her shoulders to pool around her waist. He eased back a bit, a low, masculine sound of awe coming from his throat as he took her in.

At this point she normally would have withdrawn into her head and escaped more into the role she was playing. Now there was only anticipation and enjoyment of the way he looked at her.

Then his hands closed around her waist, his dark head bending to nuzzle the valley between her breasts. Kiyomi's heart squeezed as he kissed her there, right over her pounding heart, his beard prickling her skin, and slid her hands into his hair.

The connection she felt with him was overwhelming. She'd never imagined feeling this way, had never imagined being able to truly give herself to someone.

Those big hands cupped her breasts, pushing them up slightly as he nuzzled first one, then the other. She squirmed restlessly, sucked in a breath at the first brush of his lips across a straining nipple, the anticipation nearly painful.

Then warmth, followed by a streak of sensual fire as he took it into his mouth. A soft moan escaped when he sucked gently, his tongue caressing, sending streamers of pleasure through her.

The sensation triggered an automatic reaction to withdraw physically, shut off the sensations, but she fought it back, desperately craving this experience with him. The pleasure he offered.

Releasing one breast, he stroked his hand up and down her ribcage while he tended to her other nipple. She arched her back and pulled him closer, the pulse in her core making her hotter, wetter.

The moment he lifted his head she dove in for a deep, urgent kiss, her tongue sliding along his while her hands roamed his back. She wanted to touch all of him, couldn't get close enough as he turned them and laid her on her back beside him.

Her arms wound around his neck and she rolled into him, only to have him still her with a firm hand on her hip. He abandoned her mouth to nip at her chin, her jaw, one hand trailing down the plane of her belly.

Kiyomi shut her eyes and fought to stay present rather than retreat mentally, focused on the sensation as his fingers neared where she needed them so badly. His kisses gentled, trailing across her cheek, then his hand settled over her mound, warm and solid.

She pulled in a shaky breath and forced her body to relax. She'd fantasized about this for so long, she didn't want to ruin it. Her thighs trembled slightly as she parted them, the warmth of his hand reassuring and arousing at the same time.

Restraint. Marcus was all about restraint, and it was driving her deliciously crazy.

She bit down on her lower lip to stifle a whimper when he at last moved his hand, his fingers sliding along her wet folds. It felt so good, yet it wasn't nearly enough.

She tried to grab his hand and move it to where she wanted it, but he evaded her, nipped her bottom lip softly while his fingers traced a torturously slow path up to her throbbing clit. Her entire body tensed when he finally made contact where she needed it most. He caught her mouth with his, eased his tongue inside to play with hers while his fingers caressed gently.

An incoherent sound of pleasure and need came from her. She could barely breathe, her heart pounding out of control at the knowledge that she was giving him complete access to her body, that he would be the one giving her the orgasm she craved.

His mouth trailed hot, nipping kisses down her chin to her chest, closing around her nipple at the exact moment he slid two fingers into her. Kiyomi cried out and bucked into his hand, holding his head to her. She was quivering, pulled taut like a bowstring in the hands of a master archer, and only Marcus could send her flying. But she was so close now, and when she came she wanted him inside her.

She pushed at his shoulders. He stopped instantly and raised his head, concern in his dark eyes. She grabbed his face in both hands to kiss him, telling him without words that she was more than okay, that she was loving everything he did to her.

"Want you inside me," she gasped out, then grabbed for her robe lying discarded on the far edge of the bed and took the condom from the pocket. They didn't need one, but explaining why might kill the mood so she'd brought it with her anyway.

Marcus eased his hand from between her legs but dipped down to torment a breast as she tried to sit up and see all of him. She nipped at the side of his neck, her whole body humming with anticipation. He'd gone so long without any kind of intimate contact. She wanted to get him as worked up as she was, give him all the pleasure she could.

His fingers speared into her hair as she kissed her way across his chest, pausing to tease his nipples, earning a hitch in his breathing when her hands eased over his belly and hips. He was fully erect, his cock standing proud against his belly. She curled her fingers around him, reveled in the low growl he made, and stroked him.

She followed the cues he gave her, adjusting her pressure and speed, but when she would have slid to her knees and taken him in her mouth, he stopped her.

Face taut with pleasure, his chest rising and falling, he took the condom from her, rolled it on with an economical motion and pressed her down flat on her back. Settling between her legs, he rocked his hips slowly, dragging the hot length of his erection over her swollen clit while he covered her mouth with his.

With a murmur of pleasure she wound her legs around his calves, pushing up to meet his lazy thrusts as she sucked at his tongue. Her entire body was suffused with warmth, desire pulsing in her core.

Marcus raised his head to stare down at her, eyes blazing, breathing fast. She set a hand on the side of his face, overcome with need and the trust she had in him. Holding his gaze, she shifted beneath him, one hand sinking into his muscled ass as she pulled him forward.

With a low groan he came up on an elbow to reach his free hand between them, found her clit and caressed it while the head of his cock lodged thick and hard just inside her. Instant pleasure suffused her, melting her bones like chocolate left out in the sun. Her eyes fluttered shut, a lovely floating sensation filling her.

She allowed her body to surrender to it, let herself drift on the tide. This was Marcus touching her. His weight pressing her into the bedding. And it changed everything.

His muscles bunched beneath her fingers, then he slowly thrust inside her. The fullness, the incredible heat magnified the pleasure. She squeezed her eyes shut, unable to control her reaction, helpless as his every movement pushed her closer to the edge. All she could do was cling to him and trust him not to stop as he stroked her inside and out, hitting all her sweet spots at once.

Release rushed at her, taking her off guard. She shoved aside the need to distance herself from it, focusing on the feel of him, his scent. "Marcus…"

He lowered his head, brushed a tender kiss across her mouth. "Aye, love." His voice was deep, almost guttural, and though she couldn't open her eyes she could feel him watching her. Watching over her as he took her to the edge.

That image seared itself into her brain. She held onto it, to the way it intensified the sensation, and then she soared into oblivion, her cries drowning out the thud of her pulse in her ears.

MARCUS FOUGHT FOR breath, gritted his teeth at the need to plunge harder, faster, the need to come burning like fire at the base of his spine. Sweet Jesus, the look on her face just now, the feel of her clenching around him and the way she'd let go so completely in his arms, destroyed him.

She relaxed into the bed with a soft moan, her eyelids fluttering open. Her cheeks were flushed, those liquid dark eyes drowsy with pleasure, and the sated smile she gave him had his heart trying to punch out of his chest.

Leaning up to kiss him once, she unwound her legs from around him and pushed at his shoulders. "I want to watch you," she whispered.

He feared he wouldn't last as he withdrew and allowed her to settle him on his back. She pushed her hair over one shoulder and swung a leg across his body to straddle him.

Marcus didn't know where to look first. He settled his hands on her hips, his muscles tight as tripwires as she leaned forward to tease his mouth with hers. He slid his hand into the cool silk of her hair, groaned into her mouth as she wriggled into place, closing a fist around him to bring him into position.

Then she sat back up, her eyes gleaming with pure female intent. He grabbed hold of her hips again, held his breath and bit back a throttled shout as she eased down on him, taking him deep inside her.

Pleasure ripped into him, brutal and swift. He didn't remember closing his eyes, but then he was forcing them open, unwilling to miss a second as her teeth sank into her plump lower lip and she began to move. A slow, sinuous motion that was like some insanely erotic dance.

She swayed and undulated, pumping up and down his aching cock while the firelight kissed her smooth, golden skin. Her breasts bobbed with each movement, taut, dark coral nipples topping each one. Her belly was flat, the delicious outline of her abs flexing, and the soft, bare mound between her legs was so damn hot—

She planted her hands on his pecs, that inky dark stare locked with his as she rode him.

Christ, she was the sexiest, most incredibly beautiful thing he'd ever seen in his life, and the pleasure she was giving him already had him sweating and panting for breath. She'd wanted to watch him, and Jesus it was incredible, a soul-deep connection solidifying between them as he struggled to hold her gaze.

Each time she sank down on him she squeezed, pushing him closer to release. Unable to stay still, needing to touch her, he released one hip to cradle her breast in his hand, rolling the nipple between his thumb and forefinger.

"I'm close," he ground out.

She hummed and pushed him flat, dark eyes gleaming. "Let me watch you come."

Helpless to resist, he seized her hips, his last sight of her before his eyes slammed shut burned into his mind for all eternity. The slick sound of her sliding up and down his cock, the feel of her so tight and warm and wet, were too much.

His fingers bit into her backside, a cry of surrender wrenching from his throat as the orgasm hit. He held her fast, bucked up into her, holding as deep as he could get while the pulses tore through him. When at last they began to fade, he slumped back against the pillow, his entire body lax and the blood rushing in his ears.

Kiyomi eased off him for a moment, then stretched out over top of him and blanketed him with her weight. He groaned and wrapped his arms around her back, cradling her to him. She was so small and soft, the scars between her shoulder blades and the Valkyrie mark on her left hip aberrations he couldn't wait to avenge.

Tomorrow he could begin to do something about it. Tonight, he didn't want anything to come between him and the incredible woman in his arms.

After a while he turned her onto her side and snuggled up behind her, one arm banded around her ribcage as he drew the covers over them. The fire had burned low in the grate. Karas was fast asleep in front of it. Marcus kissed the top of Kiyomi's head, filled with a tenderness and contentment he'd never experienced before.

Cuddled up tight together, they both fell asleep. He awakened to darkness sometime later when Kiyomi jerked against him. She twitched, a low sound coming from her that he recognized all too well.

He drew her tighter into the curve of his body and hugged her close. She gasped and went rigid, her heart thudding wildly against his palm. "You're okay. It was just a dream," he murmured.

She pushed away from him and sat up, her back to him as she exhaled and ran a hand through her hair.

Marcus reached out to curl a hand around her hip, his thumb rubbing gently over a dimple at the base of her spine. "Okay now?"

Another exhalation. "Yes." She turned toward him and lay back down, immediately flattening herself to the front of him.

Marcus wrapped his arms around her, one hand cradling the back of her head. Her skin was damp with sweat. "Was it the same one?"

Her hair caught in his beard as she nodded, her breath warm against the front of his throat. "It's always the same. Always him."

Rahman.

"I'm always helpless." She cuddled closer yet, wedging a leg between his.

"You're not helpless anymore. And you never will be again." He hugged her tight. "Because we're going to get him."

She didn't answer, her body still tense. Then, after a minute, "I need you to promise me something."

"Anything."

"I can't go through that again. So if something goes wrong, if he captures me and you can't get to me—"

Denial burst inside him, fierce and strong. "He's not going to get his hands on you ever again."

"But if he ever did, and you couldn't save me. I need you to promise that you'd kill me rather than let him take me again."

Marcus's heart seized, his entire body going rigid as cold swept through him like an arctic blast. "Jesus Christ, don't talk like that."

She pulled back a few inches to look into his face, and there was just enough light from the glowing coals in the grate to make out her deadly serious expression. "Marcus. Promise me. Please. I need you to promise me."

He would do anything to protect this woman. He would kill to keep her safe. But take her life to do the same? It was unthinkable. Horrifying.

"Please," she whispered, her voice ragged, eyes tormented.

He wanted to say no. That he would never harm her under any circumstance. That it would kill him to fulfill her request.

But her demons ran deep, and they were headed to enemy territory tomorrow to take on the man responsible for all her suffering. He never wanted her to suffer again.

So if the worst did come true and Rahman managed to capture her…if Marcus had her in his sights…if he had a clear shot and it was the only way to spare her more terror and pain…

It was something he wished he could have done for his troopers. If it ever became necessary, he owed Kiyomi that final act of mercy.

"Aye," he finally said, shaken even though he knew it would never come to that. They had an entire team going after Rahman. Marcus would make sure she was safe.

Kiyomi sighed and snuggled up to his chest once more. "Thank you," she whispered, her fingers drifting lightly over his back.

Marcus squeezed his eyes shut and gathered her close to banish all the ghosts between them. "Sleep now."

Chapter Twelve

Fayez hurried from his vehicle into yet another safe house—the third one he'd been moved to in the last twenty-four hours. His security team wasn't taking any chances with his safety. If not for the last-minute tip the previous night, he would have been in that camp during the British assault and either be trapped in a cell or dead right now.

"Sir. In here." His head bodyguard came out of the back room he'd just checked, holstering his weapon.

Fayez moved straight into it and stood in the middle of the floor as the door shut behind him. The metallic clang of it reminded him of a prison cell door closing. Fitting, since until the threat against him died down, he would be more prisoner than free man.

Someone had sold him out. And someone had saved him with that anonymous tip. Both needed to be found and dealt with accordingly.

His phone buzzed in his pocket. When he saw the number, his pulse jumped. Only one person had ever called him from that area code. It had to be *her*. He'd tried to find her, to no avail. It was like she'd simply vanished.

He activated a customized app that would record the

conversation before answering in English. "Hello?"

"So you managed to dodge another bullet last night, did you?" the female voice said. His people had previously traced her calls and only found a general location—somewhere in the Atlanta, Georgia area. Never anything more specific, and no one knew who she was, referring to her only by her moniker. The Architect.

A mix of relief and excitement shot through him. It was definitely her. "Yes. And I'm guessing this call means I have you to thank for that?"

"Maybe."

No maybe about it. "Why did you do it?"

"Because you and I have a business transaction that still hasn't been completed."

Kiyomi.

He paced the room, restless as a caged tiger. He hated being penned up like an animal. "Do you have any news on her?"

"Yes, as a matter of fact."

He stopped walking, his entire body drawing tight as a cable. "Tell me." His heart thudded in his ears as he awaited her answer.

"I've just received an alert that she was spotted crossing the Turkish border into Syria. Facial recognition puts it at a ninety-two-percent certainty that it's her."

A wave of heat suffused him. "When?"

"Four hours ago."

If it was true, Kiyomi could be anywhere by now. "Was she alone?"

"Yes."

Mind whirling, he resumed pacing again. "What is she doing here?"

"What do you think?"

A slow, savage smile spread across his face. "She's come back for me."

"To kill you."

He smothered a laugh. A single woman against him and his security team? He didn't care if she was a Valkyrie. "She's welcome to try." The idea made all kinds of fantasies spin in his head. Her naked, on her knees in front of him.

He pulled in a calming breath, willing his heart rate to slow down. His security was the best in the business and he paid them well. They were loyal, motivated, and skilled. She would never get past them.

"I'll get her." His groin tightened at the thought. He had a vast network of contacts and other resources to help him locate and capture her. "If she comes anywhere near Damascus, I'll know." *And then she'll be mine.*

"My original terms still stand. And may I remind you, she was to be delivered to me undamaged. The way you treated her the last time you had her was untenable."

She'd used that word before, so he'd looked it up. It meant indefensible, not to be tolerated. Well, fuck her.

"She's not for sale this time." The words burst out of him in a low growl. The Architect had never told him why she wanted Kiyomi in the first place, but that had been *before*, and there was a reason she wasn't going after Kiyomi herself. Was she under surveillance and couldn't risk detection?

He didn't give a shit. Kiyomi was *his*, and when he got her, he would do whatever he wanted with her.

"No?" The sly, almost bored edge to her tone sent a sliver of warning through him as she continued. "Did you wonder how I knew about the raid on the camp last night? Or that you were heading there? Because I know everything about you, Fayez. Including your exact location right now."

He paled when she recited the exact coordinates and address of the safehouse he was in right now. The slippery bitch was watching him via satellite or drone, it was the only way she could know where he was.

"But as long as you give me what I want, I'm no threat to you," she went on. "I'll even up the price on her from three million to four. Wired to your offshore account the moment I have her safely in my possession. *Without* any further damage this time."

A hot rush of anger and outrage blasted through him. He reined it back with effort. She was forcing his hand. He'd killed people for less. He had no choice but to capitulate, since she currently held the upper hand in their negotiations. "I'll sell her to you, but she won't be untouched. Not after what she did to me."

"You maim her, you get zero money. I'll take her from you and then kill you myself."

The threat would have made him scoff until ten seconds ago when she'd told him where he was standing in the safehouse. Who the hell was this woman, and how did she have access to that sort of technology? Why did she need him to capture Kiyomi?

Because she knows Kiyomi will come to you. And when she does, the Architect will be waiting to take her.

Fury exploded in his gut. The Architect would no doubt have a team on the way. They might already be here. He needed to move again, but not until he had Kiyomi. *No one* was taking her from him.

"Five million," he finally snapped, "and I'll try not to disfigure her." Much.

A few seconds of silence passed. "Done."

Yes. They were. "I'll be in touch when I have her. Unless you plan to…*architect* something else?" He said it just to piss her off, because he wasn't supposed to use her moniker in any communications that could be monitored. Tough shit. She had as much at stake here as he did.

"Oh, don't worry. If you find her, I'll know long before you call."

He disconnected and shoved the phone back into his pocket, his entire body amped up with restless energy and frustration. After all this time, Kiyomi was finally close, and might be coming right to him.

Unbidden, an image of her in that ruby-red gown filled his mind. The first time he'd ever laid eyes on her, in that hotel lobby. Their eyes had met across the room and in that instant he'd felt something shift inside him.

That old cliché about the world falling away was true, because he'd experienced it that night. He'd abandoned his security and the man he was making a multi-million-dollar business deal with just to go over and introduce himself.

She'd been arresting. Alluring. Intelligent. Demure and submissive. And her lack of inhibitions in bed still left him hard and aching whenever he remembered it.

No. Stop it. It was all a lie.

She'd deceived him. Betrayed him. Now she would finally pay.

He turned for the door, wrenched it open and began barking orders to his men. It had been months since he'd had her. Months since he'd first learned of the level of betrayal she'd dealt him.

She'd purposely made him fall in love with her, manipulating him all the while and playing him for a fool. He'd treated her like a queen, had been prepared to share his life with her, even give her his heart and unswerving loyalty.

Until he'd found out she was nothing but a lying whore who'd used him for her own personal agenda. Leaving him heartbroken and humiliated.

The rage expanded in his chest, spreading down into his gut. *No* one made a fool out of him. *No* one used him and got away with it. Not even the Architect.

He might not be able to kill Kiyomi when he captured her, but there were plenty of other ways to make her suffer for the pain she'd caused him.

****

A few hours after everyone arrived at the safehouse outside of Damascus, Kiyomi found Marcus stretching on the floor in his room upstairs. They'd all flown to Turkey early that morning on a private jet, then individually crossed the Syrian border using fake IDs Amber had cooked up for them.

"Here," she said, offering him a small bottle of water. Though it was November, the weather was unusually hot and dry here in Syria.

"Cheers." He chugged it then set it down beside him, wrapped his arms around his upraised left knee and pulled it toward his chest, his features tightening.

"Can I help?"

The ghost of a smile tugged at the edge of his mouth. "I wish."

She smiled back, thinking of last night. She'd crept out of his room before dawn and gone back to hers so that no one would know they'd spent the night together.

Not because she was ashamed or embarrassed. But because this was her first consensual relationship and she wanted to keep it all to herself. Marcus was a private man. She hadn't wanted to make him the topic of any gossip or questions. They'd both maintained a careful distance on the trip here as well, for the same reasons. "I stand ready to assist you in any way I can, Mr. Laidlaw."

"That right?" He lowered his leg to the floor and held a hand out to her. When she placed hers in it, he tugged her forward.

Kiyomi went to her knees in front of him, her heart turning over as she gazed into those chocolate-brown eyes. This man had dropped everything, left his quiet, peaceful life behind at a moment's notice and returned to the very place that haunted him most —for her.

"I don't think I've said it yet, but thank you for being

here. It means a lot to me."

He curved a hand around the back of her neck and drew her in for a kiss. "I don't want to be anywhere else."

Though he was a man whose actions spoke more loudly than any words he ever could have said, he continually surprised her with just how romantic he was, deep down. She kissed him, humming in enjoyment as his lips molded to hers, those powerful arms wrapped around her.

The truth was, being here again spooked her too and rattled the cage she'd locked some of her demons inside. But the prospect of capturing and then killing Rahman once they extracted the necessary intel from him made facing her past all worthwhile.

Marcus's cell phone went off. He pulled it out, frowned, then answered, watching her. After a moment he put his hand over the bottom of it and spoke to her. "Can you get Amber?"

She jumped up and rushed to get their resident tech wizard. "Marcus wants you."

Amber looked up from her laptop. "What for?"

"Someone just called him. Must be important."

They stepped into the room and shut the door just as Marcus was lowering his phone. "What's up?" Amber asked.

"That was a former teammate. Rory McFadden, the team leader from last night's raid on the camp. He had a tip from an intel source here in Damascus. They got a signal intercept on a recent phone call that appears to match Rahman's voice. Apparently he used the term 'architect' during the call, and the way he said it referenced a special significance to the person he was talking to."

Kiyomi's heart leapt. Was this it? Did Rahman have a direct lead to the Architect?

Marcus held out the phone so Amber could see the screen. "This is the number that received the call. Rory didn't have a location for me."

"I'll run it now." Amber took his phone and hurried from the room.

Kiyomi stepped in front of Marcus. "*Thank* you," she whispered, then lifted on tiptoe to kiss him.

He gripped her shoulders, his expression stopping her cold. "He knows you're here."

Rahman. "Does he know where?" The team had decided that she should purposely not wear a disguise while crossing the Syrian border, counting on facial recognition alerting Rahman to her presence—along with anyone else hunting them, like the Architect.

They'd been hoping to learn he'd been tipped off, and then try to track his location that way. But this scenario was beyond anything they'd hoped for, a way to kill the proverbial two birds with a single stone.

"Not yet. And that's the way it stays." A frown creased his forehead. "There's more than a bounty on you. Whoever the caller was offered five million U.S. if Rahman turned you over."

She smiled, the first real hope of nailing Rahman's oily ass to the wall starting to bloom in her gut. "He won't get the chance."

The frown disappeared as he smiled back, but it didn't reach his eyes. "No, he won't. But that's more than enough money to tempt a lot of people to start hunting you."

Kiyomi didn't respond, unfazed by the increase in the bounty. They went downstairs into the kitchen where the rest of the team was gathered around the table. All except for Jesse and Ty, who were currently outside keeping watch. Everyone waited while Amber ran the phone number through her custom laptop, Lady Ada, and waited for the software to do its thing.

A few minutes passed, then the frown of concentration on Amber's face eased. "I found something."

Kiyomi and Marcus crowded in on either side of her

to look at the screen. It was hard to follow. Amber had at least a half-dozen programs open, all doing different things. She pointed to the one on the far right. "The call was received here." She indicated a building in an industrial area on a satellite map.

"Can you verify whether it was him or not?" Marcus asked.

"Already running his voice through my software. But there's something else interesting here as well." She paused, looking up at them. "The caller's number originated in the Atlanta area."

Where previous calls in their investigation on the Architect seemed to have originated as well. "Rahman used the term architect during the conversation. Who was he speaking to?"

"Rory said the other voice was synthesized. They couldn't determine the gender."

Amber shook her head, typing more commands in and checking a different tab. A voice recording came up, two different graphs tracking similarities as the person spoke. "I can't tell either."

The program stopped, the red lines on the graphs suddenly turning green. "Wait." Amber typed some more, muttered under her breath as she read to herself, fingers racing over the keyboard.

Kiyomi studied the graphs, waiting.

Amber sat back. "It's a woman."

Everyone looked at her sharply. "You're sure?" Megan asked.

"Lady Ada is, so yeah, I'm sure."

Kiyomi stared at the screen. "So the Architect's a woman?" She'd been so certain it was a man.

"Looks that way." Amber typed something else. "I can't get a location for where this most recent call originated. The signal's been scrambled just like all the others, bounced around all over the globe. I've tried to triangulate the previous calls and there's just no pattern to go by."

"Now we can take out Rahman," Kiyomi said, excitement burning in her chest.

"No," Trinity said firmly, cutting her a sharp look. "That's not the mission."

Kiyomi straightened, frowning. "Yes it was, we—"

"We were going to capture Rahman to get a lead on the Architect. Now we might have one. And since she knows you're here, we can't assume she's going to sit back and depend on Rahman to capture you. She'll probably send a team after you too."

"So? We'll be in and out before they can get there."

Trinity's expression hardened. "I know you want him dead. I get that. We all do. But we don't know yet whether we still need him or not. If we don't, we'll take him out—together—before we leave the country. And as of this moment, putting you or any of us at further risk by going after him now, is just reckless. We need to wait and see before we move on him, give Amber time to analyze this further."

Kiyomi stared hard at her friend, argument piling up on her tongue. But she knew Trinity better than she did any of the others. One look in those deep blue eyes, and she could tell that arguing was pointless. Trinity was team leader. Her word was final, and this decision was not up for discussion.

"He's going to run," she warned, desperation clawing at her insides. "He'll disappear again and next time we might not find him."

"We'll find him."

Dammit, no, they might not if they let this chance slip away. Didn't Trinity and the others see that? Of all people, didn't Trinity understand how important it was to kill Rahman now?

Kiyomi wanted to scream. This wasn't how it was supposed to happen. This wasn't the way she'd imagined it going.

"We will get him eventually, I promise," Trinity said in a softer tone. "But the Architect takes priority, because that's the only way we end this thing for all of us."

Meaning, Kiyomi's personal revenge was a distant second and would just have to wait—if it happened at all.

Resolve crystalized in the pit of her stomach. She was done waiting. And targeting Rahman as a team wasn't what she wanted anyway.

It wasn't enough for him to just die. It had to be just him and her in the room when it happened. He had to think he was triumphant first. That he'd won and she was defeated, cowed by fear and helplessness.

Frustration burned in her chest. They had his probable location. After last night's raid on the camp, he'd be more paranoid than ever about his security. His team would move him soon, likely sometime in the next few hours once it was dark, and then she might not get another chance.

If she was going after him, it had to be now, before it was too late.

She stayed quiet, lost in her thoughts as the others began talking amongst themselves while Amber pulled up the satellite view of the building Rahman was in and enlarged it. Kiyomi quickly assessed the security surrounding it, the entry and exit points, making mental notes.

"I'm starving," Megan announced a while later. "Anyone else in for kabobs?"

Ty went out and got them all dinner, and the whole time he was gone, Kiyomi continued to formulate her plan. Two minutes after he walked through the door with the takeout bags, Amber got another alert from Lady Ada.

The entire room went quiet as everyone focused on the laptop screen. "I've got a possible location for where the call to Rahman originated," Amber murmured, eyes scanning rapidly across the screen as she analyzed the data.

Next she pulled up a satellite map and entered an address. A residential neighborhood appeared on screen. She zoomed in on the target house. A large, private mansion surrounded by manicured grounds.

"Where is that?" Eden asked.

"Newnan, Georgia." Amber looked at Trinity. "Suburb of Atlanta."

A bubble of hope rose inside Kiyomi. Maybe this was the break they needed to get the Architect. Maybe now they could go after Rahman, seize his cell and other electronics.

Then put him down like the rabid animal he was.

Trinity nodded once. "We'll start the search there. I'm sending Briar and Georgia there to do recon."

Two Valkyrie snipers Trinity was close with, and they were both recon experts. Kiyomi and the team were lucky to have them to lend support back in the States.

Pulling out her phone, Trinity started to dial a number then stopped, her gaze slicing to Kiyomi. "Rahman's still a no-go for now."

Dammit! It took all Kiyomi's restraint to bite back an angry retort. Arguing now was not only pointless, it would also tip her hand. Trinity was right about one thing, though. Risking the team's safety now *was* reckless.

But Kiyomi didn't need a team for what she had in mind.

She'd made her decision. All she had to do now was put her plan into action.

After Ty handed out the food, Kiyomi sat quietly beside Marcus and ate, ruthlessly shoving aside the twinge of guilt and did what she had to. A chill swept over her at the thought of confronting Rahman again if her plan worked. The increase in bounty for her made every move she made here more dangerous.

She brushed it aside, because there was no help for

it. This might be her only shot, and he wouldn't dare kill her because he was too afraid of the Architect and wanted the bounty money so he could buy and sell more women, weapons and drugs.

As everyone finished their meal she glanced around at the others. She and her Valkyrie sisters had been subjected to too much throughout their lives. They all deserved their freedom and their lives back. If she could secure that for them by getting a definitive lead on the Architect from Rahman before killing him, then she was duty bound to do so.

They'd all risked so much to save her. She owed them. And Marcus too, enough that she would spare him what came next.

"Who's on watch next?" Jesse asked across the room before popping a bite of chicken into his mouth. "Amber and me?"

"No, I want Amber to keep working on these leads," Trinity said. "Eden and I'll take the next shift. I'm still finalizing the op in Atlanta with Briar and Georgia."

And there it was. The perfect excuse.

Kiyomi waited until Trinity and Eden went upstairs. While they grabbed their gear, she gathered what she needed and quickly tucked it away in the bathroom. As soon as she heard the back door close, she jogged back downstairs and made sure the others could see her as she checked her pistol.

"What are you doing?" Marcus asked suspiciously.

She holstered her weapon at the small of her back. "I'm watching the northwest side for Trin while she finalizes things with Briar and Georgia."

The look he gave her told her he didn't believe a word of it. Summoning her acting skills, she shot him an annoyed frown. "Look, they're waiting for me, and I need to keep busy right now. At least this gives me something to do instead of sitting around being pissed off."

He didn't say anything. She sighed in frustration and held her phone out. "Wanna call her yourself and check?"

He stared at her for a long moment, so long she worried he might actually check with Trinity. But she maintained her expression and finally he relented with a nod. "When I check in with you, you'd better answer," he said.

She narrowed her eyes at him. "I'm a grown-ass woman. Don't ever treat me like a child." As she strode for the door the other four didn't even look up at her.

Slipping out the back, she made sure Trinity and Eden were gone before going to the fence. She wasn't sure when Marcus planned to check in with her, but all she needed to make this work was a twenty-minute lead.

Scaling the fence, she hopped down and hurried out of view, whispering under her breath as she thought of how Marcus and the others would react when they learned she was gone. "You left me no choice."

Chapter Thirteen

Marcus made himself wait a full fifteen minutes before texting Kiyomi, so it didn't seem like he didn't trust her at all on this. *Are you in position?* he asked.

She responded seconds later. *Yes.*

Relief slid through him. He'd pissed her off earlier, but he wasn't sorry. His whole purpose for being here was to keep her safe, even if it meant protecting her from herself.

He started to put his phone in his pocket. A niggling sense of unease made him text Eden, not wanting to interrupt Trinity while she was sorting out the Atlanta op. *You in contact with Kiyomi?*

No. Why?

Dread trickled through him. *Is she watching the northwest?*

No. She's still at the house.

The dread turned to fear.

He dialed Trinity, his pulse thudding in his ears. "Is Kiyomi with you?" he demanded when she answered.

"No. Why, what's going on?"

She'd lied to him. Looked into his eyes and fucking

lied to him. Christ! "Did you ask her to pull security with you?'

"No. Marcus, what—"

"She's gone." A shot of adrenaline burst through him. Ty, Megan, Jesse and Amber were all staring tensely at him now. "And we all know where she went."

Fucking hell. She'd gone after Rahman. Alone.

"Christ," Trinity hissed.

Marcus dragged a hand over his face, thinking fast. Shite, he'd known she was too quiet at dinner, and she'd given up arguing with Trinity much too easily.

"When did you last see her?" Trinity asked.

"About eighteen minutes ago, give or take." Shite. Way too long. Kiyomi had an almost twenty-minute head start on them. They wouldn't be able to stop her in time.

"We're heading back now. Be ready to move when we get there."

"Aye." As soon as he rang off, he dialed Kiyomi's mobile. It kept ringing, didn't even go to voicemail.

Fear ground in his gut, eclipsing the anger. He hated that she'd done this, even though he understood it on a personal level. Revenge was a powerful motivator.

Crossing the room in three strides, Marcus pulled Amber's laptop toward him. "We have to stop Kiyomi. This is the fastest route to Rahman. If he's still there," he added, tracing the route on the satellite map on screen with his finger. She would have stolen a vehicle. Something small, nondescript and maneuverable.

"Holy shit," Ty muttered, shaking his head.

"She didn't trust that we'd take him out later, so she's going to do it on her own," Megan answered, reaching for her weapon. "We better haul ass."

"I'll drive." Marcus snatched up the keys to one of the vehicles and the others followed him out back.

By the time Trinity and Eden jumped in the back seat, almost twenty-five minutes had passed since Kiyomi left. He took the lead, speeding down the darkening streets while the last, weak rays of sunlight faded in the west.

The sights, the scent of the dust and the smell of grilled meat took him right back to his final deployment here, triggering a gut-deep anxiety he couldn't shake. The back of his neck prickled, a subconscious warning he couldn't ignore as he thought of the blast.

His men screaming all around him. Then the pain. The torture.

He shoved the memories back. He'd take on hell itself to save Kiyomi. Saving her was all that mattered.

They *had* to reach her in time. Because if they didn't, Marcus couldn't bear the alternative.

****

Now or never.

Kiyomi had waited as long as she dared. For the past twelve minutes she'd watched Rahman's security come in and out of the gated property. Just as she'd thought, they were getting ready to move him.

No way she was going to let that happen.

The growing shadows swallowed the alley as she snuck down it and toward the privacy wall surrounding the house Rahman was in. She'd just checked the interior yard from a balcony across the street. He had to still be in there because she recognized two of his personal body-guards patrolling the inside yard. He didn't go anywhere without those two.

Two well-placed shots from her silenced pistol took care of them. Security cameras would likely pick them up, but it didn't matter. By the time anyone noticed what she'd done, it would be too late.

Her hand closed around the grip of her weapon as she chose her moment. She'd planned everything out as best she could on the way here, confident that Rahman and his men wouldn't kill her on the spot when they saw her.

Ironically, for the moment, the Architect was her best protection. Kiyomi could endure anything short of death until her team got here—and she was betting that wouldn't be long. Even if they were pissed as hell about what she'd done, they would still come for her.

In the meantime, she had a personal score to settle.

Blocking out the rage and hatred, she slipped into stone-cold op mode as she scaled the wall and landed lightly in a crouch in the yard. As she'd hoped, no other security rushed her.

She hugged the shadows as she ran across the yard for the window at the side of the house she'd chosen for her entry point, making sure the camera mounted there didn't spot her.

By the time she'd pried open the window and started to boost her body through it, they must have seen the camera footage. Because just as her foot touched the floor, two men rushed toward her from the back, Rahman's head of security in the lead.

She shot them both in the chest. Both fell, but the head bodyguard was still moving, trying to raise his pistol.

Kiyomi walked up and stood over him, staring into his ugly face for a moment before she put a bullet through it. She shifted her attention to the room at the back of the house. If Rahman was in there, he might have seen everything from a laptop.

The bedroom door was closed tight. She stopped a few feet from it to gather herself, then attacked.

She kicked the door open and burst into the room, her heart jolting when Rahman whirled to face her in his desk chair.

He froze, that eerie, dark gaze locking on her. His stunned expression faded as he stared at her in the sudden silence, then a fanatical gleam entered his eyes, contorting his handsome features into a cold smile that sent a shiver up her spine.

"Well, well," he said in heavily accented English, raking the length of her body with eyes filled with a sickening mixture of lust and hatred.

Her stomach contracted into a hard ball even as she held her pistol steady, the barrel aimed at his head.

"Where are my guards, Kiyomi?"

"Dead. And soon, so will you be."

Rather than look afraid or even concerned, he laughed softly. "You came back."

"To kill you." Her finger was on the trigger. Something held her back from pulling it. A shot to the head was too easy. No. When she killed him, she would make it hurt.

He smirked, the rage taking over the desire in his eyes. "I don't think so, pet."

Pet. God, she wanted to puke. He'd called her that before he'd realized she was more than she'd seemed.

Kiyomi's pulse thudded in her ears as she confronted the monster before her. This was what she'd wanted. To face him alone. She let the anger and hatred coalesce into a fire in her gut, giving her strength to endure what was about to happen.

"You really thought you could do it, didn't you?" he mused, sneering as he stared into her eyes. "You thought you could break in here, take out my men, and kill me?" He laughed again, raking that chilling gaze over the length of her. Still arrogant as ever, confident in his power and his training even though he was the one at gunpoint. "I find that…untenable."

"You were going to sell me," she hissed.

He raised a taunting black eyebrow. "Oh, I'm still going to sell you, pet. After I've had my fill of you. The buyer's going to pay even more than our original agreement."

She might be able to get the intel out of him verbally. "The so-called 'Architect'?" she said in disdain.

His stare burned into hers. "So you do know about her. I wondered."

Idiot had just confirmed it was a woman. After she killed him, Kiyomi would take his phone and any other electronics she could find in here and let Amber work her magic. "What does she want with me?"

He shrugged, the smirk reappearing. "She recognizes perfection when she sees it." Then his expression shifted. Showing a glimpse of the monster beneath the mask. "No one betrays me, Kiyomi."

His hand flashed up, a pistol in it. She dropped into a battle roll as the bullet slammed into the tile behind her, swung out a foot and knocked his chair off balance. He caught himself and swiveled to face her again, but too late.

She kicked the weapon from his hand and moved in close to grab his wrist, taking away his leverage before he could reach for anything else. They stared at each other, both breathing fast, her weapon inches from his face. Rahman's eyes burned like glowing coals as he stared at her in a terrible mixture of fury and lust.

Snarling, he wrenched her wrist down and broke her grip, twisting her pistol free. It clattered to the floor beside them.

Kiyomi didn't move. Didn't look away from him. She waited for the triumph to show on his face. For that arrogant look she hated so much, and thought of her Valkyrie sisters. Of Marcus. They gave her strength. "You're mine," he growled at her.

He thought he had her. That he had won.

She was about to show him just how wrong he was.

Grabbing the clip in her hair, she split the two halves of the butterfly apart and slammed one stiletto through the back of his hand, pinning it to the armrest.

His eyes bulged, his mouth opening on a scream of agony she muffled instantly with a hand clamped across his mouth as he struggled to pry the blade free with his other.

"How's it feel to be this helpless, you evil mother-fucker?" she snarled, then drove the second blade up and under his jaw, jamming it through his carotid pulse. She twisted it while he screamed and flailed at her with his free arm, his right hand still pinned to the chair.

Blood spurted as she yanked the thin blade downward with a savage jerk, opening his carotid and jugular wide. He clapped his free hand over it, screaming into her palm as he tried to bite her.

Ripping his phone from his pocket, she leapt back and landed on her feet with the second blade in hand, ready to stab him again. Her heart pumped fast as she tucked the phone into her pocket.

Rahman was already sagging in the chair, his eyes already growing unfocused as he slumped sideways, his hand falling away from the slash in his neck. The sound of her rapid breaths was harsh in her ears, the powerful lash of adrenaline and triumph making her muscles quiver.

She'd done it. She'd killed him. Now his reign of terror was over.

A distant slam in the background was her only warning before the unmistakable crack of gunfire shattered the silence. She whirled to face the wide-open door, then dove for the pistol Rahman had dropped.

The shooting was coming from outside, toward the rear of the house. Men shouted. More gunfire came from the rear and then the side, then the faint sound of running footsteps.

Kiyomi raced to the wall beside the door and waited, centering herself, ready to fight for her life with everything she had left. She had what she'd come for. She wasn't going to die now that he was finally dead.

Something slammed into the front doors. Twice. Three times.

Kiyomi tensed, prepared to fight to the death for the chance to live.

One more slam and someone burst inside. Kiyomi waited until the intruder got close, then ducked through the doorway to fire.

She froze.

But it wasn't more of Rahman's security rushing in to kill her.

It was Marcus in pure operator mode.

Chapter Fourteen

W eapon up, Marcus swept past Kiyomi to check the entire room, searching for other targets. "Clear," he called out to the others.

Willing his heart to climb back down his throat, he holstered his weapon and spun to face Kiyomi, ignoring Ty and Jesse as they rushed forward to check the rest of the place. Kiyomi was covered in blood and he didn't know if it was hers.

"Are you hurt?" he demanded, stalking forward to seize her by the shoulders. Her face was pale, her eyes dilated, a pistol in her hand.

"No. I'm fine."

On the other side of the room Rahman was slumped in the chair, stone dead, a vicious wound in the side of his throat and a blade pinning his hand into the wooden arm-rest.

Shoving out a breath, Marcus grabbed her and pulled her into a fierce hug, closing his eyes on a hard exhale. He'd rip into her later for what she'd done. Right now he just needed this reassurance that she was okay.

She was trembling a little, her breathing shaky. It was warm in the room and he was pretty sure the shaking wasn't from shock, but from a backlash of adrenaline after killing the bastard who had tormented her day and night for the past several months.

He bent and scooped her up in his arms.

"No," she protested, "I'm—"

"Quiet." No damn way he was letting her out of his sight for an instant. The others could retrieve her blades and try to minimize any evidence that might lead back to her.

He strode from the room, his limp more pronounced, the additional weight sending pain shooting through his hip and thigh. Bloody hell. Before his injuries he could have swept her up in his arms and carried her for miles.

"I got his phone. But we need all the electronics," she said, turning to look behind her. "There's a laptop on the desk."

Trinity stood outside the bedroom door, her stare glacial as she locked eyes with Kiyomi. "I'll get it." She walked past without another word, and Marcus swore the temperature dropped several degrees from the amount of frost Trinity was giving off. Not that he blamed her.

"Who did you engage?" Kiyomi asked as he carried her to the front doors.

"Hit team. Not Rahman's." Four men dressed in black, armed with rifles and pistols. "We killed three, wounded and captured the fourth."

Her attention sharpened on him. "The Architect sent them?"

"Don't know." Right now, he didn't even care. All he wanted was to get her the hell out of there safely before they had any more surprises.

"Rahman confirmed it was a woman," Kiyomi said to Marcus as he carried her out of the house. Ty and Jesse were standing guard in the yard where two more of Rahman's men lay dead. Kiyomi had taken out two others earlier.

"He told you that?" Outside the wall, Eden and Megan had both vehicles pulled up as close as possible.

"Yes. But I don't think he knows her identity."

He grunted and kept going. Amber was waiting by the side gate, watching the sidewalk. She waved them forward, rushed ahead to pull open the back door of the second van. Marcus bundled Kiyomi inside it and climbed in beside her.

She turned toward the door. "Wait, what about the prisoner—"

"He's already in the back of the other van," Marcus growled, anger beginning to bleed through the relief.

He pushed it aside, focused on keeping the team safe as the rest of the members rushed out of the house and climbed into the vehicles. Trinity jumped into the front passenger seat of their vehicle just as the first van pulled away from the curb. Eden followed it.

A cold, brittle silence filled the vehicle as they raced away from the scene. Law enforcement would no doubt be on the way, the shooting reported by the local residents. As soon as word got out about the attack and Rahman's death, security forces would be alerted.

Getting the team out of Syria was now ten times harder.

Marcus squeezed his hands into fists and took a slow, deep breath to take the edge off the anger eating at him. He waited until he was sure they were in the clear and heading back to the safehouse before speaking. Just as he opened his mouth to tear into Kiyomi, Trinity beat him to it, swiveling in her seat to nail Kiyomi with a hard stare.

"I told you we'd get him. I gave you my word. But that wasn't good enough. You ditched us so you could go off on your own and take care of your vendetta. Do you know how fucking furious we are at you right now?" Her deep blue eyes snapped sparks at her. "I'm so disappointed in you."

Kiyomi's chin came up, a flush hitting her cheeks. "His security team was in the process of getting ready to move him. I wasn't losing my chance."

The fury on Trinity's face was something to behold, and Marcus approved. Kiyomi deserved to be reamed out for this stunt she'd pulled. "Well, lucky for you, Marcus figured out you were missing soon after you'd left, otherwise you'd be dead right now," Trinity continued.

"I could have handled the others," Kiyomi argued. "I had it under control."

"Jesus Christ, that's not the point," Marcus snapped, drawing her dark stare. "You took off to go after Rahman by yourself, when you were expressly ordered not to by your team leader. You didn't want to wait, so you lied to me, went behind our backs and did what you wanted anyway. That's not only reckless as hell, it's bloody selfish, yet you don't give a shit because you got what you wanted."

Hurt flashed in her eyes. "If I'd waited, he'd have disappeared again," she shot back, color flooding into her cheeks. "He'd have wriggled off the hook and escaped justice yet again, and then we'd have spent God knows how long trying to track him down again—if we ever did. I couldn't let that happen, and you of all people should understand why," she flung at him.

Marcus shook his head, suddenly weary now that the edge of his temper had been dulled. "I told you, I didn't kill any of the men who captured me." Just two guards on the way out of the compound with Megan.

Her dark stare bore into his, hard, unflinching. Showing him the steely core he'd always known lay inside her. "But they're all dead, aren't they. You got justice. If some, or even one of them had still been alive right now in the city, you're telling me you wouldn't have wanted to settle the score?"

She didn't get it. She was too blinded by hatred to

see the truth. "Killing them wouldn't change what they did to me. And no, I *wouldn't* have gone after them, because unlike you, *I* would never risk my team to settle a personal score," he finished with a pointed look.

She wrenched her gaze away, a muscle flexing in her jaw as she folded her arms. "I wasn't risking any of you. Just myself. That's why I took off on my own. None of you were supposed to know what happened until it was all over."

"From where I'm sitting, you're damn lucky we *did* know and got there when we did."

He was well aware that she was highly skilled and deadly in a lot of ways. But taking on that many armed and highly trained security personnel alone, then Rahman, and making it out of the fortified compound while she ran through the neighborhood looking for a vehicle to steal?

It still made his blood run cold to remember her standing there covered in Rahman's blood and not knowing if they were too late. Wondering if that bastard had touched her again.

A few minutes later, the van in front of them turned left and drove off. "Where are they going?" Kiyomi asked as Eden kept driving straight.

"To a different location," Trinity snapped, not having softened her stance even a little. "Amber's trying to access Rahman's security system remotely to scrub it of all evidence of us being there, but it might be too late. Now we have to split into two teams until we can get out of the country."

Kiyomi was silent a moment, then released a hard sigh. "All right. I'm sorry you guys were dragged into this. But I'm not sorry for going out on my own and killing Rahman. I had to."

Nobody said anything else for the rest of the drive to the original safehouse. The brittle tension between Kiyomi and the rest of them remained as everyone went inside.

"Here's his cell," she said, handing it to Trinity. "Hopefully Amber can find a way to get the whole conversation with the Architect from it. Oh, and tell her he used a particular word that stood out during our short conversation. Untenable."

"So?"

"So, it was out of place. English is his third language. And the Architect used it in the recorded clip between them earlier. Amber's using linguistic forensics as a tool in the investigation. Thought it might be significant." She shrugged.

Trinity walked past her without another word and dialed someone on her mobile.

Eden started to follow, then stopped and faced Kiyomi with her hands on her hips. "I get why you did it. I really do. But we're not just your backup, Kiyomi. We're your family." She shook her head, a pained frown drawing her eyebrows together. "What if you hadn't made it? What if we'd all gotten there and found you dead?"

Kiyomi's cheeks flushed again. "Then you would have moved on and finished the mission to expose the Architect without me." Eden gaped at her in astonishment but Kiyomi stalked past her, her shoulder brushing Marcus's on the way down the hall.

Shaking her head, Eden met his gaze. "She talks like she doesn't think she matters to us at all."

That's exactly how it sounded.

He stood there a moment after Eden went into the next room with Trinity, gathering his thoughts. What a shit show.

He ran a hand over his face, unsure what to do. What was done was done, no one on the team had been injured, and they were dealing with the aftermath as best they could. They'd have to get out of this place by morning at the latest, and with luck they might get some actionable intel from the electronics or the captured bodyguard that would lead them to the Architect.

For now, Marcus's hip was killing him, and he wanted a hot shower. His shirt and hands had Rahman's blood all over them.

In the bathroom attached to his room upstairs, he stripped and stood under the hot spray for a few minutes, letting the heat of the water ease the tension in his neck and shoulders.

After scrubbing himself down, he got out, toweled off, and wrapped it around his waist. He brushed his teeth, took a couple anti-inflammatories and paused to run a hand over his beard, contemplating at least trimming it.

The door behind him opened. He watched, unmoving as Kiyomi slipped inside and locked the door behind her. She wore that plum-colored satin robe, her hair wet from a recent shower.

She met his gaze in the mirror, and there was a surprising amount of hesitancy in her expression. As if she was assessing him. Trying to figure out how angry he still was.

The answer was, he was still mad as hell. But not for the reasons she probably thought.

He stood where he was as she crossed to him, turning only his head to look at her. She was so beautiful and strong and talented in so many ways. But she didn't have a fucking clue when it came to relationships, romantic or otherwise.

Still watching him, she boosted herself up to sit facing him on the edge of the vanity. Without any makeup she looked younger than her thirty-one years, but the timeworn look in her eyes was much older than that.

He didn't say anything, somehow resisted the urge to take her face in his hands and kiss her senseless, and finally she spoke. "I meant what I said earlier. I'm sorry for going behind your back, but not about the rest. It had to be done, and I'd do it all over again."

She looked tired. Fragile, although he knew better than anyone how untrue that was. "You understand that, right? Rahman had to die by my hand. I had to be the one. It's the only way I could ever move forward."

He searched her eyes for a long moment. "And now? Did it magically heal you like you thought it would?"

Sadness and a pain he understood all too well and would have done anything to remove filled her eyes. "No. But at least that part of me can rest now. It's like a weight has been lifted."

He couldn't stand that she was still hurting. Couldn't stand that he might have lost her today, when he'd only just found her. But most of all, he couldn't stand her thinking she didn't matter to him or any of the others.

He curled his hands around the edge of the vanity, not daring to touch her yet. She was addictive. One touch, one kiss and she went straight to his brain like a drug.

He wasn't a man who wore his heart on his sleeve, or had fancy words to flatter her with. But she meant a great deal to him, so for her he was willing to try. "When I realized what had happened, my heart stopped."

She didn't look away, didn't try to stop him or plead her case, just watched him intently.

"What you did scared the hell out of me, and it wasn't just selfish because you put yourself and the rest of us in danger. It was selfish because you didn't stop to consider how the rest of us would feel if you'd died."

He paused to let that sink in a moment. Then, unable to stop himself, he curled a hand around her nape, his thumb rubbing over the side of her neck, emotion welling up inside him. "Do you know what it would have done to me if I'd gone in there and found you dead?"

She started to shake her head. "Marcus—"

"No," he snapped, his eyes drilling into hers. He had

to make her understand. Had to get this out. His fingers tightened slightly. "We care about you. *I* care about you. More than I've ever—" Only Megan had mattered to him on this level before, but for entirely different reasons, none of them romantic. "You matter to me. And if anything happened to you, I'd…"

He didn't know what the fuck he would do. Aside from going back home to Laidlaw Hall and hole up there for the rest of his bleak, lonely existence, grieving for her until the day he finally stopped breathing.

Torment filled her face for an instant before she lowered her gaze. "No, don't."

He pulled her toward him, leaned his forehead on hers. "You *matter* to me," he repeated in a rough whisper, his heart pounding. Why wouldn't she accept it? "I would walk through hell for you. I would do anything for you, except sit back and watch you recklessly risk your life. I won't do it. I can't," he finished in a taut whisper.

Kiyomi drew a shaky breath, her hands coming up to settle on his cheeks. He didn't know if he'd gotten through to her, but at least she'd heard him.

She angled her head, settling those soft, full lips on his, and it was like lightning striking tinder. He kissed her back with all the desperation still pumping through his system, one hand buried in her hair while he wrapped his other arm around her waist to haul her close.

Marcus drove his tongue into her mouth, needing to claim her, show her without words what she meant to him. How much he needed her.

Kiyomi moaned into his mouth and pulled her robe open. Her naked breasts plastered to his chest as she rubbed them against his skin. He gripped her hair and pulled her head back to kiss his way down her throat, earning a gasp and a shiver as his tongue found a sensitive spot.

He was hard as stone beneath his own towel, his cock

aching to sink inside her soft heat, make her his again. He forced the need aside and focused on loving her instead, giving her pleasure even when she pulled his towel free and slid a hand down his belly.

He groaned when her fingers curled around him and pumped, his mouth now an inch from her right nipple. He took the hard point into his mouth and sucked, rubbing his tongue over it while she stroked him. Her touch was too much and yet not enough.

Holding tight to his control, he pulled her hand from him and sank to his knees before her, putting his face close to the tender place between her thighs. She put a hand on his shoulder as he pulled her hips toward him with a hand on the base of her spine. Marcus paused to look up at her, making sure she was okay with this.

Her eyes were dark with need, her teeth sunk into her bottom lip, and she didn't try to stop him. He kissed the soft skin just above her mound, inhaling the mix of soap and the scent of her arousal, nuzzling her before kissing the smooth flesh at the top of her flushed folds. She sucked in a breath and waited, watching him.

Wrapping both hands around her hips, he bent his head and touched his lips there, adding a gentle stroke of his tongue. Her thighs clenched around the sides of his shoulders and she gasped, arching toward him.

He wanted more. So much more. But not here on the bathroom counter.

Growling low in his throat, he pushed to his feet, scooped her off the counter and carried her through to his bedroom, his mouth busy on hers. He set her on the foot of the bed, leaned over her to push her to her back, then sank to his knees before her, bringing her shapely legs across his shoulders.

She was perfection spread out before him like that. His stare riveted to the wet, silken folds before him, the swollen bud of her clit peeking out at the top.

With every bit of reverence in him he lowered his mouth to her and began worshipping her with his lips and tongue. Kiyomi wound her hands in his hair and whispered his name. She tasted sweet yet tangy, and her soft gasps and moans made him drunk. Drunk on her, on her response to every caress.

When he plunged his tongue inside her she grabbed at the quilt and arched. Her head came up, those dark, sexy eyes watching him while he tasted her. He pulled his tongue out slowly then thrust back in, reveling in the way her mouth opened, a soft cry spilling from her lips.

He would gladly do this all day. Stay here on his knees pleasuring her this way, ignoring the pain in his hip and leg. He wanted to worship her. Show her exactly what she meant to him, let his actions prove his feelings in a way his earlier words might not have.

"Stop," she finally gasped out, and pushed his head away.

He sat back on his heels, breathing fast. Before he could say anything she leaned forward to cover his lips with hers. Marcus wound his hands in her damp hair, sliding his tongue along hers, his cock trapped between them.

A second later Kiyomi suddenly released him to turn around and face the bed. Tossing her damp hair over her shoulder, she looked back at him with smoldering eyes as she slid a hand between her legs and wiggled her hips. "Get in me."

His tongue stuck to the roof of his mouth for a second while his brain caught up. Then he glanced around. *Shite*. "I don't have any—"

"We don't need one. I didn't tell you before, but I got tested on my way to the UK."

At the American military hospital in Germany when they'd stopped at Landstuhl to get her checked out and refuel.

153

She licked her lips. "I'm clean. And I can't get pregnant." She leaned forward onto one elbow, closed her eyes for a moment as she stroked herself, then nailed him with that sultry gaze that made his brain short-circuit. "Now get in me before I come without you."

It was a miracle he didn't explode on the spot.

Stepping up close behind her, he leaned forward, covering her back with his chest. His cock pressed tight to her slick core, all but killing him with the promise of the heated pleasure awaiting him.

Wrapping one hand around her hip, he guided himself into her, then gripped her other hip and leaned over her, his mouth on her neck. "Ready for me now, love?"

"Yes," she breathed, pushing backward.

Closing his eyes, Marcus buried his face in the side of her neck and slid slowly inside her.

They both moaned. His hands tightened on her hips. He kissed her neck, the curve of her shoulder, scraping his teeth over the tender spot as he eased back and then surged forward again. A slow, steady rhythm, using her reaction and motions to guide him.

Her eyes were closed, soft, throaty moans filling the quiet as he worked her core, her fingers gliding over her clit. He reached around to help her and she grabbed hold of his hand, pressing his fingers to the slick nub.

"Oh, God, just like that," she whispered, her hips surging in time with his.

It was incredible. The closeness, the slow, sensual build to explosion.

He lifted his chest from her back to watch through heavy-lidded eyes as the muscles along her spine flexed, the perfect heart-shape of her arse moving with him, her soft, slick folds closing around his cock with every thrust. *Ahh, Christ...*

Her thighs began to tremble. Kiyomi laid her cheek against the bed and closed her eyes, an expression of pure bliss on her face as she neared the edge. She was panting now, tiny groans coming from her as she thrust back to meet him a little faster, a little harder. Her core clenched around him, then her cry of ecstasy set him loose.

Marcus leaned back and gripped her hips as he thrust in and out, watching his cock disappear into her while she clamped around him. His eyes slammed shut as pleasure blasted up his spine. He threw his head back, barely managed to stifle his roar of release as the orgasm hit.

Still breathing hard when he could finally open his eyes again, he eased out of her and quickly turned her as he scooted her up the bed on her back. After grabbing a towel to clean them both up he crawled up beside her and pulled her into his arms with a groan of mingled contentment and relief.

Kiyomi draped a thigh across his middle and burrowed in close as the quiet hum of the ceiling fan registered and a wash of cool air bathed their damp skin. "Are you still mad?" she asked after a minute.

"Aye," he murmured, eyes closed.

She kissed his chest. "I like makeup sex, though."

He chuckled. "Me too."

She cuddled closer, tucking her head beneath his chin. She fit so damn perfectly against him. Like she'd been made for him. "You matter to me too, you know."

"Good." He kissed the top of her head and hugged her tight. He was quiet a moment, thinking of what she'd said earlier now that his brain had blood supply again. "When you said you couldn't get pregnant. Are you taking something?"

"I had a hysterectomy when I was seventeen."

His eyes snapped open and he jerked his head around to stare at her. "What?"

"A tubal ligation wouldn't take care of the messy business of monthly biology, and trying to regulate my cycle out in the field was a hassle, so they went for the more convenient option." She sighed, didn't protest as he rolled her to her side to look at her abdomen. "There's no scar. They did it internally. Wanted to take care of the problem without damaging the goods, you know?"

He forced his gaze back up to her face, reeling and unsure what the hell to say. "Love, I'm so sorry."

She lowered her gaze. "Thanks. It's okay. I accepted it a long time ago. And it's not like I ever expected to want kids someday." A frown wrinkled her brow. "We were so vulnerable when they put us into the system. And then into the Program. No one did anything to stop them from exploiting us. That's the part I hate the most. I want to stop it from happening to other vulnerable girls."

He didn't dare ask more, not wanting to upset her. But dammit, it infuriated him to know what they'd done to her. Those bastards had taken away her childhood, then her adult life, and they'd taken away her choice to have children one day as well.

Rolling her back into him once more, he wrapped her up in his arms and held her close, her cheek resting over his heart. "You all right?" A lot had happened in the past few hours. It would be hitting her hard now.

"Yes." She drew a deep breath, let it out slowly. "I thought I'd feel different. I know he's dead, but it still doesn't seem real."

He made a low sound and squeezed her tighter. "He's gone, and can never touch you again."

She nodded. She was so still in the minutes that followed, he thought she'd fallen asleep. But a few moments later her breathing hitched slightly, then her shoulders jerked.

He knew before he felt the wetness on his chest that she was crying, and his heart twisted. He drew her even closer, one hand on the back of her head and the other banded tight around her back. She needed to let this out.

"I've got you, love," he murmured, and held her

through a different kind of release than the one he'd given her before.

Gradually her little shudders and gasps subsided. She melted into him with a sigh and her breathing grew deep and even as she slid into sleep. He dozed off too, awakened sometime later by the ringtone of his mobile in the bathroom.

"Stay here," he whispered when Kiyomi stirred, and got up to see who was calling.

Megan. He dialed her back. "Everything okay?" he asked.

"Yes. How's Kiyomi?"

"Better."

"Good. Tell her we're finished interrogating the prisoner. Didn't get much, other than some messages on his phone. We dumped him at a certain location and left him for the local security forces to deal with. Briar and Georgia are en route to the target house in Atlanta now. Rahman recorded the conversation with the Architect. Amber is analyzing it now, then she's going to tackle the recovered laptop. Trin's working on getting us a flight back to the UK before first light."

Good. "I'll tell her."

Kiyomi was sitting up on the bed watching him when he came back into the room to tell her. "Amber's analyzing data now," he told her. "We're flying out in a few hours."

A leap of excitement flashed in her eyes, then her expression hardened. "Good. I can't wait to hunt this bitch down."

Chapter Fifteen

"Rahman's dead."

Janelle laid down her pencil on her drafting table and sat up straight, burner phone to her ear. "When?" she asked the young woman on the other end. One of her most trusted members of her personal guard.

"Last night. Murdered in his bedroom at the compound."

"How?"

"Stabbed through the neck while sitting in a chair. Killer used another blade to pin his hand to the armrest."

Interesting. The team sent on her orders to intercept Kiyomi had all been killed. "What kind of blades?"

"I don't know yet. There's no security footage. I only found out from a source in the medical examiner's office." A pause. "Did you order it?"

She snorted. "Don't be ridiculous." Though she'd been tempted more than a few times. If Rahman hadn't been so committed to finding Kiyomi, he would have been a liability. With all his military and security connections, under different circumstances she might have regarded him as a threat.

"Was it one of us?"

"No. It was our target."

A kill like that, up close and personal, signified a strong emotional connection to the victim. She had experienced that phenomenon herself several times, most recently when she'd killed that asshole Glenn Bennett, the CIA officer she had fucked once upon a time to get what she needed.

He'd known too much. Then he'd panicked, and talked too much. So she'd slit his throat and left his severed tongue lying on the floor for talking too much.

Rahman's killer had hated him too. Janelle felt a rush of pride and affection.

Ah, Kiyomi. So full of fire and resolve even after all you've been through.

Was it any wonder why she was Janelle's favorite? And if Janelle was right about everything she'd hypothesized so far, then now that Rahman had been dealt with, Kiyomi would be going back to the UK as soon as possible. To where she and the others seemed to feel safest right now. Janelle's hired team had failed, but this might give her a way to finally track her prized target.

"So we're not implicated in any way?" the woman asked her. "There's no way for them to trace anything back to you? One of the men you sent is still missing. Rahman might have talked."

"It doesn't matter." She wasn't worried. Rahman never knew her identity. But for precaution's sake, she needed to be proactive and act accordingly. "What about the surveillance team in the UK?"

"They haven't seen anyone coming or going from the estate yet."

"Tell them to drag it out for another few days. We may see something by the end of the week." If the Valkyries had been staying there, it was possible that a team of them had flown to Syria to provide Kiyomi with backup.

Janelle would have to search recent flight data in and out of airfields near Damascus. "Inform me if you find out anything more. In the meantime, I'm initiating the next phase and mobilizing the others. Stand by for further orders."

Disconnecting, she began packing up her designs. She'd always lived a nomadic and somewhat Spartan existence, never knowing when she would need to move, and not wanting to leave any damning clues behind.

The trio of framed photos on the windowsill were the only indications as to her true identity. Two were links to her past, and the most likely key to her future. The third represented the dream she'd longed to achieve for almost thirty years.

She packed them away where they wouldn't be seen amongst her things. Moving quickly, she gathered up her sparse belongings and her weapons while her next moves formulated in her mind.

In her closet she paused, her eye catching on her reflection in the mirror hung on the back of the door. The image was still somewhat of a shock, almost as if a complete stranger was staring back at her.

The woman in the mirror bore no resemblance whatsoever to the one she was inside. In her mind's eye she was still young and beautiful with a hard, toned body, able to seduce any man she wanted. All that might be behind her now, but the future was more promising than ever.

No one knew what she was capable of. The only ones who had, were all dead.

Her gaze hardened in the mirror. Green eyes that reminded her too much of people from her past. They turned cold as she fought the rage that had been her constant companion since childhood. Her entire life had been a competition. A fight to prove she was the best.

Eliminating competition came as naturally to her as

breathing. Once she set her mind on something, nothing would stand in the way of achieving her goal, and it was no different now. If she could do what she'd done to start the Program in the first place, nothing else even came close.

Sacrifice was necessary—as long as she was the one who came out on top. And she always would, because she was a survivor.

She drove out of the garage and closed the remote-controlled door behind her. A cleanup crew was en route. By the time they arrived, she would be waiting to board her plane to the UK.

Her Valkyries were proving a difficult target thus far. That only made the hunt more enjoyable, the outcome more satisfying. Now it was time to join the hunt in person.

Janelle smiled fondly as she drove toward the freeway. She was so damn proud of them all. It would hurt to kill the thing she loved most, but nothing worthwhile ever came without loss.

As the original Valkyrie, she knew exactly what it cost to come out on top. Once she had the final piece she required, she would begin her lifelong ambition of creating a new force of the most perfect female assassins the world had ever known.

****

Was this real? Sometimes it was still hard for Kiyomi to believe.

She had never dreamed that she would ever allow her heart to get involved when it came to a man, but Marcus made it impossible not to.

In the safehouse living room she quickly packed up the last of her gear into her duffel and caught herself watching him as he did the same. The moment she looked at him, a sharp pain pierced her chest.

In the space of a few days, everything had changed for them. He'd unlocked something inside her she hadn't known existed, and now the thought of losing him tore her up inside.

No, she told herself sternly. *You know there's no choice. It's safer for him if you go. You knew when you first slept with him that this was only temporary.*

She laced up her boots and picked up her bag. Shutting off and compartmentalizing her feelings wasn't so easy where he was concerned. Every time she looked at him she remembered what it was like together, the way he touched her. Like magic. With him she never had to pretend, be someone else.

He straightened, duffel in one hand and cane in the other. Tall and strong. Proud. "Ready?"

"Yes—"

Trinity rushed into the room, her expression grave as she held her phone to her ear. "Understood. We're moving now." She ended the call just as Eden stepped into the room. "That was Megan. Some of Rahman's people are on their way here."

"What? How?" Kiyomi demanded.

"Probably CCTVs around his compound. We've got two minutes to vacate the premises."

Kiyomi snatched the keys from the counter. At this point it didn't matter how the enemy had found this place. "Let's go."

There wasn't time to wipe down the place properly. Everyone grabbed their gear and hurried to the van. Kiyomi slid into the driver's seat and had the engine running while the others piled in. Trinity got in beside her, Marcus and Eden in the back.

"Go," Marcus said as he slid the side door shut after him.

Kiyomi hit the gas. "Where am I going?" she asked

Trinity.

"Just head east for now."

Kiyomi turned right and began to weave her way through the residential neighborhood. Trinity was checking the GPS on her phone. "Left at the light up ahead."

She did as she was told, but a few hundred yards after she'd made the turn, in the rearview mirror she spotted a black SUV weaving erratically through traffic behind them. Whoever it was, was in a helluva hurry. "Someone's coming up fast on our six," she said, and ducked down a side street just in case.

Sure enough, the SUV skidded around the corner seconds later.

"Hang on," Kiyomi said, and stepped on it. She veered left at the next street. The traffic was light, but a high-speed chase through an area like this was still dangerous. "Get me to a highway," she told Trinity.

Marcus and Eden were both swiveled around in their seats, looking through the back windows. "He's still back there," Marcus said.

"I see him." Searching for a place to lose them, Kiyomi was forced to slow to maneuver around other vehicles.

"Straight ahead three blocks, and then a hard right," Trinity told her, eyes on her phone.

Kiyomi darted around a delivery truck, then slammed on the brake to avoid a head-on collision with a bus. Horns blasted as she yanked the wheel, narrowly missing both vehicles. Behind her, the SUV jumped onto the sidewalk to pass the snarled traffic.

"Two more blocks," Trinity said.

Kiyomi saw the turn up ahead. "Get ready," she told the others, then hit the brake and made a sharp right turn, accelerating as the back end of the van swung around. "Now where?" she said to Trinity.

"Right at the light, then first left. Highway's right

there."

There was too much traffic backed up at the light. Kiyomi turned into an alley before the intersection. It was narrow, with only a few inches of clearance on either side of her mirrors.

When they were partway up it, the SUV tore around the corner. Sparks flew as it lost its mirrors on the walls of the first building, but it kept coming.

"Front passenger's lowering the window," Marcus said. "Rifle. He's getting ready to fire."

Kiyomi floored it. Up ahead she could see traffic passing the end of the alley. She couldn't afford to slow down. Had to risk a collision and burst through the intersection. "Brace," she snapped.

She shot the van out of the alley. Swerved to avoid the truck coming right at her, then darted between two other vehicles going the other way as she crossed the intersection. Tires screeched and horns shrieked. "Left?" she said to Trinity.

"Yes, then immediate right."

Kiyomi made the left turn, caught sight of the SUV to the left as it sped past them up a different street. Losing sight of it sent a wave of cold through her gut. "You see it?" she asked the others.

"No," Marcus said, looking around intently.

She kept going, driving as fast as she dared. If she could get to the highway, she might be able to lose them.

The van's tires squealed as she took a fast left. Ahead, the SUV was coming right at them. "*Shit*."

Throwing it into reverse, she whipped them into the next alley she found, skidding into it backwards. She hammered the brakes. *Dead end.*

"Stop here," Marcus commanded, reaching for his door handle.

She brought the van to a rocking stop. Marcus

jumped out, Eden diving after him. Kiyomi put the transmission back into drive and crept forward, following them.

Near the end of the alley Marcus crouched down on one knee, gripping his pistol in both hands. Eden was off to his right, mirroring his pose. "They gonna try to shoot out the tires?" Kiyomi said to Trinity.

Before Trinity could answer, Marcus and Eden raised their weapons almost in tandem and fired a quick burst. A second later they both stood and hurried for the van, Eden in the lead, while Marcus faced the street with his weapon still up, his gait uneven as he moved backward toward them.

An instant later a loud impact reverberated just out of view. Eden jumped in the open door. Kiyomi sped forward to meet Marcus, who practically dove inside. "Go right," he barked, reaching for the door to slide it shut.

Kiyomi stomped on the gas, yanking the wheel to the right when they reached the street. The SUV was a crumpled heap behind them, its front end smashed into the brick building. Men were climbing out of the wreckage, weapons in hand as they turned toward the van.

"Down!" Marcus commanded.

They all ducked as shots cracked into the back of the vehicle. The rear window shattered but they didn't hit the tires. Kiyomi raced for the next road and turned a hard right, veering out into traffic. As soon as she'd steadied the vehicle she looked in the rearview.

Trinity whipped around to look in the back. "Everyone okay?"

"Yes." Eden popped upright, then Marcus, and Kiyomi's heart began to beat again.

She kept her eye on the mirrors as she finally got them to the highway and put distance between them and the shooters. There might be others coming. "Where to now?"

"Airport, eight miles out," Trinity replied, dialing someone from the other part of the team.

Thankfully the rest of the journey was uneventful. The others were waiting when they arrived, and the jet was fueled and ready. "What happened with the prisoner?" Kiyomi said to Megan as they climbed aboard.

"He's currently being transported to a secure holding facility by the Brits for further interrogation," Megan said, then cut her a look sharp enough to slice through metal. "He didn't know the Architect's identity either, but the data on his phone has the same Atlanta number that was on Rahman's. You're lucky," she said with a bite to her tone. "Lucky you're still alive after that stunt you pulled, and that you didn't blow our best shot at finding the Architect."

Kiyomi bit back the argument that sprang to her tongue. Being defensive was a dick move right now. "You're right. I'm sorry."

The apology seemed to take the wind out of Megan's sails, because she closed her mouth and frowned. "Good. But you just burned up a lot of the trust we had in you."

Kiyomi nodded. "Understood." She would apologize to Amber, Jesse and Ty once they were airborne. "What about the address in Atlanta? Did you verify it?"

"Amber did. Briar and Georgia will be checking it out. It'll be at least five or six hours before we hear anything. Hopefully by the time we land in the Cotswolds, we'll know something."

Megan moved down the aisle to find Ty. Marcus was sliding into a window seat in the middle of the plane. He grimaced, grabbed hold of the armrests as he lowered himself into it.

Kiyomi made her way over to him, shoved her duffel under the seat in front and sat next to him. "You okay?"

He nodded and slid his arm around her, pulling her snug into his side. "Be glad to get airborne and put this place behind me forever."

"Me too." Kiyomi curled into him and wrapped her arms around his ribs. "I'm glad you're here with me." She planned to stay just like this for the duration of the flight. Because once they got back to Laidlaw Hall, everything would change.

He kissed the top of her head and squeezed her in answer.

Once they were in the air everyone relaxed visibly. Kiyomi closed her eyes, memorizing the feel of Marcus's arms around her before dozing off. She woke minutes before landing in the Cotswolds, and then it was a forty-minute drive to the manor.

They arrived just after noon, the sky a solid, leaden gray and a cold wind gusting over the hills. Marcus slowed as they approached a work crew up ahead on the side of the road, working on what looked like the water main.

Marcus picked up the handheld radio and contacted Ty, who was driving the other vehicle behind them. "Go 'round and come in through the east pasture, just as a precaution."

They passed through a narrow gate at the eastern entrance to the property and drove across the pastures. Several minutes later, Laidlaw Hall appeared nestled in the small valley, the golden-toned stone a welcome sight in the gloom.

A bittersweet pang hit her, part nostalgia, part grief. She'd grown so fond of this place, and now she had to leave it and its owner behind forever.

Inside, she found the hall and entry full of bags and boxes. Zack was the only one waiting there for them, as Chloe and Heath had moved into their new flat near Coventry the previous night.

Zack pulled Eden into a big hug, kissed her, then looped an arm around her waist as he spoke to the rest of them. "We got everything packed up except your bedrooms. Didn't want to invade your privacy."

Even though she'd known this was coming, Kiyomi's heart twisted. Seeing everything packed up made the finality of imminent departure hit home, leaving her more torn than ever.

A sharp pain knifed her chest as she met Marcus's gaze across the foyer, followed by a lick of panic. She wanted to stay. Didn't want to leave Marcus.

But they'd never made any promises to each other and she couldn't make one right now anyway—not with the future so uncertain. More importantly, she didn't want to place him in further jeopardy, and he'd gone so far above and beyond for her and the others already.

He deserved peace and security after all he'd been through, and she could never give him that. She would only bring him more chaos, danger and pain.

Just as she turned for the stairs to go pack the few things in her bedroom, Trinity walked out of the kitchen, talking on her cell phone. She spoke to whoever it was, then motioned for the others to gather around her. "Briar, hang on. I'm putting you on speaker so everyone can hear. Go ahead."

"Hey," Briar said. "Georgia and I are at the target house in Atlanta. It's empty. And I mean, empty. No furnishings, no artwork, nothing in the drawers or closets. As far as we can tell, everything's been wiped down professionally. Couldn't get a single print off anything—light switches, drawer handles, fridge, nada. Whoever was here is trained and incredibly efficient because she left no trace behind. The only thing we could dig up on the house is that it's owned by some corporation you'll need to look into. I've sent Amber the details."

Kiyomi released a frustrated sigh. Great. So even with the new intel, they'd hit yet another brick wall. "Did the prisoner give us anything else we can use?" she asked

Megan.

"Nothing that helps us at the moment," Trinity replied, then thanked Briar and ended the call before speaking to the rest of them again. "Rycroft's got his Stateside analysts working on a couple leads, trying to find out who the woman on the last call to Rahman was, and if she's connected to the address in Atlanta. He's in the air right now, should be touching down soon. I'll know more once he gets here, but we'd all better finish packing and be ready to move."

With that Trinity turned to Marcus, smiled and held out a hand. "Marcus. I can't thank you enough for what you've done for us."

"It's been my pleasure." He shook it, paused to look at Kiyomi, then turned and headed into his study, Karas limping at his heels.

An acute sense of loneliness hit her. She fought it back, glancing around at the others. Everything was happening too fast now. She wanted to slow time down, make these final few hours last forever.

Eden and Zack were already heading upstairs, with Megan and Ty right behind them. "Are you guys leaving tonight as well?" Kiyomi asked Amber, who was next to Jesse.

"Yeah, but we're not going to Coventry yet."

"No?"

She shook her head. "That second cousin I told you about is a total busybody and found someone that could be our aunt. She's apparently in London on business, and heading for a work conference in Birmingham in the morning. She contacted me via email, asking to meet up early, before it starts. I've only replied to her the once via the encrypted email account, for obvious reasons, but everything about her checks out on my end."

"So are you going to meet her?"

Amber shrugged. "Trin says she doesn't need us until tomorrow afternoon, so Meg and I've agreed to a quick meeting before we head to the next safehouse."

"Did she say anything about why she gave you both up? Or why she never tried to contact you?"

Amber's eyes were flat. "She says she was told Meg and I both died soon after entering foster care, and that's why she never tried to find or contact us after we were taken away. A fire or something." She shrugged. "Whatever, I just want to see if it's really her. If it is, I want some answers. Well, what I really want is to yell at her for abandoning two scared little girls when we needed her most. After that, we're done, and we'll go to our place in Coventry."

Kiyomi nodded. "I hope you get your closure."

Amber's smile was weary. "Closure would be nice."

Yes. They all deserved the closure they were looking for.

Amber and Jesse headed upstairs to finish packing, leaving just her and Trinity at the bottom of the staircase. Kiyomi wished her friend wasn't still angry with her. An uneasy tension filled the space between them, then Trinity walked up to her.

After a moment of silence, Trinity's set expression melted into one of fondness and she sighed, reaching for her. "Come here, you."

Kiyomi's throat closed up as her friend's arms came around her. She returned the embrace, a staggering sense of relief hitting her to know she was forgiven. "I'm sorry."

"Sorry/not sorry," Trinity accused, and Kiyomi couldn't help but smile. Then Trin pulled back and took her by the upper arms. "I'm leaving to get Rycroft soon. After our meeting, you and I will need to go soon." She nodded at Marcus's study door. "Go and say goodbye while you can."

Kiyomi covered a flinch, not wanting to accept that

she was down to her last few hours with Marcus.

Trin gave her a sad smile. "I know it hurts. But this doesn't mean it's goodbye forever. Maybe one day, after all this is behind us, you can—"

"Yeah. Maybe." Though she couldn't allow herself to believe that. This hurt too damn much already without adding false hope that would crush her later on. She was too much of a realist, and she hadn't asked for anything either.

Right now a shadowy figure known only as the Architect stood between her and any hope of a future. Kiyomi refused to allow herself to think beyond the mission.

As Trinity started up the staircase, Kiyomi turned to face Marcus's study door. There was only one thing within her control at the moment, and she was going to make the most of it while it lasted.

Chapter Sixteen

The end was here, and it hurt like hell.

Heart heavy, Marcus smiled as Karas set her front paws in his lap and tried to lick his face. Zack had been taking care of her while they were gone.

"I missed you too," he told her from the chair behind his desk, ruffling the top of her furry head while dodging her tongue. In spite of his smile, a mix of sadness and dread pressed down on him. It was raining now, the drops lashing the windows with each gust of wind. "Tomorrow it'll be back to just you and me, lass."

He was dreading it with every fiber of his being. This place had been his refuge ever since his ordeal in Syria, but soon it would only amplify his aloneness. He couldn't ask Kiyomi to stay here, it was no longer safe. And the past two days had forced him to acknowledge what he'd been afraid to admit for so long.

He no longer had what it took to be effective on ops. He wouldn't jeopardize Kiyomi's safety by asking to go with her.

The study door opened. Kiyomi stepped inside and shut it, and just the sight of her made his heart pound and his body tighten. She had changed into jeans and a cherry-red sweater that hugged her breasts.

Smiling, she crossed the room toward him, the fire-light gleaming on her shiny black hair. "How is she feeling? Any better?"

"Aye." He patted Karas's side. "Moving much better."

Karas hopped her front paws off his lap and turned to Kiyomi, white tail wagging, grinning her doggy grin as Kiyomi reached down to stroke her head. "You'll be back to yourself in no time." Karas licked the back of Kiyomi's hand, back end swaying with each tail wag. "I know you adore him, but if you don't mind, I'd like to have your master all to myself for a while now."

Straightening, she pointed at the bed in front of the fire, then snapped her fingers. "Bed."

Karas stared up at her in astonishment for a moment, as if shocked that anyone other than him would dare to give her a command, then her ears lowered and she limped off to her bed as if she'd just been banished to the ends of the earth for all eternity. She flopped down on her bed, chin resting on the edge of it, giving Kiyomi a reproachful look that made him chuckle.

"Total drama queen," Kiyomi said with a grin, then sauntered around the edge of Marcus's desk.

His blood pumped hot and hard through his veins as her scent reached him. He inhaled, released it on a soft growl when she gripped his shoulders and straddled his lap in the chair. Her soft weight settled over his hardening cock. He pulled her close, one hand on the middle of her back and the other sliding into her hair.

"Everyone else is gone now, and Trinity's left to pick up Rycroft," she murmured, trailing her fingers over his jaw. "Which means two things."

"Which are?"

Her eyes twinkled with sensual mischief. "We've got the entire place to ourselves for a while. And we don't have to be quiet."

Don't go. The words were right there in his mouth. He swallowed them back. This was hard enough, he didn't need to make it any worse. "Kiyomi, I—"

She laid a finger over his lips. "No talking. Just this," she whispered, and leaned forward to settle her mouth on his.

Marcus tightened his grip and put everything he had into the kiss. It started slow and tender but quickly grew heated, both of them desperate for closer contact. He wanted to imprint himself on her, somehow leave part of himself inside her forever so she'd never be without him again.

He started to lift her off him, intending to set her on his desk so he could strip her and bury his face in the soft folds between her thighs, but she stopped him with a soft sound and her hands on his chest. She kissed her way down the left side of his neck, her hands reaching for the bottom of his shirt.

Marcus lifted his arms so she could pull it over his head and toss it aside. She settled back over his cock again, her fingers trailing gently down the scars covering his neck, left shoulder, chest and side. The nerve endings there were dead but his body didn't seem to notice, her touch radiating all over him, right down to his aching cock.

The soft silk of her hair brushed across his chest as she bent her head and followed her fingers with her mouth. She kissed his scars, ducking to reach the ones over his ribs, then started at the top on the other side and worked her way down.

His pulse thudded in his ears when she looked up at him with those liquid dark eyes, her tongue darting out to lick his skin. "Stay still," she whispered, then shifted back and scooted off him to kneel between his splayed thighs.

She murmured appreciatively and rubbed her palm

over the bulge in his jeans. Marcus grabbed hold of the armrests to keep from reaching for her, unsure if he wanted to make her go faster or draw the anticipation out forever.

His mouth went dry as she undid his jeans, opened the denim and pulled the fabric down to expose him. His cock sprang free, lying thick and hard against his belly, and the sight of her face so close to his throbbing flesh had his thigh muscles bunching.

"Don't move." Kiyomi leaned forward, her hair brushing his cock as her lips touched the skin just above his navel. She darted her tongue into it, flicked the tip of it against the thin line of hair that led down to his groin.

Christ, she was killing him. His breathing was uneven, his fingers clamped around the armrest for fear that he'd seize fistfuls of her hair the moment she touched his cock. He released a throttled groan when her cheek touched the sensitive crown.

Her dark gaze lifted, holding his as she placed a soft, agonizingly slow kiss to the tip. Somehow he held still, fighting for breath. A tiny smile tugged at her lips, telling him she was enjoying tormenting him. Then it faded and she slid her tongue around the sensitive underside.

He tensed, the breath leaving him on a gust of air. He couldn't look away, spellbound, dying from the promise of pleasure in her eyes, and then she finally parted those gorgeous lips and enveloped the head of his cock in her hot mouth.

His eyes slammed shut as pure pleasure rocketed up his spine. That silken tongue ran around the crest once more, then her mouth slid down farther.

Unable to stop himself, he blindly grabbed for the back of her head, his fingers closing around a fistful of hair. "Kiyomi," he managed to get out, his heart ready to explode.

She ran a hand up his chest and sucked him with

slow, luxurious pulls that threatened to undo him, the other dipping low into his underwear to tease his balls. Marcus pulled in a ragged breath and held on, tremors racking him under the exquisite lash of pleasure.

With superhuman effort he pried his eyes open, unwilling to miss a single second of this. Her kneeling before him, the firelight playing over the side of her face and hair while she sucked him, her velvet tongue teasing the most sensitive spot just under the crown.

It was incredible. So unbelievably hot, but he wasn't going to last much longer, and he wanted to bury himself in her one last time. "Stop," he rasped out, tugging on her hair.

She resisted him for a moment.

"No, stop." He pulled in a breath. "I want inside you. Want to feel you come around me."

Meeting his gaze, she slowly pulled off him, making sure to give him one final, luscious lick along the head of his cock. With a low growl he grabbed her under the arms and lifted her, rising from the chair with effort because of his hip and the pleasure she'd weakened him further with.

Cupping her delectable arse in his hands, he made the awkward walk around the desk to the sofa, his movements hampered by the denim rolled down to his thighs. He laid Kiyomi down on her back on the leather sofa, paused only to give Karas the command to stay, then set about getting his woman naked.

Another shot of arousal burst through him when he saw the sexy things she wore underneath. A lace bra and panty set in black and crimson, so sheer he could see her nipples through the fabric.

He ran his fingertips over them, entranced by the sight, then tugged the cups aside and took one rigid peak into his mouth. Her sigh mixed with a groan as he sucked at her, his free hand trailing down to the lace between her thighs. "Are you wet for me, lass?"

"Find out."

He intended to.

Sliding his fingers under the edge of the fabric, he brushed them across her smooth, bare flesh. Silken heat coated his fingertips. He growled against her breast and switched to the other as he began to stroke her softly. She whimpered and spread her legs apart more, giving him room.

Dying to taste her again, he kissed his way down her flat belly and tugged the knickers down her legs. Setting a hand on the inside of each thigh, he pushed them wide and lowered his face to the glistening folds between them.

Her fingers knotted in his hair as he stroked her with his tongue, a plaintive moan coming from her as he zeroed in on the swollen bud at the top. He kept going until she was panting and trembling, moving restlessly beneath his mouth.

"Now," she begged. "Now."

Keeping his tongue right where it was, he released her thighs and shoved his jeans and underwear off. With one final caress over her rosy clit, he knelt on the soft leather.

He grasped her legs and draped them over his shoulders before coming down on top of her, his weight braced on his hands as he stared down into her face. Her cheeks were flushed, her eyes molten with desire.

You're mine, lass, and always will be.

He didn't say it. Didn't want to spoil this last time with her. But he let his eyes say it for him, let his body chant the words to her as he dropped a hand down to tease her clit and then drove into her in a single, smooth thrust.

Kiyomi gasped and clutched at his shoulders, her eyes closing as her head kicked back on the tufted leather. With her legs over his shoulders he was so deep, buried to the hilt in her warmth. She clenched around him, her silken heat sending pulses of ecstasy up his spine.

He would never feel this way about anyone else. Only her. And maybe it made him a selfish bastard, but he wanted her to feel the same way.

With each stroke of his fingers and slow thrust of his cock, he told her how much she meant to him. How much he…

I love you. I'll never stop loving you.

He was frantic with it, a sudden, sharp spear of grief threatening to pierce the rising pleasure. Kiyomi was the most incredibly beautiful thing he'd ever seen as she moved beneath him in the firelight, her face taut while she moved with him, seeking her pleasure.

He could tell when she reached the edge. Her breath halted. Her fingers dug into his back. Then her lips parted and she cried out, her core clenching around him, hips bucking.

It was too much. Marcus buried his face into her neck with a hoarse shout and let himself go, pumping into her until he shuddered. The sound of his ragged breathing was harsh in his ears as he crashed back to earth, cradled by her warmth.

Lifting his head, he propped his weight back up on his hands to gaze down at her. The sight of her like that, gazing up at him so trustingly, split his heart wide open.

"Come here," she whispered, drawing him down for a kiss. He went willingly, all but melting into her, unable to tell where he stopped and she began.

Only when his arms began to ache did he stop and ease her legs from his shoulders. His hip burned like fire but it was worth any amount of pain to make love to her.

Awareness of the room began to settle in. Rain hitting the window panes. The crackle of the fire in the hearth and the quiet ticking of the clock on the mantelpiece. He didn't know how much time had passed. "How long have we got left?" he murmured.

"Trin should be back soon. After that…I don't know.

A few hours, maybe."

He sat up on his knees, locking an arm beneath her back to bring her with him. "Come up to bed with me."

The house was still and silent as they went up the staircase hand in hand, Karas trailing a few treads behind them. Upstairs his room was dark and cold, rain pelting the roof while the wind moaned in the eaves.

The sudden emptiness around them registered as a lump of dread in his gut. He led Kiyomi straight to the bed and tucked her under the covers to keep her warm.

"Will you light a fire?" she asked when he started to climb in beside her.

He would do anything for her. "Aye, if you like."

"I'll never see a fire again and not think of you."

Or him, her.

A sharp blade of agony pierced his chest. He turned toward the fireplace where Karas was already curled up on her bed, laid and lit the fire, then crawled in beside Kiyomi.

She smiled and slid over top of him, blanketing him with her silken weight, her hair draped across his chest. He stroked his fingers through it and pulled the covers up to her waist so he could still run his palm over her bare back.

Sudden pressure swelled in his chest. Rising and rising until the words he'd been holding back burst free. "Come back to me when this is over." He fucking hated that he was begging, but couldn't hold back any longer. "Or I'll come to you, wherever is safest for you."

"Marcus." She slid her arms around him, burrowed in tight. "I wish I could promise you that, I truly do. But I can't. Because…I may not live through what's coming—"

He sucked in a breath, crushing her to him. "Don't say that. Don't even *think* it." Christ, it chilled him to the bone to even imagine it.

"I wish it could be different," she whispered. "I wish *I* was different."

"I don't. I wouldn't want you to be anything other than who you truly are." It was why he'd fallen for her in the first place. "When this is over, I'll come for you."

They lapsed into silence, both of them lying there wide-awake, greedily soaking up the comfort of their last intimate embrace while the minutes ticked past.

Marcus held her close as he stared into the fire, dreading the moment Trinity returned and took Kiyomi from him.

****

Trinity pulled her hood up before exiting the car as the Lear jet came to a stop on the runway of the private airport.

She jogged toward it through the rain, hunched against the cold wind, hoping Rycroft had brought good news with him. It felt like they were close to finding the Architect, and it couldn't happen soon enough. Trinity wanted all of this to be over so she and the others could finally move forward with their lives.

The jet's door opened and the staircase lowered. A man's silhouette appeared in the doorway above it. Tall, broad-shouldered.

She smiled, slowed as she reached the bottom of the steps, rain drilling the tarmac around her. "You made good time."

"Yeah, team emergencies tend to make things move fast," Rycroft said dryly as he opened an umbrella and came down the stairs. "Everyone on the move now?"

"Everyone but Kiyomi and me. I wanted her to have a few more hours to unwind before we leave."

He nodded, silver eyes knowing. "She and Laidlaw together?"

"Would it matter if they were?" Kiyomi deserved every bit of happiness she could squeeze out of this life, even if it was short-lived. Trinity would give her friend every last moment possible with Marcus, but the end result was inevitable. By first light, they had to be out of here.

His lips curved a bit. "No." The smile faded. "Did you read her the riot act for going after Rahman?"

"Yes, and she apologized to everyone. Though I have to admit, I'm glad that son of a bitch is dead. Even more so since she got to be the one to end him." Hopefully that would give Kiyomi some measure of closure and peace, because she needed all the positive things possible to help her through the broken heart she was about to be nursing.

"I'm not as thrilled as you about it, since I'm the one left dealing with cleaning up the mess you guys left in Damascus," he said in a wry voice. "It's not easy protecting your identities when you leave a body count like that behind." He angled the umbrella to cover her better, placing his body between her and the wind. "Got a call on my way over, so there's been a change of plans. I'm flying to London right now to meet with MI6 and see if I can smooth things over there."

"Right now? You could have just called and diverted there. And what about—"

"Oh, almost forgot. Brought you something." He turned toward the plane.

Another male silhouette appeared in the doorway, a duffel in hand. Broader than Rycroft's. Then the man stepped into the light and Trinity's breath caught, happiness flooding her. "*Brody*."

Her fiancé grinned and jogged down the stairs as she rushed for him. He caught her to him with a groan, lifted her off the ground with his powerful arms wrapped around her back. "Surprise," he murmured. "Guess this means you're glad to see me?"

181

She hugged him tighter, burying her face in his throat. He smelled incredible. Like evergreens and Brody and…home. "I'm so happy you're here."

Her throat tightened, a telltale burn pricking the backs of her eyes. She didn't care that Rycroft was right there watching, didn't care that she normally wasn't this emotional or demonstrative in front of others. They'd barely seen each other over the past few months and she'd missed him so damn much through the craziness of this whole thing.

Brody chuckled and set her on her feet but didn't let go, upping the pressure of his arms. "Glad to be here. I missed you."

"Missed you too." Oh, dammit, she was going to cry.

"Okay then," Rycroft said in amusement behind her. "You're in good hands, so I'll be off to London now."

Winding her arms around Brody's ribs, she leaned her head on his shoulder and aimed a wobbly smile at Rycroft. He liked the world to think he was a heartless bastard, but she and a few chosen others knew better. He'd made this happen for her. "Thank you."

One side of his mouth kicked up. "Welcome. Contact me when you leave the manor. Briar and Georgia are heading here from Atlanta as we speak. I'll be in touch when I know more."

She nodded, stood there pressed tight to her man as Rycroft jogged back up the steps and started to raise them.

"I know I'm asking the impossible, but tell everyone to behave," he called down.

"No promises," she answered, all giddy and warm in spite of the cold rain and wind. She smiled up at Brody as they turned for her vehicle. "I can't believe you're here." There was so much she hadn't been able to tell him about what was going on. But she wanted to.

He hugged her to his side, carrying his duffel over one shoulder. "Lucky for me, I'm on the end of a really short and extremely well-informed grapevine, so I heard all about what's happening from DeLuca, then Rycroft." He gazed down at her, his brown eyes somber. "There's no way I would let you face this alone."

She didn't need his protection, but him coming here and offering it willingly meant the world to her. "I love you."

He stopped and gazed down at her, uncaring of the rain soaking his hair and shoulders. "I love you too." Cupping her cheek in his hand, he kissed her.

Trinity took his bearded face in her hands and poured all her emotion into it, her heart full enough to burst. Even with her unconventional and ugly past, this incredible man loved her. Loved her enough to have her back and fly halfway across the world even when it placed him in harm's way.

Enough to want to spend the rest of his life with her.

The solid gold ring pressed into her finger as she held him, a symbol of his promise and commitment. But him showing up tonight was more testament of his love than any ring or vow could ever be.

Deep inside her, those old insecurities she'd carried throughout her life—about her not being whole, not being good enough for someone like Brody—suddenly seemed to weaken. The ever-present fear of rejection and abandonment receded. Because tonight had given her the proof she'd needed to accept what Brody had been telling her all along.

He wasn't ever going to wake up one morning and decide she was too much trouble. That her past was too much for him to handle. Or that he deserved a better life than she could give him.

"So," he said, holding her close as they approached her vehicle. "What have you guys been doing to fill your time out here in the idyllic English countryside?"

She laughed softly at his teasing tone. "You'd be surprised."

He gave her a knowing look. "Doubt it."

That made her smile. The man knew her too well. And she *was* worthy of him, no matter what she'd done, or what dangers they had to face going forward. They belonged to each other. Trinity would take on any threat, take any risk to ensure she spent the rest of her life with this incredible man at her side.

Including setting a date.

"Where to now?" Brody asked as they got into the vehicle.

"To pick up Kiyomi at the manor." Trinity was sorry to end her friend's time with Marcus, but there was no help for it. "It's time to move on."

Chapter Seventeen

Janelle grabbed her bags and rushed out of the rental house to the SUV idling in the driveway, excitement fizzing inside her like the finest champagne as she approached the trunk of the vehicle.

This was it. After years of waiting and planning, this was finally it.

She tossed her gear into the back then slid into the front passenger seat with her cell pressed to her ear. "You're certain?" There could be no mistakes. They had only one shot at this. In order for this to work, both operations had to take place simultaneously.

"The drone captured three separate vehicles leaving between midnight and six this morning. And when we checked the entrance off the east side of the property, we found the tire tracks. It has to be them."

Janelle shut her door and motioned for the driver to move. "You're positive Kiyomi's still there?"

"Unless she was hidden in the back of one of the vehicles. The cameras our team posing as the construction crew installed identified Kiyomi in a vehicle with Laidlaw yesterday afternoon, and she hasn't been seen since."

It would have to do. Janelle couldn't afford to wait now. She had to act. "I'm en route with team alpha." Her best unit, though not nearly the caliber that her operatives would be after she'd finished the next phase of her new program. Her objective wasn't possible without Kiyomi, however. She was the blueprint, the inspiration behind everything. "Is bravo team in place?"

"They reached the meeting point ten minutes ago. No sign of Amber or Megan yet."

"I'm almost sorry I'm going to miss the reunion." But her top priority was waiting for her at Laidlaw Hall.

Today would erase her past completely and give her the future she'd always dreamed of.

****

"Stop picking."

Megan rolled her head from side to side and shot an annoyed look at her sister beside her in the backseat as she lowered her hands into her lap. "I can't help it." It wasn't that bad. Most of the raw spots and scabbing around her nails were from the other night when they'd realized Kiyomi was missing.

"Yes, you can." Amber kept clicking away on her keyboard, doing whatever it was she was doing.

"I'm nervous. Aren't you nervous?" About meeting the woman who had abandoned them so long ago. And she was also sad. Leaving Marcus behind had been hard.

After saying a perfunctory goodbye she'd snuck out the back like a coward so he wouldn't see the tears in her eyes, afraid she would break down and embarrass herself if she'd lingered. If it had been that hard for her, she couldn't imagine how devastated Kiyomi must be right now.

"A little. But you don't see me picking all around my nails until they bleed."

She gave her sister an annoyed look. "It's my one flaw, Amber. Can't you just let me have my one flaw?"

Her sister looked up to arch a brow at her. "Only one?"

Ty swiveled around in the front passenger seat to give them a hard look. "Am I gonna have to come back there and break you two apart?"

"No." Megan huffed and tucked her hands beneath her arms to resist the urge to keep picking. Thank God he and Jesse were going to be with them—nearby at least— during the meeting, or she would have been twice as nervous.

What if this person wasn't even their aunt? They'd only agreed to this meeting because the timing suited them, and it would be quick. The whole point was to find out if it was her, and if so, find out exactly why she'd dumped them into the system rather than become their guardian. Anything else was a bonus, though if their aunt had dreams of spending Christmas together, she could fuck right off.

Ty reached a long arm out and squeezed her knee. "Hey. It's gonna be okay, dimples."

A tiny smile tugged at the edges of her mouth. She loved it when he called her that. "Yeah."

He grinned and turned back around to face front. "Jesse and I'll be there through the whole thing, and the others will be nearby just in case. If the meeting turns to shit, you just pull the chute and leave."

"What if I want to punch her?" There was a good possibility she might.

"No punching. Just walk away."

"Easy for you to say," she muttered.

After their second cousin had so *helpfully* interfered in all of this, they were taking every precaution for the meeting. Chloe, Heath, Eden and Zack were stationed two blocks away from the meeting point in case their paranoia was justified and this proved to be a trap of some sort. Having the other four as backup was overkill on top of having Jesse and Ty close by, but so be it.

"Okay, she got my message saying we're going to be a bit late," Amber said, still typing. The excuse gave them more time to watch the meeting point before approaching it. Just so there weren't any last minute surprises when they went in.

Megan had lost track of the things Amber was working on at once. "And?"

"She said it's fine and she'll see us when we get there."

A second later Amber suddenly stopped typing and stared hard at the screen. Megan glanced at her, worry bursting inside her when she saw her sister's deep frown. "Something wrong?"

"I don't… No," she said slowly, then shook her head. "Nothing. Just ignore me."

Megan scowled and punched her sister in the shoulder. "Don't scare me like that."

Ignoring her, Amber went back to typing. Currently she had three different screens open on Lady Ada, one of them searching up and comparing words from various sources.

Megan had no clue what network Amber had hacked into out here as they drove, but then she didn't understand most of what her sister did with her tech. And in her opinion, it was a sign of just how desperate they were to discover who the Architect was that Amber had resorted to trying linguistic forensics as a tool to crack the mystery. It might have worked to bring the Unibomber down, but that didn't mean it would help in this case.

All too soon they neared the outskirts of Coventry. Jesse pulled off the motorway and drove past the café Amber had chosen for the meeting. It was in a busy area close to several hotels, about a thirty-minute drive from the conference their aunt was attending in Birmingham.

"Busy place," Jesse commented as he slowly drove past, giving them a good look at what they were dealing with.

Megan counted about a dozen bistro-style tables set out on the sidewalk. Only a handful were occupied, and no one sitting at them made Megan's internal radar ping.

Jesse continued to the end of the block and made several turns in quick succession to make sure no one was following them. "See anything?" he asked Ty.

Ty checked his mirror again. "Nope. We're good to go." He got on his phone and called Zack to let the others know Megan and Amber were about to go in.

Jesse turned right at the next corner and pulled to the curb in front of some row houses. "You taking Lady Ada with you?" he said to Amber in a dry voice as Ty hopped out.

"No. So guard her with your life while I'm gone."

"My life," he agreed solemnly, taking it from her. Amber leaned between the front seats to kiss him, then got out.

Megan climbed out with fake glasses on and her hair tucked under a knit cap. She and Amber had disguised their appearances a bit to make facial recognition harder when the CCTVs in the area picked them up.

Shutting the door, she faced Ty. He was so damn good looking, he distracted her all the time. "Okay, wish us luck." This was it. She just wanted this done with so she and Amber could lay this part of their past to rest and get on with the mission.

"You won't need it, but good luck anyway." His face softened with an easy smile. "Don't worry. Jess and I've got your backs." He drew her close to kiss her, then lowered his voice to a sensual rumble that made her toes curl in her boots. "Hurry back, Mrs. Bergstrom."

It sill sounded weird, but she was grinning like an

idiot as she walked up the sidewalk with her sister.

"Wipe that lovesick smile off your face and focus," Amber said.

She shoved her hands in the pockets of her leather jacket, her weapon a comforting weight at the small of her back. "I *am* focused. I can smile and still be focused." And she'd smile about her husband if she damn well wanted to.

They approached the café from the west, walking up the alley beside it. "We still good?" she murmured so Ty and Jesse could hear via her earpiece.

"Affirmative," Ty answered.

"Mmm, I love it when you use military speak."

Amber jabbed her with an elbow. "Now's not the time." She pulled her phone from her pocket to study it, probably having received an alert of some sort from her laptop.

The café was in view now. Megan studied the sidewalk again as they approached, searching for someone who resembled her hazy memories of Aunt Jane. She should be here by now.

"Oh, shit," Amber breathed. She stopped, staring at her phone.

"Oh, shit what?" Megan demanded, drawing up short beside her. They were almost at the doors now. She cut a glance around them and then across the street, searching for possible threats. Nothing jumped out at her.

Then she met Amber's gaze, and Megan's stomach dropped as she watched the blood drain from her sister's face. "The profile's a match," she said, her gaze fixed on the glass front door of the café as she scanned the interior.

Ice slid down Megan's spine. "A match to what?"

"The Architect. Linguistic forensics identified her education level, where she went to school. It all matches what we thought Aunt Jane's should be."

Megan's pulse thudded. "You sure?"

"The word *untenable*. It's not common. Using it in everyday language would stand out."

Megan's heart thudded faster. "The Architect used it in the conversation with Rahman."

"Yes." Amber's eyes were full of a terrifying mix of anger and fear. "And Lady Ada just found it in the court documents. Jane used it to explain why she couldn't take care of us. 'The situation is untenable,' she said in her original statement."

Megan stared at her, unease tying her insides into knots. "Oh, shit. You mean…"

Amber nodded, her green eyes stricken. "Lady Ada projects it's a 95% probability that Aunt Jane's the Architect."

Shock reverberated through her. Megan whipped around to scan the people around them with new eyes. Her gaze halted on two new guys across the street with faint bulges beneath the arms of their jackets. *Shiiiiit.* "It's a trap."

"Get behind cover," Ty said urgently in her ear, having heard everything.

Before either of them could move, the café door opened and an employee came out. The young girl looked around, spotted them, and started toward them. "A gentleman just asked me to deliver this to you," she said with a smile, handing over a folded piece of paper.

Megan grabbed it and read the note typed inside it, delaying her innate instinct to run.

Sorry I couldn't make it, but tell my sister I said hello when you see her.

The horrifying words played through Megan's mind, too terrible to comprehend. Their aunt was the Architect, and she'd been planning this all along—planning the moment she could isolate and kill them so she could go after Kiyomi.

She started to crush the paper in her hand. A red laser

dot appeared on the back of it.

"Get down!" She grabbed Amber, wrenching her off her feet and reached for the closest table, overturning it. They dove behind it a heartbeat before a bullet punched through it, spraying slivers of wood.

People gasped and screamed, overturning chairs as they bolted. In the confusion she and Amber scrambled behind a large concrete planter and drew their weapons. "Contact, your one o'clock," she said.

"Megan! What's going on?" Ty demanded.

"Under fire. Two shooters," she answered, ducking as more shots struck inches above their heads, this time spraying bits of concrete and dirt.

"Hang tight," Ty said curtly. "We're coming."

"How far away are you?"

"Two minutes."

In two minutes they could be dead if there were more shooters coming. "They gotta be moving toward us," she said to Amber over the chaos and noise around them. "We can't sit here."

Amber nodded, face set. "Head south. I'll cover you."

"You mean you'll be right behind me."

"Yeah."

She pushed out a breath and shifted her grip on her weapon. The instant she left cover, she needed to identify the shooters and neutralize at least one of them. "On three." She counted down, tensed, then burst from cover.

Shots rang out. She turned, spotted a man coming at her with a weapon aimed. She fired even as Amber did the same. Their rounds struck the man in the chest, then one in the throat.

He fell, clutching at the wound in his throat. Megan whirled and ran for the corner of the building. Ducking around it, she heard Amber returning fire.

Megan whipped around the corner, found the other

shooter. There were too many people in the way, running in panic. She had to step out into the open to fire. She hit the shooter in the back. He fell to his knees, tried to raise his arm but Amber shot him in the head and ran toward her.

"This way," Megan said, and sprinted down the alley.

Someone darted around the corner at the other end of the alley. Megan cursed silently and dropped to her knee as the person fired, striking the wall where her head had just been. Amber returned fire an instant before she did. The person disappeared from sight.

Amber glanced behind them. "Now what?"

"We're one minute out," Ty reported.

Still too far away to get them out of this. Megan looked left, then right. Their options were limited, and equally shitty. Going back the way they'd come was too risky. Running toward the shooter was just as bad.

Megan shook her head, knowing her sister was thinking the same thing she was. "We have to go for it." The panic and confusion of the crowd would give them at least a chance of concealment. "We have to be fast."

Amber waited a beat, then nodded. "I take point."

"Why do you get t—"

"I'm older. I make the rules." Amber got up and hugged the wall as she made her way back the way they'd come.

Megan guarded their six as they hurried back the way they'd come. No sign of that last shooter, but they were still out there. Amber paused at the entrance to the alley and looked around, then back at Megan. "Ready?"

She blew out a breath. "Ready."

Amber bolted out of the alley and turned left. Megan followed, weaving in and out of the frightened people cowering in groups on the sidewalk. They raced across the street, darting between traffic to veer right around the next corner.

Back pressed to the brick wall as she panted, Megan glanced over at her sister. "Clear?" Ty and Jesse would be tracking them via their phones. They should be here or at least within sprinting distance in a matter of moments.

Amber nodded. "Think so."

No sooner had she said it than she pivoted and aimed past Megan's head. Megan spun just as Amber fired. The female shooter fired too, narrowly missing Amber. Amber and Megan didn't miss. Their bullets hit home. Two in the belly, one in the upper chest. The woman collapsed, her weapon falling to the alley with a clatter.

Megan shoved her sister forward. "Move."

They ran toward the downed woman, weapons up. She didn't twitch, her sightless eyes only partially open as they reached her.

While Amber kept watch, Megan crouched and began checking the body. She found a cell phone, yanked off one of the woman's gloves and used the thumb to unlock the screen.

The text messages she found made her blood run cold. "Oh, shit—the Architect's going after Kiyomi." Who now only had Marcus, Trin and Brody to stand with her.

Amber bent close to read the messages. "It's divide and conquer. The bitch must have been watching the manor. She split us all up to isolate Kiyomi."

The sound of an engine behind her made her whip around to find a vehicle roaring around the corner. She raised her weapon to fire through the windshield, but Amber grabbed her arm. "It's Heath," her sister said.

Megan expelled a sigh as Jesse's vehicle came around the corner a second later. The cavalry had arrived.

The back door of the first SUV swung open as the vehicle screeched to a halt in front of her while Amber ran past to Jesse's. Ty grabbed Megan and pulled her inside, crushing her to him.

Chloe peered at her from the front passenger seat, scanning her anxiously. "All right?"

"Yeah." Megan pulled away and fished out her cell, frantic as she dialed Marcus. "But the Architect's going after Kiyomi."

Chapter Eighteen

He'd faced plenty of goodbyes in his life, but this one was the most painful yet.

Marcus had lost both his parents young. Later, he'd lost men he'd served with, men who'd been like brothers to him. Last night he'd said goodbye to Megan. But knowing that in the next minute or so Kiyomi was about to walk out his back door and out of his life forever was more than he could bear.

Karas sat at his feet as he said his goodbyes to Trinity and Brody. He shut the door behind them, giving him and Kiyomi one final bit of privacy.

They stared at each other in wordless silence. Marcus's heart pounded so hard against his ribs it felt bruised. It hurt to breathe. So many thoughts crowded his mind, begging to come out.

"So this is it," she said with a wistful smile.

He wanted to pick her up, carry her back upstairs to his room and lock her in it with him. Refuse to let her go. Force her to stay. Take her somewhere they could never find her.

But none of that was possible, and she'd hate him for it anyway. "Aye."

She fidgeted with her hands. "I wanted to thank you, for every—"

He pulled her to him and wrapped his arms around her in a fierce embrace, his face pressed to the side of her neck. "Don't." He couldn't bear it. He was barely hanging on to his last shred of control as it was. Hearing her thank him for letting her stay here, or for their time together, or whatever she'd been about to say, diminished everything they'd shared.

She clung to him in turn, holding on tight. "I never meant for this to happen," she whispered in a rough voice.

He nodded, understanding what she meant. She hadn't expected to develop feelings for anyone, least of all him, and she wouldn't promise a chance at a future together. Not until this was all over. Maybe never.

Much as he hated it, there wasn't a damn thing he could do to change that. "I'm glad it did." As much as this hurt, he wouldn't have traded a moment he'd shared with her to spare himself the pain of losing her.

Finally, she eased back, took his face in her hands and kissed him. Hard. Then softer. Slower. Full of so much tenderness and longing that his throat tightened.

Her eyes shimmered with unshed tears as she gave him a heartbroken smile. "I'd better go."

He cradled her head in his hands, rubbing her hair in his fingers. The urge to tell her he loved her was so powerful it was burning a hole in his chest. But he couldn't say it. Wouldn't do that to her when she had no choice but to leave, and he to let her go.

"You be careful. And when you can…if you can, at least tell me you're okay." He desperately wanted her to come back to him. Prayed that she would one day. It was all that was keeping his heart beating.

She nodded once. "I will."

He lowered his hands, fighting the urge to grab her again. This was wrong. All wrong. He'd only just found her, he'd barely had any time with her, and now she was being torn from his life. "Take care of yourself."

"You too." She sniffed, ran a hand over her wet cheek. "Well. Bye."

I love you. Don't go. "Tarra, love." It took an act of will to make himself turn and open the door for her. An aberration, him aiding in her leaving.

She hurried down the gravel path running along the rear of the house and got into the back of the vehicle with Brody and Trinity without looking back. But as it drove away, she turned to look back at him through the rear window and lifted a hand.

Marcus did the same, his whole chest being crushed in an invisible vise. Somehow he managed to remain standing there until the vehicle disappeared from view.

Quiet settled around him. A quiet he'd once craved with every cell of his being. Now, it was oppressive and suffocating.

He walked back through the door on autopilot, numb all the way through. Karas followed him into the study where he lowered himself into the chair at his desk to stare into the cold, dark fireplace.

He couldn't bring himself to light a fire. He'd never look at one again and not think of Kiyomi. The way the light danced over her features, and shone on her inky black hair.

He dropped his head into his hands and sucked in breath after breath, struggling to hold on. He didn't know how long he sat there fighting to overcome the tidal wave of grief, but eventually it registered that his mobile was buzzing in his pocket.

He pulled it out, hope leaping inside him for a moment, then he saw it was Megan and frowned in concern. "All right?" he answered.

"No. Marcus—"

"What's wrong?" The fear in her voice had him shooting up from his chair. Megan didn't get scared.

"The Architect is our aunt. She's coming for Kiyomi,

will be there any minute with her team."

His stomach dropped. "How many?"

"I think at least seven. Maybe more. Where's Kiyomi?"

He grabbed his keys, started running for the door. "She just left with Trinity and Brody."

"We're calling them now but you need to get them back to the house and arm up until we can get there to reinforce you."

"I'm going after them," he said, grabbing a rifle from behind the secret panel before wrenching the study door open and running for the front entrance. "Alert me when you get close."

"Okay."

He disconnected and dialed Kiyomi's number. Throwing open the door, he rushed for his Land Rover, mobile to his ear and fear twisting his insides like a snake as it started ringing.

Answer the phone…

****

Kiyomi bit down on the inside of her cheek and stared unseeingly through a haze of tears as Brody drove along the country road away from Laidlaw Hall.

The urge to look back at it one last time before it disappeared from view was overwhelming but she didn't dare. She was barely holding on right now, the pain in her chest making it hard to breathe.

She'd hated hurting him. Wished there was some way they could stay together, but under the circumstances it was impossible. And it wasn't fair to let him wait for her, to give him false hope that she'd come back to him one day. There was a good chance she wouldn't survive to the end of this mission.

If by some miracle she did, she was coming back to

Marcus.

Her cell rang in her pocket. She pulled it out, only because it might be important, and joy leapt inside her when she saw Marcus's number. "Hey, miss me already?"

"*Come back*," he said, the urgency in his voice making her insides twist.

She closed her eyes. "Marcus—"

"The Architect is Megan and Amber's aunt, and she's coming with a team to get you."

Her spine snapped taut. Up front, Trinity was on her cell now too, speaking in an urgent tone. "What?"

"Come back *now*. We need to kit up and hold them off until Megan and the others arrive."

"Brody, stop," she ordered. He hit the brakes, his head swiveling around to look sharply between her and Trinity. "The Architect is coming for us. Go back to the manor *now*."

"Hurry," Trinity added, phone still to her ear.

Brody pulled a tight U-turn and sped back the way they'd come.

"We're on our way. Two minutes out," Kiyomi told Marcus. The manor came back into view as they reached the crest of a hill. Marcus's old Land Rover was roaring down the driveway toward the gate. Coming after them. "Go back," she urged him.

"Stay on the line with me."

"I will." She turned to look through the rear window. "No sign of anyone so far."

"Just get here."

Brody was speeding along the road, the engine revving. "We'll be there in thirty seconds," she told Marcus.

"Which entrance?" Brody asked.

"Main one," Kiyomi answered. They were coming to the bottom of the hill now.

Up ahead, a vehicle came into view at the top of the next hill. Coming toward them fast. Large. Maybe an

SUV. The back of her neck prickled. "That them?"

"Not sure," Trinity answered in a tense voice.

Marcus had his vehicle parked just inside the open gate. He stood behind the open driver's side door, a rifle to his shoulder as he faced the oncoming vehicle, waiting for it to come within range.

"Behind us too," Brody said, racing for the driveway.

Kiyomi glanced behind them, and sure enough, another SUV was hurtling after them. "They're going to try to box us in." They had to get through the gate and close it, buy themselves what little time they could to get back up to the manor. It was made of solid wrought iron and should withstand a good ramming.

Brody swore and swerved as a bullet hit the front of the hood. Kiyomi faced front. Ahead, the passenger side windows of the SUV in front of them were down, two rifles pointed at them.

Two rounds slammed into its windshield a moment later. Marcus.

The SUV lurched to the side for a moment but kept coming, its bullet resistant windows still intact.

Kiyomi gasped and ducked as the rear window shattered behind her. They were almost at the driveway. She could hear the sound of Marcus returning fire. She popped back up in time to see the SUV behind them veer toward the ditch, one of its front tires damaged.

"Hang tight," Brody muttered, and hit the brake for a skidding turn into the driveway. Gravel flew everywhere as the vehicle fishtailed before Brody regained control.

Kiyomi caught only a glimpse of Marcus returning fire as they neared him, then jumping into his vehicle as they raced by. "Let me out," she ordered.

"No." Brody floored it, roaring toward the manor.

She spun to face the shattered rear window, heart in her throat. She couldn't see through the shattered glass.

Couldn't see what was happening to Marcus. "But Marcus—the gate—"

"It's already closing and he's hauling ass up the driveway," Trinity said, watching anxiously in her side mirror.

Kiyomi closed her eyes a moment, trying to take everything in. "Why the hell does she want *me*?"

"I don't know," Trinity answered, "but she's not getting you."

"Pull around back," she told Brody, rolling down her window to look back now that they were out of range of the shooters. Marcus was reversing after them, and the SUVs were just pulling up to the gate. The first one rammed it, but the wrought iron held. The SUV reversed and tried again.

"They're going to be through it any minute," Trinity muttered. "We need to get to the loadout room."

"He's got one in the house?" Brody asked in surprise.

A secret arsenal tucked away beneath the study. "Yeah," Kiyomi answered. "But I doubt he imagined using it because of an attack like this."

Brody wheeled around the side of the house and came to a lurching stop near the west garden wall. Kiyomi leapt out and ran the opposite way as Trinity and Brody raced for the back door of the manor.

Marcus roared up a moment later and jumped out. His face was taut, his gaze burning with intensity as he rushed toward her in a limping run and grabbed her to him. "You all right?"

"Fine," she promised, and hurried with him toward the house.

"I counted at least seven in those two vehicles, and there are probably more coming around to the eastern entrance." His tone was as grim as his expression. "We won't be able to hold them off long, so we're going to have to figure out a way to buy ourselves the time we need to get out of here."

Chapter Nineteen

Janelle stepped out of the SUV and reached up to activate her earpiece. All around her, rolling hills in various shades of green spread out in every direction. A beautiful spot for a mission. Her forces were already deployed and closing in on the targets.

Now, it was finally her turn to take action.

"I'm on scene." She strode through the gate on the east side of the property, flanked by two female bodyguards. The op in Coventry had failed. Megan and Amber were both still alive. But that didn't matter for the moment, because this op was her priority, and it was going perfectly so far.

Thirty yards into the field she stopped and took her toy out of her ruck, placing it at her feet on the damp grass. "Activating drone now."

Stepping back, she started up the battery and piloted it into the air using the small remote control. Within seconds they had a bird's eye view of everything they needed.

The two other elements of her force had deployed exactly as ordered. One was positioned to the north of the house, the other to the west. All her operatives were en-circling the front and back of the main house, awaiting her word for the attack.

She flew the drone over the manor house, circled it, and zoomed the camera in. There was no sign of Kiyomi and the others. Not even her custom infrared device was picking them up inside.

They had to be hiding beneath the house in an old cellar. "Check under the first floor and flush them out of the house."

With the north and east entrances blocked, the only options for escape were south or west. And the only good cover near that fence line was the woods to the southwest. "Once they come out they're going to head southwest. Follow them."

"Copy."

She watched the screen as she spoke. "Remember what I said. Kiyomi is to be captured alive. And if possible, unharmed."

"And the others?"

"Kill them all." They were dead weight and liabilities for her.

"Roger."

"Extraction is in eighteen minutes. Synchronize timers…now." She hit a button on her wristwatch, activating the stopwatch function, then turned south and started for the thick band of woods near the southwest fence line.

In just a matter of minutes, Kiyomi would be hers, and then she could finally begin the most important work of her life.

****

"Where's Karas?" Kiyomi asked as she and Marcus hurried through the study to the bookcase.

"Already inside," he answered, pulling her through

the opening into the secret passage beyond it and shutting the bookcase behind them. Trinity and Brody were already down the ladder and in the old priest hole that he and Megan had converted into a loadout room.

Kiyomi quickly climbed down the ladder. Marcus followed, cursing the pain and weakness in his left hip and thigh. It was still flared up from the attack on Rahman's headquarters.

As soon as he reached the bottom Kiyomi was there, handing him a ballistic vest. He strapped it on as the others did the same. "They're going to try to flush us out," he said. "Our best chance at getting out is to use the escape tunnel."

"It lets out on the east side of the garden wall," Trinity added for Brody and Kiyomi. "There's some cover there, but not much."

"How far out are the others?" Kiyomi asked, taking a rifle from where it was mounted on the stone wall.

"From Coventry it's at least forty-five minutes by car," Marcus said, typing out a text to Megan. There was no reception down here but hopefully it would send once they got outside. He didn't know when he'd get the chance to stop and text again, so better now and hope for the best. They couldn't involve the local cops. They'd be slaughtered against this kind of enemy.

Silence met his words, the gravity of the situation hitting hard. They were outnumbered. There was no way they could hold off the enemy force for that long, so escape was the only option.

"We stack up just inside the tunnel exit," he told them, grabbing extra ammo and shoving it into the pockets on his vest. "Then we make a break along the garden wall and head for the stables."

Kiyomi stared at him. "We're going to escape on horseback?"

He nodded. "The ATVs are too far away. We'd be

exposed trying to get to them, and they're too loud even if we could." Reaching for the sniper rifle on the top shelf, he pulled it down and handed it to Brody. "You'll be wanting this."

Brody took it. "After we get on the horses, where are we riding?"

"Woods on the southwest side." He loaded a full magazine into his rifle, then checked his sidearm and holstered it, urgency beating at him. They had to hurry. Get out before they became trapped. "There's an eight-foot stone wall there. We need to get the women over it, and find a place to hide until the others can get here."

"Oh no," Kiyomi argued, spinning to face him with an annoyed look. "We're not damsels in distress. If we go over that wall, you're both coming with us too."

"The Architect wants *you*," he told her, a wave of protectiveness blasting through his system. "It's my job to make sure that doesn't happen."

"You—"

He held up a hand, his attention riveted to a monitor attached to the far wall. The camera showed a split image of the front and back entrances to the hallway. Two slender figures were slipping inside the back door, and two more through the front. "We're out of time. Questions?"

No one said anything.

"Right. Let's move." He crouched down in front of Karas to ruffle the top of her head. "Stay. You'll be safe here." She gazed up at him with confused brown eyes, but this was the safest spot for her and she had food and water put out. If he didn't make it back, she would be all right until Megan or one of the others could come for her.

Standing, he hid a wince and turned Kiyomi by the shoulders, then pushed her toward the opposite side of the room and the bolted steel door. He opened it, paused to listen, then nodded at Brody. "Go."

Brody disappeared into the darkness, then Trinity.

Kiyomi followed them. When Marcus reached back to shut the door behind him, he found Karas at his heels, ears back, head lowered in a submissive posture. Not understanding why he was abandoning her here.

"No," he told her firmly. "Stay."

He stepped into the tunnel after Kiyomi and shut the heavy door once more. The shooters in the house would be hard-pressed to find the entrance to the secret passage. Marcus hoped it would give them the chance they needed to get to the stables.

The passageway was dark and narrow, and he had to crouch down to avoid banging his head on the stone roof. He kept one hand on Kiyomi's back, staying close to her as they made their way under the garden. His hip screamed at him with every step, his eyes slowly adjusting to the faint light coming from the opposite side. After a minute the tunnel began to rise and the light grew brighter.

Brody and Trinity were waiting at the exit. "I'll go out first," Brody whispered. "Wait three seconds. If you don't hear anything, the coast is clear."

"Roger that," Marcus said, adrenaline pumping hard and fast.

This was risky, but it was riskier still to stay here. Sooner or later the enemy would discover them. Their only real chance of escape was to get to the stable and take the horses as close to the southwest wall as possible, then pray the others got there in time to extract them before they were overrun.

The rest of them were silent as Brody slipped outside. Marcus counted down the seconds. When a five-count passed without any warning from Brody, Trinity slipped out of the tunnel.

Marcus squeezed Kiyomi's shoulder. "I'll be right behind you," he said in a low voice.

"Just don't you dare sacrifice yourself to save me," she warned, "or I'll never forgive you."

No promises. She was worth everything. He squeezed her shoulder again. "Go, love."

He was right behind her as they burst out of the tunnel and veered right into the cold November air. Brody and Trinity were thirty yards ahead of them, hugging the garden wall as they kept watch. So far they appeared to be undetected, and Marcus prayed it stayed that way.

At the end of the wall they stacked up again. Marcus squeezed Kiyomi's left shoulder and she did the same to Trinity. Trinity signaled Brody and he took off, darting to the next bit of concealment offered by the yew hedge between the wall and the stable.

The rest of them followed, Marcus last, his limping gait slowing him down. With every step Marcus expected to hear shots ring out. He didn't know where the rest of the enemy force was, but they had to be close and it was only a matter of time before he and the others were spotted.

They ran for the stable where the daylight streaming through the far door cast long shadows over the floor. The stableman had brought the horses in several hours ago. Marcus hurriedly began opening the stable doors. There was no time to tack up or even put bridles on the horses.

He pulled Rollo around by the mane. "Brody, get on." An expert horseman who had grown up on a horse farm, Brody grabbed a fistful of Rollo's mane and swung himself onto the animal's back.

Grabbing Lucy next, Marcus helped lift Trinity onto her back. Then it was Kiyomi's turn. He lifted her onto Maple, gripped her thigh gently in reassurance as she adjusted the rifle slung across her chest. "Just hold onto her mane and squeeze her ribs with your legs," he instructed.

She'd only ever ridden once before, never at a gallop, and that had been with full tack and a helmet. But she could do this. She had to. "Don't worry about steering her. I'll lead with Jack, and the others will all follow." She

209

wouldn't be able to shoot and keep her seat, but he prayed it wouldn't come to that.

"Okay," she said without hesitation.

God, she would never know just how bloody amazing she was to him, facing everything that was thrown at her with incredible courage.

He put a hand on base of Jack's neck and jumped up, biting down at the searing pain in his left hip as he swung his good leg across the horse's back. They were about to run the gauntlet.

Without looking at the others, he drove his heels into Jack's sides. "Hyah!"

Jack leapt forward and bolted out of the stable like someone had fired a starter pistol. Marcus leaned over his mount's neck and glanced back. Kiyomi was right behind him, face tense but managing to keep her seat in spite of the breakneck pace, followed by Trinity, and Brody guarding their six on Rollo.

Marcus caught only a flash of movement in the distance out of the corner of his eye, then the report of a rifle echoed in the morning air as the clump of grass and dirt kicked up several feet from Jack's front right hoof.

Marcus steered him to the left using the pressure of his legs. The other horses scrambled to follow, hooves thundering across the damp grass.

Another shot whizzed past, striking the ground to the left. Marcus veered right, glanced back, and put the stables between them and the shooters.

It bought them several seconds, enough time to gain them the distance needed to be at the end of regular rifle range. To hit them now, the enemy would either have to chase them or to use a high-powered sniper rifle, which would take time to set up.

He turned slightly to check on Kiyomi again. She was plastered to Maple's neck, her body hugging the horse, holding firm.

Good lass. Hang on.

Facing front once more, Marcus aimed Jack up the slope of the next hill and down the far side. At the top of the next rise, the woods finally came into view in the distance.

He rode straight for it, not daring to slow down. The enemy would be scrambling for their vehicles and would catch up to them in a matter of minutes. Only the distant trees would stop them, and hopefully give Marcus and the others concealment.

Jack's sides heaved, his nostrils flared wide open as they galloped over the fields toward the thick trees that were still half-cloaked in red, yellow and orange. Marcus made a judgment call to split up. Staying together presented too much of an easy target.

When they were several hundred yards away from the trees he shifted slightly, looked behind him and waved Brody and Trinity off. Brody expertly turned Rollo to the right. Trinity's horse followed.

Marcus urged Jack to the left and checked to make sure Maple followed. The mare was tiring now but anxious to keep up with Jack.

Finally they reached the edge of the forest. Marcus brought Jack to a plunging stop close to the trees. Slinging his rifle out of the way, he threw his leg across Jack's rump and hopped off, the impact sending a hot jolt of pain through his left hip.

It started to buckle. He grabbed at Jack's mane to steady himself, then stepped away and held up his hands to Maple to stop her.

The mare tossed her head and drew up short, skidding in the damp grass. Kiyomi lost her balance. Marcus lunged for her as she jumped free, catching her around the ribs as she landed in front of him. "All right?" he asked.

"Yes. Hurry."

He whirled to face the horses and waved his arms to

scatter them. Jack and Maple shied away, tossing their heads and snorting nervously. He whacked Jack's rump with a hard hand. "Hyah!"

Jack bolted away, ears pinned flat to his head. Maple scrambled after him.

Marcus grabbed Kiyomi's hand and rushed for the comparative safety of the woods, cursing his bad leg as they darted through the trees. The wall was beyond the woods. His priority was getting her to safety, at all cost.

As the woods swallowed them, it suddenly hit him. For so long he'd wondered why he had survived the op in Syria when seven of his men had not. Now he knew.

It was for this moment. To protect Kiyomi and get her to safety.

Whatever those fuckers coming after them did next, he was ready to lay down his life in order to make sure she got out of here alive.

Chapter Twenty

T he amount of noise they made as they raced through the trees made Kiyomi cringe, but there was no help for it. Without the benefit of camo clothing or time to be stealthy, they had to get as deep into the woods as possible before the enemy arrived, which would be any minute. How many were coming after them, she had no idea.

She'd lost sight of Brody and Trinity. They were somewhere to the right, but they didn't have earpieces for comms and cell reception out here was shit, so texting likely wouldn't work either.

A few yards ahead, Marcus was leading her deeper into the woods. He was limping badly now but didn't slow, didn't let up.

She hated that he was putting himself in more danger for her, that his home had been attacked because of her and the others. What the hell did the Architect want with her, anyway? What was so important about her that the woman would go to these extremes to capture her?

The sound of vehicles moving in the distance came from behind her. Her pulse kicked up a notch, her nape prickling because she could feel the enemy back there, hunting them.

She dove behind a thick oak trunk when the first shot rang out, landing on the carpet of fallen brown leaves as a shower of bark exploded a few feet to her left. She got to one knee and brought her rifle up, scanning the trees for a target. She couldn't see anyone…

Glancing over her shoulder, she found Marcus mirroring her position back and slightly off to the left. After a moment he signaled to her to come toward him.

She trusted his judgment enough to override the instinct telling her to stay put. Holding her weapon at the ready, she got up and darted toward him. Marcus fired, the report echoing through the naked trees. She flew past him, searching for another place to hide.

A large boulder was sticking out of the earth a dozen yards away. She ran for it, ducked behind cover and stretched out flat on her belly, bringing the butt of her weapon to her shoulder, ready to fire.

Marcus was still out in front of her, poised, ready to fire again. He waited several seconds, then turned and rushed toward her. Kiyomi automatically covered him, and spotted movement through the trees beyond him. "Down!" she called out, loud as she dared.

He dove to the ground and rolled behind a tree just as a bullet tore into the one he'd been standing in front of a heartbeat earlier. Kiyomi searched the area where she'd seen the muzzle flash through the undergrowth, hunting for the shooter.

Come on, you bastard. Show yourself.

A flicker of movement slightly to the left caught her attention. She aimed and fired a split second before Marcus did the same.

Three shots answered, one passing so close she heard it go past her. A chunk of rock hit her right shin.

She risked a look over her shoulder to find Marcus giving her hand signals. Telling her to get up and move past him while he laid down covering fire. She flashed him a thumbs up then placed her palms flat on the ground, ready to spring up as soon as he began shooting.

The deep bark of a sniper rifle sounded off to her left. Brody.

Higher-pitched rifle fire answered, but not in her direction. Then Marcus fired a burst.

Kiyomi shot up and ran in a crouch, leaping over a fallen tree trunk in her path. Marcus fired another burst, then another as she darted to the right, moving toward where Trinity and Brody were hidden somewhere in the tangled underbrush.

Finding a broken, rotting trunk to hide behind, she zipped behind it and hunkered down on one knee. The damp, sweet smell of the rotting wood and fallen leaves filled her nostrils.

Marcus was still somewhere out ahead and to her right but she couldn't see him. She put her weapon to her shoulder and scanned the forest in front of her, her pulse beating fast in her ears. He wasn't falling back. Why wasn't he moving?

Someone fired a rifle to her left. Closer now. She thought she saw something moving in the shadows. Her finger stayed on the trigger but she didn't fire, waiting to get a positive ID because she couldn't risk shooting Trinity.

She jerked the barrel of the rifle to her right at a sudden flash of movement. Man. Light gray T-shirt.

Marcus. She switched her focus beyond him, tracking his movement through the trees as he came toward her. Someone fired at him. He grunted and went down.

She shot to her feet, her heart rocketing into her throat. *No!*

More movement in the same vicinity. She aimed and fired twice. The shooter dropped out of sight. Had she hit them?

She couldn't see Marcus. She had to get to him.

Breaking from cover, she raced toward where she'd seen him fall. Splinters of wood exploded near her left shoulder. She flinched as they peppered her face and neck, fired blindly toward where the shot had come from as she raced for Marcus.

A branch as thick as her wrist landed five feet in front of her. She skidded to avoid it, darting behind the nearest tree trunk wide enough to hide her. Marcus lay on his belly to her right, watching her. He shook his head at her, thrust a finger behind him, his expression set.

"Are you hit?" she whispered, loud as she dared.

He lowered his brows in warning and thrust his finger in the direction she'd just come from.

No freaking way she was leaving him.

Kiyomi didn't move, scanning him from head to toe. She couldn't see any blood, but he was in visible pain as he pulled himself to one knee. And then she glanced up as a muted, rhythmic thumping came from overhead. Helicopter rotors.

Shit, what if the shooters had more reinforcements on board? She couldn't see it through the dense treetops.

Looking over at Marcus, she shook her head. *Not leaving.* Too bad if he didn't like it.

His expression foreboding, he stared back at her, his eyes promising hell if she didn't do what he said. "*Go,*" he mouthed.

Torn, she hesitated, then whirled when something moved behind her. Marcus fired two rapid shots at whatever it was. A soft grunt answered, then something hit the ground with a thud.

Her gaze darted back to Marcus. He was definitely hurt. She needed to help him up and get over the wall beyond the trees.

He nailed her with a livid look. "*Go,*" he mouthed again, his expression all kinds of pissed off.

Satisfied he at least wasn't in imminent danger of bleeding out, she reluctantly turned and ran in the direction he'd ordered. The distinctive crack of the sniper rifle boomed off to the right as she ran.

Soon the trees began to thin out slightly. The light changed, the drab gray brightening a bit, and she got her first glimpse of the stone wall standing beyond the trees.

"Kiyomi!"

She whipped her head around to see Trinity running toward her from the right.

"This way! Come on!" Trin waved her over.

The thump of the approaching helo was growing louder now. Kiyomi angled toward Trinity and kept running while more gunfire broke out behind them. The urge to stop and go back to protect Marcus was overwhelming.

"Marcus is hurt," she panted when she got close enough that she didn't have to shout.

"Shot?"

"Don't think so." Had to be his hip or leg. She crouched behind a tree several feet from where Trinity was hiding behind another, and looked up. "How many shooters are left?"

"At least six."

"That helo's getting close." How many more shooters were coming?

She glanced behind her at the wall, now less than twenty yards away. It was an easy jump to grab the top of it, but swinging over it would leave them exposed. "I'm not going over it without the guys."

Trinity nodded, her gaze trained on the terrain ahead. "Brody's coming in from our nine o'clock."

Kiyomi shifted her body to look in that direction, but whipped back around when something rustled off to her left. "I hear something," she whispered, taking aim. Trinity did the same. They both stared through the trees, searching for movement.

A shot rang out from somewhere in front of them. Trinity grunted and cursed.

Horror ripped through her when she whipped around to see her friend lying on her back, face contorted in pain as she grabbed at her chest, her legs writhing in the dead leaves.

Without thinking Kiyomi lowered her weapon and raced for Trinity.

A flurry of gunfire erupted through the woods, twice the volume than anything they'd had before.

"Trin!" Kiyomi skidded to her knees beside Trinity, reached out to pry her hands away from her chest. Had the vest not stopped the—

Something hit her in the back of her thigh. Pain shot up her leg and through her entire body, stealing her breath. She was already convulsing as she hit the forest floor. Her vision went black, her body arching and twitching.

She lay there, unable to move, unable to cry out a warning to the others, the pain stealing the air from her lungs. Somehow she forced her eyes open, her blurry gaze landing on someone stepping out from behind a tree thirty feet away. A middle-aged woman approached her, weapon pointed directly at Kiyomi.

The woman's eerie smile made Kiyomi's heart kick hard against her ribs as the woman knelt beside her. Kiyomi struggled to suck in air, fought to reach for her sidearm.

The woman's hand flashed out. Something sharp pricked Kiyomi's neck. The pain receded, a strange floating sensation taking over.

Disbelief slammed into her as her eyelids began to fall. The woman looked like an older version of Amber.

The Architect had gotten her after all.

****

"Got her."

Forcing back the rush of elation flooding her, Janelle tossed the empty syringe aside, seized the straps of Kiyomi's tactical vest and began to drag her backward across the leaf-strewn ground.

Ten yards away, Trinity lay where she'd fallen. No longer a threat, and unimportant.

"Roger," a female voice answered in her earpiece. "You're clear. Helo's moving to LZ now."

"Copy."

After a tense start to the operation where they'd lost sight of their targets for a precious few minutes, everything had gone perfectly. She'd lost several operatives, but that was a small price to pay to get Kiyomi.

A steady barrage of gunfire filled the forest as she dragged her prize backward to the wall. Her remaining operatives were keeping both Laidlaw and Colebrook busy, giving her more than enough of a diversion to take Kiyomi.

Two of her operatives swung over the top of the wall and landed lightly in front of her. Together they lifted Kiyomi over the top, where two more of her people waited to receive her on the other side. Janelle jumped up, caught the top of the stone and swung her body over it.

"Another helo's coming toward us."

Janelle glanced up to see a black outline in the distance. Possibly military. "We'll be gone before they can get here. *Hurry.*"

As she landed on the damp grass on the other side, the tallest female operative hoisted Kiyomi across her shoulders and started off down the hill at a lope. Janelle followed at an easy jog while the others fanned out behind her to form a protective semicircle. Not that Laidlaw or Colebrook would be coming anytime soon.

In the clearing a hundred yards away in front of her, her helo was lowering into a hover. The rotor wash kicked up a flurry of dirt and grass, frightening a handful of sheep into scattering. There was no one else for miles around. No one to stop her.

Another thrill of triumph hit her, and this time she didn't try to suppress it. She'd done it. Another couple of minutes and she'd be in the clear, on her way north with Kiyomi finally in her grasp.

Chapter Twenty-One

White.

Marcus flattened himself on the ground as bullets peppered the trees around him. The sudden increased volume of fire had him pinned in place.

At the first break, he raised his head and searched for a target, desperate to clear the shooters so he could find Kiyomi. His patience was rewarded a minute later when the underbrush at his two o'clock moved slightly.

He fired two shots. The brush jiggled, then stilled. The sniper rifle fired somewhere off to his left. Colebrook, still in the game.

Let's finish it, then.

Sudden silence filled the forest, broken only by the sound of the helo's rotors, turning somewhere out of view behind him. He needed to get Kiyomi, needed to head east to find another place to scale the wall.

Except moving was going to be a problem.

Carefully getting to his knees, he grimaced as he struggled to his feet. That fall had aggravated his hip. Jagged shards of glass stabbed through the joint and down his whole thigh with every movement. His already weakened muscles gave out, threatening to send him sprawling on his face.

Movement to the left.

He swung the barrel of his weapon toward it, finger on the trigger. Then a weak whistle sounded, barely discernable over the noise from the helo.

A second later, Brody called out. "Marcus. We're clear."

Keeping his rifle to his shoulder, he cautiously moved out from behind his meager cover and limped his way toward the sniper, now practically dragging his left leg behind him.

No one fired at him. Finally daring to look over his shoulder, he spotted Brody hunkered down nearby, covering him. "Where are Kiyomi and Trin?" Marcus said curtly.

"Hopefully over the wall, but the helo's on that side too."

They fell back together, each scanning half of their field of fire. Soon the wall was within sight. Brody let out another whistle.

A weak, wobbly one answered.

Brody's head jerked around. He angled toward it, whistled again.

The weak whistle came again.

Brody turned toward the source and ran. Marcus followed as fast as he could, his gut balling tight.

Ahead of him, Brody leaped over a downed log and put on a burst of speed. "*Trin.*"

Oh, Jesus. Trinity lay on her back, a hand pressed to her chest. She was trying to roll to her side. Trying to get up.

Brody dumped his weapon and fell to his knees beside her, pushing her flat. "Lemme see." She tried to bat his hands away from her chest. "Lemme see, sweetheart."

"Not…bleeding," she managed. "Busted…ribs. Can't…breathe."

Marcus stood back a good ten yards, weapon up as he glanced around them, growing frantic. There was no sign of Kiyomi.

Brody ripped the Velcro straps on Trinity's vest apart to look at her. She growled low in her throat, her legs moving restlessly. But there was no blood on his hands as he swept them over and under her torso.

"Where's Kiyomi?" Marcus demanded.

"She…took her," she said between gritted teeth, struggling to roll to her side with Brody's help.

His heart lurched.

He spun around, searching the ground for signs of a struggle. The leaves and forest floor had been disturbed nearby. Cleared in a pattern that indicated something had been dragged along it.

Marcus followed it as fast as he could with his limp, no longer even feeling the pain. The marks led right up to the wall and stopped near several sets of boot prints in the damp soil.

Oh, Christ. Oh, Christ, no… The helo.

Slinging his weapon, he grabbed the top of the wall and hoisted himself up on top. What he saw on the other side made his whole body go numb with fear.

The helo had set down in a clearing a football field length away, rotors turning. Two dozen yards from it, a group of women were fanned out in a semicircle, protecting a middle-aged woman in the center, and another behind her, carrying Kiyomi.

No. Please, no.

He jumped down, landed with most of his weight on his good leg, stifling a cry of agony as his injured hip gave out. He hit the ground on his right side. Rolled to his knees. Fought to his feet once more. He had to get to Kiyomi. Had to stop them.

He made it a half-dozen steps before his leg buckled again, sending him sprawling face first in the damp grass. He shoved up on his hands and knees, his gaze locked on Kiyomi. They were so close to the damn helo. Another one was coming in behind it. If he didn't stop them now, he'd lose her forever.

Two of the women guarding Kiyomi and the Architect fired at him. Dirt sprayed his face and arms. One round carved a crease through the side of his shoulder. The pain in his heart drowned it out as he brought his weapon up and fired at one of them.

He hit her in the stomach. She doubled over and went down in the grass. The others didn't stop. Two more fired at him. He ducked. One hit the plate in the front of his vest.

Looking up, he fired at another shooter. Then another. And another.

Three more shooters dropped. Two didn't move. The third started dragging herself toward the helo.

Only the Architect and the woman carrying Kiyomi remained. But he needed to get closer. He was too far away to guarantee a shot wouldn't hit Kiyomi with the way they were lined up.

Bracing for the pain, he forced himself upward once more. He bit back a scream, managed to hobble another dozen yards before he fell. He refused to give up, would never give up.

He dragged himself forward, his left leg dangling weakly behind him. Panic sliced at him.

Hurry. Have to save her. Have to stop her from getting aboard the helo.

He struggled forward, every inch sending shards of agony through his leg, the wound in his shoulder burning. He was almost out of ammo now. Only two shots left.

Raising his weapon, he aimed for the woman carrying Kiyomi. He fired, hitting her in the back of the thigh. She went down hard, she and Kiyomi both tumbling to the grass.

Immediately he aimed at the Architect, but he was too late. The psychotic bitch had already lunged forward to grab Kiyomi and dragged her in front. Kiyomi blocked the Architect like a living shield, the angle making it impossible for him to fire.

A wave of rage and despair hit him. They were steps from the open helicopter door. And he was down to his final shot.

If he fired and missed, he was out of ammo. Hitting the pilot from this angle was a low-percentage shot. The rotors, even less so. If he hit the Architect, the round would hit Kiyomi too. But he could *not* let them get aboard that helicopter. If Kiyomi was taken, she faced captivity, torture, and God only knew what other horrors.

A sickening realization formed in his gut as his only option became clear. He had one final chance to stop this. One final act of mercy he could give her.

The only way to save her was to do the unthinkable, and fulfill the terrible promise he'd made to her the other night.

Pushing past the wall of emotions that threatened to crush him, he laid flat on the grass and stared through the sight at Kiyomi's chest, anguish twisting in his heart as he adjusted his aim. Her vest wouldn't stop a round from his weapon at this distance.

I'm so sorry, love.

****

Kiyomi's heart raced so fast she feared it might burst, thudding in time with the thump of the rotors as the noise from the helo's engines suddenly increased in pitch. The drug was slowly fading from her system as the woman who looked just like Amber hauled her to the open helo door.

Her mind whirled, refusing to accept what was happening. Trinity had been shot. Was she dead? What about Marcus?

Her captor wrestled her the final few feet toward the helo, keeping Kiyomi in front of her like a shield. Kiyomi deliberately stayed a dead weight to make it as difficult as possible for her, ordering her unresponsive muscles to attack.

Then they were at the helo door, and she found herself in a fight for her life.

Summoning her remaining strength, she tried to buck. Her muscles refused to obey her, moving in an uncoordinated rush that resulted in her arm flailing into her captor's face.

The Architect dumped her on her ass for a moment but remained behind her as she dragged Kiyomi upright once more, holding her beneath the armpits.

No. You're not taking me!

Kiyomi managed to turn her head, tried to sink her teeth into the woman's neck. A sharp cuff to the side of her face snapped her head back. Then the Architect dragged her backward into the open helo door.

Someone else tried to climb in beside them. The Architect lashed out with her foot and kicked the person away, sending them tumbling out of the helo and across the grass.

Kiyomi tried another bite, missed. Flailed one hand up to try and gouge the woman's eyes. Another blow to the face stunned her for a second. Adrenaline pumped hard and fast through her veins, but still the drug had her in its grip.

It was maddening to be unable to fight back while her mind remained almost clear. She lurched as the Architect finally dragged her up onto the helo deck, pulling Kiyomi practically into her lap.

Kiyomi bucked as best she could, desperately tried to fight. "Why?" she managed to get out, her voice slurred, drowsy. "Why me?"

"Because you're going to be my blueprint." She was

panting, her voice filled with elation.

Blueprint? For what?

"Go, go!" the Architect shouted to the pilot, grunting as she continued dragging Kiyomi farther inside. "Before that other helo comes in!"

What other helo?

The vibrations in the deck changed. The pilot lifted them a few inches.

No! She wouldn't let them take her!

Kiyomi wrenched an arm up, clawed at the hand under her arm—and froze.

A red laser dot marked the front of her vest. Forcing her gaze upward, she squinted across the open field. Not far from the stone wall, she spotted him.

Marcus was lying prone, his rifle aimed at her chest. He couldn't get to her. Couldn't save her.

So he was going to end her suffering, just as he'd promised.

A sudden wash of tears burned her eyes as she stared back at him, a mix of grief and gratitude. He was alive, but this would hurt him terribly. She was sorry for that, but thankful for his strength to do what needed to be done.

"Thank you," she whispered to him, hoping he could see it.

She was vaguely aware of the helo beginning to lift, easing forward as in slow motion. The next instant, the bullet struck.

The pain was so intense it punched the air from her lungs. She couldn't breathe, the world eclipsed in an agonizing burn as she slumped forward.

Somewhere in the background a high-pitched scream filled her ears as she and the Architect tumbled out of the rising helo.

Chapter Twenty-Two

The instant he squeezed the trigger, everything stopped. Time. His heart.

Marcus thought his chest would implode as he watched the bullet hit home, then Kiyomi tumbled out of the helo. She hit the ground on her back, next to the Architect, and didn't move. The Architect writhed on the ground, his shot having gone through Kiyomi to strike her as well.

A sickening wave of horror swamped him as he stared at Kiyomi lying utterly still on the grass. Bile rushed up his throat, a grief-stricken scream sticking there.

Fuck, had he missed his placement? She'd moved at the very last second…

Numb all over, blood pulsing in his ears, he dropped his empty rifle and forced himself to his feet. He staggered forward a few steps, fell to his knees. The smaller Griffin was flying off now, abandoning the Architect because the approaching Puma was coming in fast.

"Marcus!"

He jerked his head around to see Brody leaping down

from the top of the wall. He ran to Marcus, grabbed him around the ribs and hoisted him upright. "What happened?"

"I shot her," he croaked out. She'd seen the laser dot a moment before he'd fired. He'd seen her lips move. Bloody *thanking* him for what she'd assumed would be a lethal shot. He wanted to puke.

Brody stared at him in disbelief, then horror. "*What*?"

Marcus tried to shove him away but Brody muscled him forward. "Trinity's still on the other side. I didn't want to move her."

Marcus couldn't take his eyes off Kiyomi. He had to get to her. Had to stop the bleeding, save her. The shooters were all down but more were coming. "I'm out of ammo. The Puma—"

"It's our team," Brody shouted back over the noise. "Amber called me a minute ago. They'd been trying to reach us for the past half-hour, but the reception out here's too spotty."

Marcus glanced up at the approaching Puma and recognized Megan leaning out the open door. She waved an arm to signal him as the pilots slowed the aircraft and dropped into a low hover. "Just get me to Kiyomi," he told Brody, voice ragged.

Brody clamped an arm around his back and draped one of Marcus's across his own shoulders. Marcus hopped along as fast as he could go on his good leg, his lungs tight, heart racing frantically.

"You're hit," Brody said.

Marcus didn't answer, just kept going, his gaze locked on Kiyomi. *Come on, love. Move. Please move…*

He'd aimed for her shoulder, but Jesus Christ, she'd moved. What if he'd killed her?

Grief and panic clawed at him, sharp and agonizing. The Puma set down fifty yards or so from them.

Megan and the others jumped out and raced toward them, rifles at the ready. They surrounded the downed shooters as Marcus and Brody raced for Kiyomi and the Architect, who had managed to crawl a dozen or so yards away.

When they got close Marcus pushed away. Brody immediately moved to secure the Architect while Marcus stumbled toward Kiyomi.

She lay completely still, her eyes half-open. His heart lurched, terror rocketing through him as for an unbearable moment he thought she was dead. But then she blinked and slowly focused on him.

He fell heavily to his knees beside her, ignoring the brutal wave of pain in his leg and hip, and slid a hand beneath her head. "Kiyomi," he choked out, a rush of tears blurring his vision.

There was a pound coin-sized hole in the front of her left shoulder, where the vest couldn't protect her. Blood stained her chest and arm, soaking into the grass beneath her.

Marcus rolled her slightly. The exit wound on the back of her shoulder blade was worse. But nothing was spurting—the shot appeared to have missed her subclavian artery—and she was breathing all right, no blood coming from her nose or mouth that would indicate the bullet had hit the upper lobe of her lung, but *Jesus*.

He ripped his vest and shirt off, then wadded up the T-shirt and used it to pad the entry and exit wounds as best he could. She writhed a bit when he pressed down on the front of her shoulder, her face blanched of all color, contorting with pain. She was in shock, but there was something more to her reaction. Almost as if she were drugged.

"It's all right, love, it's going to be okay," he told her, his voice rough as sandpaper. She was staring through him and it scared the hell out of him. He was hyperventilating, his hands shaking as he stared down at her.

He glanced up when someone came running toward him. Megan raced over and dropped down on Kiyomi's other side. "How bad?" she asked.

"She's breathing okay. Think she's been drugged."

Megan's lips pressed together and she cut a rage-filled look over at the Architect. Brody had cuffed the woman's hands behind her back and was pinning her to the ground, with his hands on the wound in her shoulder.

Megan's eyes cut back to Kiyomi as she tapped on her earpiece. "We need to medevac them both immediately." She looked up at Marcus. "Can you walk?"

It killed him to admit it aloud, but getting Kiyomi to the hospital and into surgery as soon as possible was the only thing that mattered right now, and he would only slow the process down if he tried to carry her. "No."

Megan nodded, eyes grave, and spoke to someone else on comms. "Need a hand carrying Kiyomi." She bent over Kiyomi and put a hand on her cheek. "Hey, sweetie. We're gonna get you out of here, okay? Just hang on for me."

Marcus kept pressure on her wounds with his left hand and stroked her hair back from her face with the other, overcome with guilt and helplessness. He might have saved her life, but in doing so he'd probably cost her the use of her arm.

His guts twisted, nausea churning in his stomach. "I'm so sorry, love," he told her raggedly, his throat burning along with his eyes and hip. "So, so sorry."

Heath ran up a few moments later, took in the situation with a sweeping glance, and ripped open his ruck-sack. "I'll put on a pressure dressing and then we'll get her loaded."

The former PJ gloved up and worked fast. Marcus stayed at Kiyomi's side, his heart breaking every time she grimaced and gasped as Heath worked. Finally it was done.

Heath looked up at him. "You need treatment too. Colebrook," he called to Brody. "Get Marcus on board."

Marcus hated to let go of Kiyomi. Hated being parted from her for even a moment, but he was useless to her now. He sank back to the bloodstained grass as Heath and Megan lifted her and rushed her to the waiting Puma.

Brody arrived a moment later, bending down to grab him around the ribs. "Come on, big guy," he said, and helped Marcus onto his right foot once more.

Marcus glanced over his shoulder to check behind them. Zack was helping Trinity to the Puma.

Ty and Jesse had the Architect. They'd put a pressure dressing on her shoulder as well. Unlike Kiyomi, she was fully conscious. Fighting them as they hustled her to the waiting helo.

From out of nowhere a tidal wave of rage rose up to choke him. He'd never wanted to kill anyone as badly as he wanted to kill her, but they needed answers. The Valkyries deserved answers *and* justice.

"Keep me the fuck away from her," he warned Brody as he hobbled toward the Puma.

Thankfully the team had moved the bitch to the rear of the aircraft as Brody helped him inside. Marcus immediately crawled over to where Kiyomi lay on the deck, surrounded by Heath and her fellow Valkyries.

Marcus was barely aware of the aircraft lifting and nosing forward, all his focus on the pale, still woman in front of him. Kiyomi's eyes were closed now, and he hoped whatever she'd been drugged with was sparing her the worst of the pain.

Heath and the others all moved aside to let him collapse onto his right hip beside Kiyomi. Marcus grasped her hand, his fingers automatically going to the pulse in her slender wrist to reassure himself she was still alive.

Someone laid a hand on his shoulder. Probably Megan.

He didn't look up, didn't utter a word, refusing to look away from Kiyomi's pale face as he clenched his jaw, the acidic burn of tears scalding the backs of his eyes. *I'm right here, love. Hang on for me.*

****

Fire. She was burning.

The pain registered at the back of Kiyomi's mind as she floated up toward consciousness.

Her eyes fluttered open to find herself in a dim, quiet room. She was in bed, blankets tucked around her. She sucked in a breath, tensing as the fiery pain suddenly took over. She glanced down at her left shoulder. Everything was covered in a bandage, her arm secured to her chest.

Plastic squeaked nearby and then a shadow loomed over her bed. Her heart seized for a moment, then a gentle hand smoothed her hair back and a beautiful, deep voice spoke in a Yorkshire accent. "You're okay, love. Just out of surgery."

She relaxed, relief flooding her. She blinked up at Marcus, his features becoming clearer as her eyes adjusted to the dim light. Her throat was sore, probably from the intubation when they'd operated.

"You missed," she said hoarsely as everything came flooding back. It was the only explanation why she was still alive.

His hand froze on her head, his face tensing. "No," he finally answered, his voice rough. "I aimed for your shoulder, but then you moved as I squeezed the trigger and I thought… I thought…"

He sucked in a ragged breath and leaned over her, his other arm coming up to slide beneath her neck. Then he pressed his bearded cheek to hers, his familiar scent filling her nose. "I'm so goddamn sorry," he choked out.

His pain distressed her. "No," she whispered, reaching her right arm up to embrace him.

His shoulders shook and he pulled in an unsteady breath. She could feel wetness on her cheek, trailing down to her neck. Her heart clenched. This strong, proud and humble man was crying because of what he'd been forced to do. "*I'm* sorry. You should never have been put in that position."

He shook his head, holding her tighter. "I couldn't get to you," he said, his voice catching on a sob that broke her heart. "I couldn't save you and I only had one shot left. I didn't know the others were coming, I just saw her take you into that helicopter, and…"

"But you *did* save me," she told him, squeezing tight, her eyes stinging. "I asked you once to promise me you wouldn't let me be taken, and you didn't. You *didn't*." Her voice broke.

She hated that he'd been forced to shoot her to save her, but he'd seen it as the only way, and even then he couldn't bring himself to take a head shot. Hadn't been able to kill her because he just couldn't.

Her pulse raced, her heart beating frantically under the tide of emotion, and suddenly she couldn't hold her feelings back for him a moment longer. "Marcus, I—"

"I love you," he told her, easing back to cup her face in his hands. "I love you so goddamn much, and because of that, when it came down to it, I just couldn't do what you'd asked."

She smiled up at him through a haze of tears, hardly able to believe this was real even as the pain in her shoulder convinced her it was. "I'm glad you didn't." Because she'd be dead otherwise, and they never would have been able to tell each other how they truly felt. "And I love you too. So much." She pulled him down to her again, wrapped her good arm around him and let the tears spill freely down her face.

Marcus held her until she'd calmed, her tears reduced to shuddering sighs. "Trinity," she said. "Is—"

"She's fine. Round hit her vest, dead center mass. Cracked her sternum and broke three ribs, but no internal damage."

"Thank God. What about Karas? And the horses?"

"They're fine. I rang the gardener and asked him to find them. He rang me back not long after to say he got Karas out, then found the horses waiting at the stable when he got there."

"That's good."

"Aye."

Every jerk of her chest made the pain in her shoulder worse. She winced and let out a groan. "So, what's my damage?"

He wiped her face and straightened next to the bed. "It's…bad, but your surgeon is one of the best in the UK. He pieced your shoulder joint and scapula back together. He said there'll be some nerve damage, but we won't know the extent until the swelling goes down."

A new fear coiled inside her. "Will I be able to use it again?"

"You'll likely have permanent loss of strength and range of motion," he said, lowering his gaze, the guilt on his face hurting her as much as her newly repaired shoulder.

She grabbed his hand, squeezed hard. "Don't blame yourself."

He looked away, snorting. "Who else should I blame?"

"The Architect."

His eyes came back to her, his expression hardening. "Aye. She's in surgery now for a similar repair."

Kiyomi frowned, revulsion shuddering through her as she remembered the attack. "She said I was going to be her blueprint."

"For what?"

"I don't know."

A knock came at the door and then it pushed open a few inches. "Hey," Trinity said, moving slowly into the room, her movements restricted. "Good to see you, sweetie."

"You too." Kiyomi reached a hand out for her friend.

Trinity came over and took it, raised it to her lips to press a hard kiss on the back of it. "That was way too damn close."

"For both of us. I'm so glad you're okay."

Trin smiled. "Okay is a relative term in this instance, but I'm glad too. Think I can let the others in now? They're dying to confirm for themselves that you're still alive."

"Sure."

"Watch your eyes," Marcus murmured. "Gonna turn on the light." He switched on the small lamp beside her bed.

Squinting as her eyes adjusted, she focused on the door as Trinity told everyone to come in. Megan was in the lead, followed by Amber. Chloe marched in next, Eden right behind her. The sight of her Valkyrie sisters gathering around her made Kiyomi want to cry again.

"So, can we all agree to never go through anything like that ever again?" Chloe said, her expression agitated as she chewed her gum. "Because that sucked big time."

"I'm down with that," Kiyomi answered, a wash of tears blurring her vision. Megan leaned over to kiss her on the forehead while the others set a hand on her legs and good arm. She looked around at them all. Her sisters. "I really love you guys, you know."

"Oh, shit, don't you dare make us cry," Eden warned with a sharp look, her dark eyebrows drawn together in a worried frown.

Kiyomi smiled and gave a watery laugh that ended

in a streak of fire through her shoulder. "Ow. Okay, this sucks."

"Yeah it does," Amber said, rubbing Kiyomi's shin through the blankets. "And I will personally shove the pain meds down your throat if you refuse to take them, so don't even bother trying that shit."

She looked between her and Megan. "So. Your aunt, huh?"

Both women's expressions darkened like thunderclouds. "Yeah," Megan muttered. "I'm only sorry we figured it out too late to stop her from getting you."

"I think I remember her."

Everyone stared at her. "From where?" Megan asked.

"The Program. Just before I graduated. Some of the cadre would come in and observe me during various tasks. I noticed her because she reminded me of you," she said to Amber. "She came in a handful of times after that. And she was there at my grad ceremony."

"During the branding?" Amber asked.

"Yes. I saw her just as she slipped out of the room. But I didn't know who she was. Never spoke to her." A shiver swept through her. "I wonder if she selected me all the way back then."

"Jesus," Megan whispered, sounding horrified.

Kiyomi shared that sentiment. "Did you get anything out of her before they took her into surgery?"

"No. Except that she's a psychopath who managed to stay under everyone's radar, even the highest levels of intelligence agencies in the world," Megan said in a hard voice. "And she orchestrated this entire thing—all of it, right back to when Amber was targeting us—to get you."

That was scary as fuck. Little wonder they hadn't found her.

Kiyomi told them about the blueprint remark. "Any idea what she was talking about?"

"No," Amber answered, eyes glittering with suppressed rage. "But I'm gonna find out."

"Rycroft's here mopping up the mess," Trinity said. "He's started the initial investigation, and we'll finish it together."

"Good," Kiyomi said with a sigh. Her gaze strayed back to Marcus, now standing off to the side of the room behind the others. He was gripping the windowsill behind him, his weight shifted onto his right foot, and there was a slight bulge beneath the sleeve of his shirt.

Alarm jolted through her. "You're hurt."

The others looked over at him but he shook his head. "I'm fine."

"What he means is," Chloe said in a sardonic tone, "he took two bullets and tore his hip all to shit trying to save you."

Kiyomi scanned the length of him intently. He'd been wounded trying to save her, and he hadn't said a thing. "Marcus—"

"I'm *fine*, love," he said, putting on a smile as he came toward her, leaning heavily on a cane. His limp was a hobble now, and it tore her up inside. He took her hand and leaned down to kiss her softly. "I'll be right as rain in no time."

Someone cleared her throat.

"We'll give you guys some privacy," Trinity said, then shooed everyone out. She moved slowly to the door, then paused to smile at them. "You guys need anything—anything—just holler. We won't be far."

As soon as the door swung shut Kiyomi focused on Marcus, drinking him in. A beep sounded close to her head, and a moment later, a warm, floating sensation took hold. The pain began to fade, her eyelids growing heavier and heavier.

She grabbed Marcus's hand. The decrease in pain was awesome, but she didn't want to lose a moment with

Marcus. "I love you." She needed him to hear it again before she slid under. "Don't leave."

He squeezed her hand, his lips pressing a kiss to her forehead. "I won't ever leave you, love. I swear it."

Chapter Twenty-Three

Rycroft was waiting in the hallway when Trinity and the others stepped out of Kiyomi's room. "Got an update?" Trinity asked him while the others all walked past.

"She's out of surgery. We're moving her to a secure facility as soon as she's out of recovery."

Might be smarter to move her while she was still unconscious, but that wasn't Trinity's call to make. Rycroft was walking a fine line while cooperating with British intelligence and authorities on this matter. "London?"

"Birmingham. How's Kiyomi?"

"She's in good spirits. Marcus is keeping watch."

Rycroft nodded. "I've got extra security posted outside and on this floor. You guys staying?"

"At least two of us will be here until she's released." Jane Allen—aka Janelle Richards—had been caught but the threat might not be yet over. She might have more soldiers planning an attack. "Think she's got any others out there, ready to stage a rescue attempt?"

"We're making sure that doesn't happen. What did the doctor say about Kiyomi?"

"We can get her released tomorrow if we want. The long-term prognosis isn't clear yet. It'll be a few days until we know more, once the swelling and inflammation starts to subside."

Those intense silver eyes scanned her face. "And what about you? How are you feeling?"

"Sore as hell." Her entire chest was on fire. They'd bound her ribs with a tensor bandage because there really wasn't anything else they could do.

She'd refused any opioid meds, wanting to keep her mind clear in case anything happened. And because between the injured ribs and sternum that wouldn't let her draw a deep breath and the opioid side effect of suppressing the cough reflex, she was wary of developing a respiratory infection.

The extra strength ibuprofen tablets weren't doing much that she could tell. Every breath hurt. And if she coughed, sneezed or laughed, it was unbearable.

He cracked a grin. "No shit."

"Yeah." No one had to tell her how lucky she'd been. The only reason she was still here was because of her vest. If that round had hit her a few inches higher or to the side, she likely would have died from hypovolemic shock from a slug that caliber. "What about the prisoners?" They'd captured two of Jane's wounded bodyguards.

"They've already been transported to different facilities around London. Initial questioning resulted in nothing."

"Did they have tats like the other ones?"

"Not the same kind. It's almost like Jane was trying out a bunch of different designs. Anyway, the interrogations started an hour ago." Keeping the tats wasn't the best idea if Jane had planned to start a new version of the Program, but what did she know?

It was scary as hell to think that Jane had not only

been behind the Valkyrie Program, but may have implemented a new one. "Any idea how many more might be out there?"

"No, but finding out's one of our top priorities." He pulled his phone from his pocket, still buzzing. "I gotta take this." He ran his gaze over her face again. "I'm going to start trying to crack Jane as soon as she wakes up. I'll call you with the location later, and you can meet me there if you're up to it."

"I'll be up to it." There was no way she was missing her chance to interrogate the bitch responsible for all of this shit they'd been through.

She followed Rycroft down the hall, heading for the waiting room where the others were all gathering. Briar and Georgia had stayed there with their men while the rest of them visited Kiyomi.

Everyone looked up when she entered, but her gaze slid right to Brody and stayed there. He'd flown across the ocean to be here for her, had voluntarily put himself in harm's way to help and protect her. Today he'd done all that and more. He was more her hero today than he'd ever been.

Before anything else happened, she had something to get off her chest as soon as they were alone.

She filled the group in on what Rycroft had said. Amber had Lady Ada open on her lap. So much of this next part of the investigation hinged on what Amber and Rycroft's analysts were able to uncover. "What do you need us to do?" Trinity asked her.

"Find any new intel you can and send it to me," she answered, busily typing away, jaw tight. "I'm going to crack that bitch open if it kills me."

"Who's taking first watch here?" Megan asked. "Ty and I can do it."

"You sure?" Trinity asked.

"Yep. Just text us when you've got a location to meet

Rycroft. I need to be there."

"Of course." She paused, looking around the room. These strong, capable women and their partners were closer to completing their mission than ever before. All they needed were a few more breaks. "Any questions?"

"Nope," Chloe answered, taking a pull from a can of energy drink. "I just wanna get moving and *do* something."

Trinity nodded, then addressed the group. "Dismissed."

Everyone got up and filed out of the room. Brody came last. She stopped him, waited until the door shut, leaving them alone in the room.

"You okay?" he asked, his brown eyes searching her face in concern.

"I'm fine."

But Trinity's heart felt bruised, and not just because of her injuries.

She'd withheld part of herself from this incredible man out of fear and insecurity, all of which she now saw as baseless and stupid. *She'd* been stupid. She'd almost died today, and she'd been cowardly guarding her heart from the one person who meant the most to her in this world.

But no longer. However things shook out with Jane Allen and this mission, Trinity was finally clear on what she wanted. She was done with holding back. She had a life to live, and the man standing in front of her to live it with.

She set her hands on his chest, wincing as the motion pulled at her sore ribs. His heart beat slow and steady beneath her palms, those warm brown eyes delving into hers. "I've been holding back from you, and I'm sorry."

His lips twitched. "Let's talk about this later, when you're feeling better."

"No. Now."

"All right. Apology accepted. Though I kinda knew what I was in for when I fell in love with you."

She couldn't help but smile a little at his dry assessment. He'd seen her at her worst and best. The crazy along with the good. And he still wanted to make a life with her. "From here on out, things are gonna be different."

He cocked an eyebrow. "Different how?"

Her sore heart throbbed faster, a mix of relief and gratitude washing over her. She'd almost lost the chance to say this to him. Somehow that made the moment even more perfect. "I want to marry you when we get home."

His eyes widened, his whole face lighting up. "For real?"

"For real. And sometime in the not too distant future, I want to start looking into the adoption process." She wanted to be a mother, and Brody would be the most incredible dad.

He laughed, that gorgeous smile warming her inside as he carefully slid his arms around her waist, avoiding her ribs. "I want to squish you so bad right now. When are we gonna get hitched?"

A hard knot of resolve tied with the joy in her gut, sending a wave of goosebumps rippling across her skin. "Right after we deal with the bitch who did all this to us."

****

Amber finished reading the report on her screen for the second time and leaned back to rub at her tired, burning eyes. It was too much.

Jesse's arms wrapped around her from behind, his chin resting on her shoulder. "Need a break?" he murmured.

"For just a minute," she relented.

He spun her chair around, scooped her up before she

could protest, and carried her over to the hotel bed. Cradling her to his chest, he dropped kisses along the side of her face, his arms tight around her.

She sighed and leaned into him, closing her eyes. Long hours didn't faze her. She was a workaholic and comfortable with it. But today had taken an emotional, mental and physical toll on her and now she was exhausted.

From the moment they'd walked into this hotel room hours earlier, she'd been busy remotely capturing and wiping everything from dear Aunt Jane's electronics. Hard as it was to believe, every new thing she found out about her aunt was worse than the last. Jane had indeed been an actual architect. The evil, twisted kind.

It was so ironic. All of it. From the court documents detailing why Jane gave them up. She'd made an excuse about not being able to care for them because of her job, because it would impede her lifestyle, and that she wasn't cut out to be a parent.

That last bit was the only truthful thing Amber had been able to uncover about her so far, and she didn't hold out much hope that she would find more. But the captured bodyguards weren't nearly as loyal as the Architect seemed to think.

They were talking.

Having seen the way she was prepared to sacrifice them to get what she wanted, that they meant nothing to her beyond being useful pawns in her scheme, they were both talking to Rycroft and the other interrogators.

Jesse rubbed a soothing hand up and down her back. "Want to talk about it?"

Not really, but the only other person she could tell this to right now was Megan. She needed to vent before she imploded. "She didn't give us up because she didn't want to raise us. She turned us into guinea pigs so she could funnel us into phase two of the Valkyrie Program—

which she was the prototype for."

Their aunt had literally been the original Valkyrie. The Program had been her idea, and she'd done everything in her power to make it happen.

He made a low sound that told her he was listening, so she kept going. It was all just so horrific. But what she'd just learned was the hardest to take. "Kiyomi told us she was supposedly Jane's blueprint. We didn't understand what that meant. But I do now."

She shifted on his lap, a hard, heavy sadness sitting in the center of her chest as she looked into his warm brown eyes. "She wanted Kiyomi because she considered her to be the most perfect of us all."

He tucked a lock of her hair behind her ear. "She's a psychopath."

"You have no idea." She cuddled into him and laid her head on his shoulder, letting his embrace soothe her frayed edges. "Between what Rycroft sent earlier about the interrogations of her bodyguards and what I just read, it's way worse than I ever imagined. I want to tell you and Megan so bad, but I feel like I need to tell Kiyomi before anyone else, and not while she's in the hospital fresh out of surgery."

"Maybe tell Marcus, and he can break the news when he feels she's ready for it."

She sighed. This was what Jesse excelled at. Cool, calm intellect in the face of any challenge. She was usually good at compartmentalizing and removing emotion from the equation, but not with this. It was way too personal. "Maybe." She thought about it a moment. "Yeah, all right. Good idea."

She slid off his lap and called Marcus on her cell. "Hey, is this a good time?" she said when he answered.

"Aye. Kiyomi's sleeping. Nurse came in and put more pain meds in her line. She'll be out for another few hours." He paused. "Everything all right?"

A hot ball of tension formed in the pit of her stomach. She exhaled and started pacing the length of the room, unable to sit still. If Megan were here, all her fingers would be a bloody mess.

She could feel Jesse watching her from where he sat on the end of the bed she couldn't wait to crawl into with him eventually. "I just found some things that I wanted to inform Kiyomi of before anyone else. I thought I could tell you, and then you can pass them on when you think the timing is right."

A creak sounded in the background, as if he'd just sat down. That saved her the trouble of suggesting he do just that. "Aye, all right. Go on then."

She rubbed at her forehead. There was no easy way to say this. "Rycroft's team has been interrogating the surviving bodyguards. Trinity is there observing. They all have stylized tats on their hips, like the ones we ran into in Virginia did, but different designs."

"So she did have her own private fighting force."

"Yes. But there's more." She glanced up at Jesse, decided to hell with trying to be tactful. "I've been digging into her personal files through her phone, and a laptop recovered from one of the bodyguards. She's good. Maybe even better than me with tech stuff, but I was able to find a back door into her server. Everything was encrypted. And do you wanna take a guess what her password was?"

"Kiyomi," he said in a taut voice.

"Yeah." Which brought her to the worst part. "There's a reason she told Kiyomi she was the blueprint. It wasn't just figurative, it was literal."

"Literal how?" he asked, his tone growing darker.

"Jane was the original Valkyrie. She was a specialist in most of our fields, rather than only being an expert in one or two, and she chose to stay with the CIA. At some point after my parents were killed, she decided we might have the aptitude to be operatives as well. Even back then

247

she was obsessed with genetics to the point where she was willing to shuttle us into the Program to see what became of us."

She drew a breath before continuing, pushing past the pain. "She considered Kiyomi the pinnacle of the Program's achievements. The most beautiful and also the deadliest. When the Program was exposed and subsequently shut down, she refused to accept it. Decided to start a different program on her own, funded by private donations and money she'd funneled away from various ops, just like we have."

"How much money are we talking?"

"Hundreds of millions. She did it the same way I did, taking it from targets and other criminal organizations, then funneling it into various companies and offshore bank accounts as tax havens. She even paid for a private facility to be built for her new project, owned by one of her shell companies."

"You're saying she set this entire thing up, right from the time Megan came to me? All to get Kiyomi."

"Yes. Because she intended to use Kiyomi to make a whole generation of the best female assassins the world has ever known."

"Use her how?" he said in a taut voice.

"By…" Jesus, this was hard to say. It was sick. Next level, compared to what had been done to them in the past. "By harvesting her DNA and eggs—"

"Jesus *Christ*—"

"And then doing in vitro fertilization using various surrogates she deemed worthy to carry the babies." Yup. Aunt Jane had planned to make Kiyomi a human lab rat to harvest all the necessary genetic material she needed.

"She meant to use Kiyomi as a science experiment to make her own force of assassins out of what would have been Kiyomi's children," he finished angrily.

That about summed it up, and it revolted Amber.

"Yes." She stopped in front of Jesse, consciously relaxed her stomach muscles when he settled his hands on her hips and drew her closer. "I apologize. I know how hard that was to hear. Did I make the right call in telling you?"

"I'm… Aye." He paused again. "You're certain?"

"I wish I wasn't, believe me. But yes. Do you want me to tell Kiyomi once she's up to it?"

"No. I'll do it. I think it'll be easier for her if it comes from me."

Jesse was so smart. "If you change your mind, just let me know and I'll do it."

"I won't, but thank you. I appreciate you calling me, Amber. I know it had to have been hard. Does Megan know?"

"She's my next call, then Trinity."

He grunted in acknowledgment. "I suppose she's going to be extradited?"

The Architect. Amber couldn't bring herself to think of her as Aunt Jane anymore. She was an inhuman monster. A stain on humanity. "Looks that way."

He sighed. "Alright. You'll call if anything else comes up?"

"Of course. Keep us posted on Kiyomi."

"I will. She'll want to be involved with the investigation as soon as they let her out. When are the rest of you meeting Trinity at the facility?"

"Tomorrow sometime." And it couldn't come soon enough for Amber. The death penalty was too easy for this monster. For a narcissistic freak show like the Architect, a lifetime sentence in a max security facility spent in solitary isolation seemed a more fitting sentence.

That bitch had stolen everything from them, and Amber was going to ensure everything was taken from her in turn.

Chapter Twenty-Four

J anelle leaned back in the plastic chair to await her next visitor. They wanted her to be uncomfortable, but if it weren't for the pain in her newly repaired shoulder, she was as comfortable here in this interrogation room as she would have been in her own living room.

The bright lights, cuffs and chains didn't bother her in the slightest, and there was no way the people holding her would allow any kind of torture. It was laughable, really, all of them standing behind the two-way mirror right now, watching her in her orange jumpsuit as they tried to figure out how to break her.

All five agents they'd sent in so far had gotten nothing from her, including Alex Rycroft, someone she had a modicum of respect for.

It didn't matter who they sent in. No one would get anything out of her that she didn't want to give.

They could interrogate her all they wanted. She wouldn't be here that much longer anyhow. She still had a few soldiers coming for her. They were loyal to her not only because she paid them disgusting amounts of money, but because they were afraid not to be. They'd seen how she neutralized traitors and threats on the periphery, like Glenn Bennett.

The single door to the room opened. She didn't move, didn't show any hint of reaction at all as Trinity and her two nieces came in. But inside, she smiled.

Finally. Someone interesting and worthy to challenge me.

Except just the sight of them stirred the rage and resentment she'd fought her entire life to control. They looked too much like her sainted dead sister. The golden child Janelle had never been able to live up to in their parents' eyes.

Trinity stood in front of the two-way mirror and folded her arms, her stiff posture due to more than anger. She was injured, though Janelle couldn't tell where.

Janelle switched her focus to her nieces as Amber and Megan approached the table. They sat in the chairs opposite her, their expressions as blank as hers. Except she knew the truth.

No matter how well they hid it, they were angry and confused. That didn't bother her. If things had gone according to plan this morning, they would both be dead right now instead of about to attempt interrogating her.

Amber sat back and folded her arms, the defensive posture screaming her uneasiness, those green eyes so like her own as hard as glass. "I'm not even gonna ask you about what your plans were, because I already know."

Janelle didn't react. Even if they did know about her plans, it didn't matter. This wasn't over. Not nearly. And with Kiyomi wounded, she was at her most vulnerable. Easy pickings as soon as Janelle found her.

"What I *do* want to know is, how you can stomach looking at yourself in the mirror."

Beneath her cool exterior, Janelle's temper flared. Twenty-five years ago, she had been a near spitting image of Amber. Not as classically beautiful as Kiyomi, but pretty enough to make men lose their heads—literally. She'd aged well. Far better than most women her age, helped along by a skilled plastic surgeon in Miami.

"You're too old to do the work anymore, so you wanted to control others to do it for you. And now you've been defeated," Megan added, her hazel eyes cold as ice. "By the very people you used and discarded. That must hurt like a fucking bitch for someone with an ego as big as yours."

Janelle stared into those frigid eyes, refusing to allow the taunt to bother her. She was the original Valkyrie. The Program had been her idea, and she'd volunteered to be the first test subject. Experience had shown her that women made the best operatives—because men continually underestimated them.

Except Megan's taunt did hit home. Somehow the words pierced all the armor, finding the one weak spot she hid away from the rest of the world. Janelle tightened her jaw.

I'm not defeated. Fuck you all, I will never *be defeated.*

"Yep," Amber agreed. "I've got the blueprints for your facility, a roster of your minions, intelligence officials complicit with your activities, a list of private donors, and —oh, what was that other thing?" she asked, turning to glance at Trinity, still at the back of the room.

Trinity smirked, holding Janelle's gaze. "All your money. Every last fucking penny. It's gone." She raised her eyebrows in an insolent expression. "Poof."

They're lying.

But against her will, her heart constricted. There was no way. No way they could have found everything. She'd been too careful.

Without her money, she couldn't finish her facility. Couldn't fund the private lab she'd gone to such lengths to secure, or conduct the experiments necessary for her plan.

"It's over," Amber said in a flat voice. "You failed. And now you're going to pay for everything you did."

Janelle didn't answer, but she couldn't stop the reflexive raising of her chin. Despite what they might think to the contrary, she'd never hated her nieces. They'd merely been a convenient means to an end.

But now she did. She loathed them with every fiber of her being. Wished she could break her chains, dive across this table and smash their too-familiar faces in.

Relax. Don't let them get to you. You haven't lost. There's still time.

Megan's jaw flexed as she stared at Janelle with utter revulsion. All these years later, the initial recruiting reports had been right. She was far more emotional than her sister and had a harder time controlling it. She wouldn't have made it past the initial screening phase in Janelle's new program.

"Anything to say for yourself, *Auntie*?" Megan taunted.

Janelle refused to give them the satisfaction of a single word in reply. They were nothing to her.

Megan snorted. "Great talk. And since you're not going to give us jack, this interview's over. You're being transferred to a max-security MI6 facility where you'll be held until your extradition to the U.S. They'll hold you there in some dark pit in solitary confinement while you await trial, and then you'll stay there until the day you get the needle."

"Yep," Amber agreed, leaning forward to prop her arms on the table as she faced Janelle. "And when they eventually strap you to that table and stick that needle in your vein? I'm going to be there watching. Smiling. Maybe I'll even do the honors myself. Enjoying every second of sending you to hell where you belong."

Megan stood abruptly, her chair scraping against the

concrete floor. Amber didn't move. She sat there holding Janelle's gaze for several minutes.

Neither one of them blinked, both refusing to be the one to give in. Janelle almost chuckled at the childishness of it. Pity Amber hadn't been as beautiful as Kiyomi. Amber had a steely core Janelle could admire. This entire effort would have been so much easier if she could just have used her own niece instead.

Finally, Amber pushed back from the table. "We're done. Next time you see me, it'll be when you die." She followed Megan to the door.

Trinity started after them, then stopped and faced Janelle. "Oh, and Kiyomi? Is gone. Flown out this afternoon to some place you could never find her—even if you hadn't been chained up like the psychotic animal you are." She walked past Amber and Megan to open the door. Two guards in body armor came in, both holding shock wands.

Amber paused in the doorway to face her one more time. "I'm glad our parents died in that accident. At least our mother never had to find out what a monster she was related to."

Janelle gritted her teeth against a cry of pain as the assholes lifting her from her chair jerked her sideways, jarring her shoulder as Amber's words reverberated through her skull. They thought they'd won?

Hardly. As soon as she got out of here and captured Kiyomi, she could create the perfect breed of female assassin on her own in a fraction of the time it would have taken to get through all the government sanctions and other bullshit. She could do it her way, following her own rules.

But that old demon of resentment rose up once again. The need to prove everyone wrong and always have the upper hand.

Lifting her chin, she gave her nieces a taunting smirk

and a parting shot. "What makes you think it was an accident?"

****

Marcus leaned forward, elbows on his knees as he watched Kiyomi, waiting for a response after he finished speaking. After helping her shower and tucking her into his bed at Laidlaw Hall, he'd just told her everything about what Amber and Megan's aunt Jane had intended.

Every evil, twisted and disgusting detail he'd learned from Amber and Trinity throughout the last sixteen hours. Things that kept him from sleeping far more than the pain in his hip and shoulder. "Say something, love."

She stared pensively into the fire, gently stroking Karas's head with her right hand. The dog wasn't allowed up on the bed, but Marcus had made an exception because Karas wouldn't leave Kiyomi's side, and Kiyomi seemed to draw comfort from her presence. "I hate her," she finally said, so softly he had to strain to hear her.

He settled beside her in the bed, fully clothed, and took her right hand. Her left arm was still bound to her chest, her fingers swollen and discolored. She had to be hurting all over, but she'd refused all but one dose of pain meds prior to the drive back here earlier. "I hate her too."

Kiyomi turned her liquid dark gaze on him. She looked almost ethereal in the firelight, the flames dancing across her face, in her eyes. There was anger there, and pain. More than from her injury. A soul-deep wound that he prayed time would heal. "I want her to suffer."

He inclined his head. "She'll get the death penalty for what she did."

Her gaze hardened. "That's not suffering. It's the easy way out."

Marcus rubbed his thumb over the backs of her knuckles. "Aye. But if you want her brought to justice, then she needs to be brought to trial, where all the sordid details will come out. For someone like that, humiliation is a form of suffering."

"I want to stab her in the neck like I did Rahman. I want her to be rendered helpless and know what's coming before she dies."

It probably said a lot about the state of his blackened soul, but that made him smile. "Then I'm glad you're not in operational condition right now."

One side of her mouth pulled up, her eyes warming a little. "But the others are, except for Trin."

"The *others* are busy doing other things, and some of them are downstairs acting as our private security force right now." Megan and Chloe. God help him, Itch and Twitch on the loose in his house while Ty and Heath did a patrol of the grounds.

Her gaze turned thoughtful. "Maybe Chloe could blow her up. But not enough to kill her. Only a small blast, so she's dismembered. Then Heath could stabilize her and stop her from bleeding out. While she's lying there in agony Eden could drug her to slow her heart rate and give her truth serum, and then Amber could get all her passwords and everything else she needs to uncover every dirty secret she has."

The woman he loved was diabolical, and he couldn't have loved her more. "Then what?" he asked in amusement.

She frowned, considering it. "Megan could steal something important to her, taunt her with it. Trinity would help me decide on the weapon and stand watch while I get to kill the bitch."

"Thoughtful of you to include everyone."

Her lips twitched, then she turned serious. "I want to see her."

He tensed, hating even the thought of it. "You're just out of the hospital. Are you sure you—"

"I'm sure." The look in her eyes told him it wasn't up for discussion or debate. "When are they transferring her?"

"I haven't heard yet." Not officially, anyway.

Moving carefully, he shifted her so that she could lay her head on his chest. They lay there watching the fire for a few minutes before he spoke again. There were so many things he needed to say. He'd been trying to wait until she had a few days to recover, but he couldn't hold them in any longer. "Are you happy here?"

She looked up at him. "You know I am. I love it here. This is more of a home than I've ever had."

"I'm glad to hear it. Because this is almost over. Once Jane is put away, and all her funds seized—"

"Stolen by Amber," she corrected.

He smiled again. "Appropriated by Amber," he allowed, "and her entire operation dismantled, you and the others will be as safe as you're ever likely to get. You'll be free."

Her lips curved, a dreamy, faraway look in her eyes. "Free," she murmured, staring again into the flames. "I don't even know what I would do with myself."

"Stay here and make a life with me." It was out before he could stop himself, and he was glad. He was done holding this inside.

Her eyes lifted to his, and a beautiful, soft smile transformed her face. "What kind of a life do you imagine we'd have?"

"A happy, peaceful one, for starters," he said.

She laughed softly. "I don't even know what that would look like."

He opened his mouth to say more, but his mobile rang. Picking it up from the bedside table, he frowned. "It's Megan," he said, then answered. "Ey up."

"Hey. How's Kiyomi?"

"She's a trooper."

"Yes, she is. So… I have news."

"What sort?"

"Put me on speaker."

"Hang on." He hit the button so Kiyomi could hear. "Go on then."

"Amber hasn't slept in two days, she's been digging up all kinds of incriminating evidence on Jane. She just called to say she's cracked all the finances. Almost two-hundred million US dollars funneled away into offshore accounts that's now mostly ours.

"And her bodyguards aren't nearly as badass or loyal as she'd like to think," she continued, "because both of the survivors agreed to a plea deal. Rycroft's got a list of people associated with her latest venture, including people within the CIA and NSA, and a few private citizens who donated money. They're all going down. Her network's totally exposed. It's going to hit the media tomorrow afternoon."

"So…it's over?" he said, hope swelling in his chest. He wanted this whole shite situation over and done with so Kiyomi and the others could move on with their lives. Lives of their own choosing, where they no longer had to look over their shoulders everywhere they went. And selfishly, he wanted a future with Kiyomi at his side.

"Not quite. The bitch still won't talk. They're transferring her in the morning, just to be on the safe side because there are rumors about random members of her cell still out there with ideas on springing her."

"What time in the morning?" Kiyomi asked.

"Oh-four-hundred."

"I'll be there."

Marcus had to bite back the argument that sprang onto his tongue. She'd been through enough. Closure or not, Kiyomi confronting Jane made all his protective instincts flare to sudden life. He ended the call with Megan and settled Kiyomi into the curve of his body again.

"Well?"

She tilted her head to search his eyes. "I need to look her in the eye and show her we've won. It's the only way I can ever move past this. Will you take me?"

He didn't want to. The last thing he wanted was to put her anywhere near that bitch again, especially when she was recovering from a bullet wound he still couldn't stop feeling guilty about. But how could he deny her this after all she'd been through at that woman's hands?

He sighed. "Aye, all right. I'll take you there, and as soon as she leaves, we come straight back here." Where he wanted her to stay with him for the rest of their lives, though he wouldn't push her any more about it tonight.

The tension in her shoulders eased visibly. "Thank you."

He kissed her forehead. "I love you." And that was the only reason he had agreed to this. "Now get some sleep. We've got an early start tomorrow."

Chapter Twenty-Five

"Y ou sure about this?"

Kiyomi gave Marcus a reassuring smile, put a hand on his uninjured shoulder and went up on tiptoe to give him a kiss. Her own arm was killing her, her entire left hand and wrist swollen so much that the skin was shiny over the purple and blue bruising. "Yes. But thank you for being here."

He didn't like this, was still in a lot of pain even if he'd never admit it, and yet he'd gotten up long before dawn to drive her here himself so she could face her nemesis. He hated that she wanted him to wait outside for her, but he was doing that too, because she'd asked.

Marcus grunted. "I'll wait outside in the car."

She nodded, more in love with him than ever, but she needed to do this before she could ever feel free of the past, and he couldn't be present—for his own good.

Unbeknownst to him, she'd had a secret phone meeting with the others shortly before leaving Laidlaw Hall. "See you in a bit."

Rather than let her go, he wrapped his arms around

her hips and carefully brought her close. His dark-choco-late eyes were stormy. He was a tightly controlled man, but there was such love and devotion inside him, and both were evident in his gaze as he stared down at her.

"I just want you safe." His deep voice rolled over her, then he took her chin in his fingers and planted a hard, claiming kiss on her mouth.

Her heart squeezed. She kissed him back, telling him without words that she was his. And when he walked out of the building to let her do what she'd come here to do, the weight in her chest didn't feel quite so heavy anymore.

Trinity, Amber and Megan were waiting for her out-side a secure room. They all looked exhausted, and Trin's restricted movements told Kiyomi she was in a lot of pain. Hopefully after today, they could all get on with the heal-ing that needed to happen for them to reclaim their stolen lives.

"The others here too?" she asked.

"Waiting in the vehicle. All of us," Trinity said. "You ready for this?"

"Yes. You're sure about everything? She's of no fur-ther use to us?"

"Positive," Amber answered, a hard gleam in her eyes. "We're never getting anything from her that we don't have already."

Kiyomi nodded. "All right. Where's my escort?"

Trinity reached over and pressed a button on the wall. "They'll be here in about thirty seconds. We'll meet you outside after."

Sure enough, two heavily armed guards appeared through a secure door at the end of the hallway. They searched Kiyomi for weapons, checking her bandages thoroughly for any contraband, and put her through a metal detector before allowing her inside.

The heavy steel door locked shut with a clang as they escorted her down the hall, giving her strict instructions.

She wouldn't be allowed in the cell. No physical contact with the prisoner. She had ninety seconds max.

Kiyomi tuned them out, focused only on what was about to happen. In spite of herself, her pulse beat faster as they stepped out of a secure elevator onto a different floor. This was just like any other op, she reminded herself.

Just get it done, and soon it'll all be over.

The corridor was lined on one side with more heavy steel doors. There were no bars in them, their small slots locked shut. Finally the guards stopped in front of one halfway down the hall. They eyed Kiyomi, then one unlocked the slot, jerked it open, and stepped back to wait.

Steeling herself, Kiyomi approached the opening.

She wasn't sure exactly how she'd imagined this would play out, but it wasn't this slender, middle-aged woman staring back at her through the hole in the door.

Jane Allen remained seated on her bunk attached to the far wall, wearing an orange jumpsuit, white socks, and open-toed sandals. She looked exactly as Kiyomi imagined Amber would in her fifties, the face shape, features and eye color the same. But the emptiness in them made the difference between her and her niece clear.

This woman was dead inside. Amber was full of life, love and devotion.

For a long moment they simply stared at each other. Jane's expression remained blank, but slowly her eyes gave her away. They held a greedy, almost desperate gleam, as though she'd been starving for the sight of her.

"I wanted to see you before they transferred you," Kiyomi began, filled with revulsion.

This evil, twisted woman had lied, manipulated, killed, and ultimately destroyed countless lives in her quest for personal glory. She was responsible for the suffering of dozens of orphaned young girls. She'd used them for her own gain, ignored their pain and added so much more to their suffering. She was responsible for countless deaths, including some of Kiyomi's friends.

Jane didn't move, but didn't look away, so Kiyomi continued. "Why me?"

The woman was silent so long Kiyomi didn't think she would respond. But then she spoke. "Do you remember me?"

"No. Only that I saw you."

"Because I wanted you to."

Whatever. "So? Why?"

Jane sat up taller, that eerie green stare fixed on her in a way that sent a tremor up her spine. "Because you're everything a Valkyrie should be."

Kiyomi held the stare and waited. Jane wanted to talk. Wanted Kiyomi to know. All she needed to do, was wait.

"Everything," Jane repeated. "I knew it from the first moment I saw your initial test scores. Your IQ was impressively high, along with the scores on your psych and physical tests. You showed the best aptitude for languages and reading people of anyone in your test group. And as I watched you throughout your training, I knew." Her smug smile made Kiyomi long to slice it from her face.

"Knew what?" she said in a flat tone.

"That you would be the most successful of the entire Program. And I was right." She paused a second, an almost fond expression forming on her face. "Congratulations, Kiyomi. You're the deadliest operative of us all. Most confirmed kills, and a ninety-seven-percent success rate on your missions. You're exactly what I needed to initiate the next phase."

Kiyomi kept her expression impassive even as revulsion twisted her insides. She was done, and her time was almost up anyway. "You've now been exposed for the true monster you are. I know what you planned to do with me. And before they take you away, I have just one more thing to say to you."

She held that eerie green stare, a ripple of power surging through her. She would never be a victim again. This woman would never inflict damage on anyone else, Kiyomi and the others would make certain of it. "I would have killed myself before allowing it to happen."

She had a moment's satisfaction when her barb hit home, a flash of anger in that fixated stare. Then she turned and walked away without another word. Behind her the steel slot locked into place and the guards hurried to catch up. They escorted her back to the front of the building and watched her leave.

Marcus got out of the Range Rover as she approached, his expression full of concern. "All right?"

"Yes." She was breathing faster than normal, a little shaky. She gave him a careful, one-armed hug, took a moment to close her eyes and rest her cheek on his chest while he curled around her.

Almost over. You're almost there. "I need to talk to the others for a few minutes. I'm going to go with them."

"Sure. I'll follow you."

Trinity waited beside a white, unmarked delivery van. "All okay?"

"Yes. Marcus is gonna follow us." She climbed into the side door and found the others all inside.

Chloe was behind the wheel. Megan and Amber both had laptops open. Eden, Briar and even Georgia were all gathered behind them, watching the screens.

"Good to go?" Chloe asked. Upon confirmation she started the engine and drove out of the secure parking lot.

Kiyomi settled herself between Trinity and Eden, now watching the laptop screens. Megan's showed a secret feed patched into the cameras posted at the highly guarded loading zone beneath the building where prisoners were transported in and out of the facility. Amber's showed something else entirely.

"Here she comes," Megan murmured.

On screen, a trio of heavily armed guards accepted transfer of Jane and took her to the back of an armored van. They opened it, put her inside, and the feed on Amber's laptop began.

Amber glanced at them all. "You ready?"

Everyone nodded.

"Then let's do this," Kiyomi said, and held her right hand out.

The others all followed suit, stacking their hands on top of hers. She smiled at her sisters. It was time for Valkyrie-style vengeance.

JANELLE KEPT HER expression impassive as the guards climbed into the rear of the armored van with her and shut the doors, hiding a smug smile at the perfection of the moment.

She hadn't expected Kiyomi to be there today. It had been surprisingly upsetting. The sheer arrogance of her, coming to gloat at seeing Janelle behind bars, and then lobbing that final insult in her face before walking away.

Kiyomi might think she would have killed herself rather than submit to Janelle's plans, but it was impossible for an unconscious person to have a choice about anything. Janelle had every intention of keeping her drugged around the clock to get what she wanted, and now she wanted Kiyomi worse than ever.

She folded her hands in her lap. Rycroft and the other intelligence idiots thought they were sending her to a secure MI6 facility, but they'd underestimated her once again. They hadn't stopped her by hauling her in. They'd merely delayed the inevitable.

She had dreams to fulfill. Important dreams, and nothing was going to stop her from getting what she wanted. She *always* won in the end.

One of the guards came over to kneel in front of her

and unlock the chain holding the wrist of her uninjured arm and feet together. As it slid off with a clatter, he immediately removed her wrist and ankle cuffs.

She flexed her sore wrist, anger seething inside her. Every single person who had been involved in her wounding and brief incarceration would die.

"You know where to go?" she asked the guard seated across from her.

"We'll transfer vehicles after we drop you off at the safehouse," her man said. "Then we'll go after the cargo."

Kiyomi. "Take Laidlaw as well. I want him alive." So she could torture him for a while and then kill him in front of Kiyomi.

The little bitch might be necessary for Janelle's plans to work, but she still deserved to suffer for her part in all of this. That final insult at the facility wouldn't go unanswered, and the same went for her nieces and the rest of the Valkyries. She'd made them what they were—they would be nothing without her. Ungrateful bitches.

She stretched her spine, letting out a sigh. She was tired, yet energized at the thought of what was to come. Closing her eyes, she let herself slide into a doze.

Her eyes shot open sometime later as she flew off the bench seat when the van suddenly lurched to the right. She barely managed to spin in time so that her back hit the opposite bench instead of her face.

Snarling at the shock of pain in her shoulder, she scrambled to her feet, grabbing for the hook in the wall used to secure restraints to steady herself. The van wheeled left, jolted hard and then seemed to slow, bumping over the road now.

"What the hell? Did that idiot hit something?" she snapped, unable to see outside because there were no windows back here.

But the two men in the back couldn't answer her. They were sprawled on the floor, eyes closed.

Alarm jumped inside her. She knelt and quickly checked one man's carotid pulse. It was weak, and growing slower every second. She glanced at the other, knowing he'd be the same. They'd been drugged, and likely the driver too.

The van continued moving, bumping along the road, the slight grinding sound beneath the tires suggesting they were now traveling over gravel.

Dread coiled like a snake in the pit of her stomach.

She shot to her feet and whipped around to face the rear door. The only way out was with a series of keys. Cursing, unsure what the hell was happening but knowing it was bad, she snatched a ring of keys from one dying guard's belt and quickly began shoving them into the locks.

Nothing fit.

She grabbed the other guard's keys and tried. Nothing worked.

Stumbling back a step, she glanced around quickly, looking for a way out. Of course, there was only the door.

Facing it, she ordered herself to calm down. Whatever shit was happening, they weren't going to get her. She would not let them win, she would escape and call on her remaining loyal followers to—

One of the guard's radios crackled to life. She jerked taut, staring at it in dawning horror as the familiar strains of a classical piece of classical music began to fill the silent interior. She recognized it instantly.

Ride of the Valkyries.

Her stomach pitched. Her skin crawled. *No.*

She whirled around in sudden comprehension, a wave of terror breaking over her. But she couldn't see a camera. Even though she knew they were watching her. The surviving Valkyries. Including Kiyomi and her nieces.

With a cry of denial and rage, she reared back and

slammed the sole of her sandaled foot into the steel doors. A sharp pain ripped through it as bone fractured. She yelled, staggering back with her weight now on her other foot.

Both guards were armed. She dove for the first weapon she could get to, wrenched it from the holster and faced the door. Fired repeatedly at the lock. The concussion of each shot ricocheted through her head, the deafening noise splitting her ears in the enclosed metal box.

The rounds rebounded, two hitting her in the legs. One in the stomach. She pitched forward, gritted her teeth as she rose to her knees and kept firing, determined to break through the doors standing between her and freedom. Refusing to accept that she was helpless while they watched and laughed on the other side of the camera.

A scream of rage burst from her as she emptied the clip into the steel in front of her.

It can't end like this.

She was too important. Her work was too critical—it was going to change the world.

Chapter Twenty-Six

Kiyomi was barely aware of the way Trinity was squeezing her hand as all of them stared at Amber's laptop, riveted to the action on screen as their teamwork paid off before their eyes. Amber had remotely disabled the security escort vehicles, leaving them stranded a safe distance away from the transport van holding Jane.

The microcamera in the back of it gave them a perfect view of the interior. The cocktail of drugs in the coffee all three of Jane's men had consumed prior to departure had taken effect at exactly the time it was supposed to.

A thrill of triumph coursed through Kiyomi when the music started. Trinity had suggested it, and they'd all agreed it was way too fitting not to include in this operation.

Jane's face went slack with shock. Then the most satisfying expression of terror contorted her features as she recognized the significance of what it meant.

Kiyomi narrowed her eyes. "We are the choosers of the slain," she said, heart racing as the woman freaked out and began trying to shoot her way out. Karma literally bit her, her own bullets striking her. "Loyal Unto Death, *bitch*."

A resounding cheer rose up from the others.

Jane fell to her knees, struggled upright and screamed as she kept firing.

"My turn," Chloe said, eyes gleaming with an almost fanatical excitement, chomping away on her gum as she pulled a detonator from her pocket. "I went old school for this, red button and all. Thought it was fitting." She held it out, glancing around at them all. "Who's gonna do the honors?"

"Has to be Amber and Megan," Eden said.

"And Kiyomi," Trinity added, squeezing Kiyomi's hand. "This is their kill."

Kiyomi looked at Amber and Megan, who both nodded at her. As one, they each put a finger on the button. "On three?"

They nodded. "One," Amber said, Jane still screaming. She was out of ammo now, punching and kicking at the doors. No one would hear her. Amber's secret little device had remotely driven the van onto a country road out in the middle of nowhere.

"Two," said Megan, her face set.

"Three," Kiyomi finished.

They pressed the button together. Amber's screen went blank, but Megan's feed from a small drone Amber was operating showed the van as it erupted into a ball of fire.

No one spoke. The only sound in the interior was the crackle of the now burning van.

"That was more humane than she deserved," Megan finally said.

"But we got our justice," Kiyomi said. "Valkyrie justice."

Trinity put her arm around her waist and leaned her

head on Kiyomi's good shoulder. Megan and Amber mirrored the posture. Then Eden and Chloe, and Briar and Georgia.

"So...it's over," Chloe murmured, and Kiyomi wasn't sure if she sounded disappointed or disbelieving.

"It's over," Trinity confirmed, smiling even though her voice was rough.

Kiyomi's throat thickened. She swallowed, blinked against the sudden sting of tears, and glanced around. It was so sudden. So hard to believe. "You guys..."

Megan's face crumpled. She dissolved into tears and reached for Kiyomi, careful to avoid her bandaged shoulder as she drew her into a gentle hug.

"Gah, now I'm crying too," Eden said with a soggy laugh. "I *hate* crying."

Tears rolled down Kiyomi's cheeks. More arms engulfed her. It still hurt even though everyone was being careful of her, but she didn't care.

The Architect was dead. Jane was no longer a threat to any of them. People within her circle had either been exposed or soon would be. She would never hurt anyone ever again.

Everyone was crying, even Briar and Georgia. Kiyomi might not know them well, but it didn't matter. They shared a bond that was unlike any other. They were sisters.

"I love you guys," Kiyomi said through her tears, wishing she had the use of both arms to engulf these incredible women.

Someone sobbed. She couldn't tell who, but suddenly she was the center of the group hug, and she was swarmed by Valkyries.

"Watch her shoulder," Eden said.

"And don't squeeze Trin," warned Briar.

"I'm okay," Kiyomi gasped out, trying to catch her breath. She didn't even know what she was feeling, but the physical pain was way off in the background. Right now there was only elation. Relief. Shock.

Hope.

A watery laugh escaped her. "Oh my God, we're finally free."

"Free," Trinity whispered in awe, kissing the top of Kiyomi's head.

It was too incredible to contemplate. Where did they even start?

They all jumped when someone knocked on the side of the van. Everyone scrambled apart, looking embarrassed at being caught unawares.

"Jeez, how sad is that, for someone to catch eight lethal assassins off guard?" Chloe muttered, climbing back up front to get behind the wheel. "Oh, it's just Marcus."

Kiyomi reached over to unlock the door and slide it open. Marcus's scowl disappeared the instant he saw her. "What the hell? What's wrong?" he demanded, reaching for her.

She stopped him from dragging her out of the van, laughing softly as she wiped the heel of her hand over her wet cheeks. "Nothing's wrong. Not anymore." She smiled up at him, dizzy with love and relief. "It's over."

His brows drew tighter together. "Why, what—"

"I'll tell you later."

Even as she said it, Trinity's cell phone went off. She answered, and from the comical look on her face, Kiyomi knew it was Rycroft. "Alex, hang on." She put him on speaker as he ranted.

"—the hell are you right now? MI6 just called to tell me the escort vehicles all stalled and now the transport van just blew up. Are you guys all okay?"

Trinity's dark blue eyes were full of mirth, and she looked like she was having trouble fighting back a laugh as she answered. "We're great. But I think Jane had an accident."

****

Kiyomi waited to tell Marcus what they'd done until they were halfway back to Stow in the Range Rover. He shot her a sharp look as she finished, his expression a mix of alarm and pride. "So you're all wanted women again," he said in a hollow tone.

"No. There's no way they can trace it back to us. Even if they could, they can't prove anything. The UK and US authorities wouldn't dare put us on trial. Not with the secret shit we can rain down on our government."

His jaw worked as he drove. "When did the lot of you dream this up?"

"While you were in the shower this morning."

"Good Christ, woman," he groaned. "You'll be the death of me yet."

"Nope. All that's behind us now. Rycroft's pretty mad, not gonna lie, but Trinity's handling it."

He shook his head. "How in the hell did you pull all that off with only a few hours' prep?"

She blinked at him. "Because we're Valkyries."

A laugh burst out of him, and the deep, happy sound made her smile. "Aye. You sure as hell are."

She reached her hand across for his left one, twining their fingers together. "I couldn't tell you. It was better for you, safer, if you didn't know anything about it. In case anyone questions you now, you can plead ignorance."

"Aye," he said with a pointed, sidelong look, "because you know I would have tried to put a stop to it."

"Well, that too."

He let out a deep breath. "So everyone got to do their part, is that it?"

"It was a thing of beauty—teamwork at its finest. Trin was team leader, of course. Briar and Georgia did the recon and provided security while the other parts happened. Amber took care of the camera, remote driving and other tech stuff. Megan broke into the van and installed everything. Eden poisoned the guards, and Chloe planted the bomb."

"Of course she did," Marcus muttered, shaking his head again, but this time his lips twitched in amusement. "And what did you do?"

"I got to press the button with Amber and Megan."

He lifted an eyebrow. "Makes a man wonder if he should sleep with one eye open next to you."

She leaned across the console to nuzzle the side of his neck. "Nah. You're safe with me. Promise."

He'd taken a different route back, choosing quieter roads and avoiding Stow altogether. As they crested a hill, Laidlaw Hall came into view nestled in the valley below. "Oh, God, I'm so glad to be back," she whispered.

Marcus smiled. "You really love it, don't you?"

She hummed in affirmation. "Almost as much as I love you."

He glanced at her, a smile tugging at his mouth. "I'm chuffed you feel that way. I want it to be your home too."

Her heart skipped a beat, then went into double time. Until an hour ago she hadn't let herself consider a future with Marcus, because it had been too dangerous for him. Now, with a single op, everything had changed. "You mean it? You want me to stay?"

He frowned as if he'd thought that should have been obvious. "'Course I do. I love you."

She bit her lower lip, unsure if she was going to burst from happiness or start crying. "Marcus…"

"What? It's true." He glanced at her again. "Will you stay?"

The others were all scattering after this. It was time for everyone to move forward with their lives. She would miss them, because they were her family. But Marcus was her future.

Her throat thickened. "Yes. I'd love to make a life here with you."

A wide smile spread across his face. Lifting her hand, he kissed the back of it. "Good. Then that's that."

Reaching the front gate, he turned into the long driveway. The stone gatehouse was dark and empty. Megan and Ty would never live there again. But the manor stood at the top of the drive, a few of its front windows glowing with warm light.

A thrill ran through her. *Home.*

Stepping out onto the gravel drive, a sense of rightness filled her. Marcus smiled and took her hand, leading her up the front steps to open the door.

"Welcome home, love," he told her, and kissed her there in the foyer as Karas limped as fast as she could up the old flagstone hallway to greet them.

Chapter Twenty-Seven

"**O**kay, is everyone else feeling totally weirded out right now too?" Chloe glanced around at them all. "No? Just me?"

Seated across the table from her, Kiyomi grinned. The bar was packed, loud and a bit smoky from all the food being cooked in the back. "It's weird, but I love it."

None of them had ever imagined going out together as a group before today. It went against everything they'd been taught. All their training and instincts.

Hard to believe that life was over now. Or that a whole world of opportunity and new experiences awaited. It was both exhilarating and a little daunting. She wouldn't ever let her guard down completely while out in public. Some things were ingrained too deeply.

"Hear, hear." Next to her, Trinity held up her beer, leaning into Brody's side. "And by the way, I hope you guys are up for a trip to Virginia soon."

"Why, what's in Virginia?" Megan asked, sipping at her pint of ale.

Trinity smiled up at Brody. "Our wedding."

Everyone gaped at her, and Kiyomi's eyes widened.

"What? When did you decide this?"

Briar ruffled Trinity's hair affectionately. "She finally came to her senses the other night."

Trinity gave a rueful grin and smoothed her hair down. "What can I say, I'm stubborn."

Kiyomi got up and pulled her friend into a hug that was way more awkward because of her sore shoulder and Trin's broken ribs. "I'm so, so happy for you," she said into Trin's hair, then dipped down to whisper, "and really proud of you for going for it."

Trin squeezed her gently. "Thanks. So, you coming?"

She gasped in mock dismay. "You need to ask? Can I bring a plus one?"

Trin glanced at Marcus. "You'd better." She looked up at Kiyomi. "Are you going to stay here?"

"Yes." She was beaming and couldn't stop because she'd never known it was possible to feel this happy. "He asked me to."

"Then I'm proud of you, sweetie."

Chloe was suddenly standing behind them. "Another group hug?" she suggested.

All the women laughed and crowded around into an awkward lump on Kiyomi's side of the table. The guys all watched with various degrees of amusement, but the level of joy around the table was palpable.

Against all odds, they now each had a future of their own choosing. They'd taken the precaution of planning a WITSEC-style program, yet now it wasn't necessary. With Jane dead, her circle exposed, files seized and assets frozen…their true identities were now safe. The threat against them had died with the monster responsible for all the trials they'd faced.

"I can't believe I'm standing in the middle of a crowded bar with my back to the room," Eden said as she got in on the hug.

It was true. Surreal, to know they were all safe for the first time in decades.

Megan laughed. "Right? Feels so wrong. Course it doesn't hurt that we've got eight badass guys here to watch our backs."

"Only eight?" a male voice said behind them. "What, I don't count?"

They turned around to see Rycroft standing there, raising an eyebrow at them.

"Yeah, you count too," Trinity said with a grin. "You want in on this hug?"

"I would, but I don't want Grace to get jealous."

"What are you even doing here?' Trinity asked. "I thought you'd be tied up in meetings for days after everything that's happened."

He seemed to be fighting a smile as he shook his head. "I should have been. But it seems that after this morning's mysterious events, I'm no longer needed, and my role in the investigation has been formally terminated."

"So you can *actually* retire now?" Kiyomi asked.

His silver eyes twinkled as he faced her. "Looks like." Glancing around at the other Valkyries, he shook his head again, his expression fond. "I don't know how you did it, and I'm not gonna ask."

"Did what?" Chloe asked, all innocence and big brown eyes as she stuffed another mouthful of steak between her lips. She'd eaten as much as Heath already and showed no sign of slowing down. Her endless supply of restless energy burned a mountain of calories.

"Uh-huh," Rycroft said, and now looked around at the men. "Just wanted to come by and wish you guys luck." He nodded at Kiyomi and the others. "You'll need it."

"Dear God, don't we know it," Heath said, raising his beer in salute.

"You want some steak? Or maybe prawns?" Trinity asked. "We've got lots left."

"Well, we did, before our human seagull swooped in to steal the leftovers," Amber said dryly, looking at Chloe.

Chloe's eyebrows drew together. "What? I'm hungry. I have a high metabolism."

"Can't stay," Rycroft said. "I'm headed down to Heathrow so I can fly home and keep my own women out of trouble."

"Have a beer with us at least," Ty said, waving the bartender over.

Marcus brought Rycroft a pint of beer. His limp was more pronounced than ever but he didn't complain about that or the healing graze in his shoulder as he leaned more heavily on his cane on the way toward them.

Joy flooded Kiyomi with warmth as he wrapped an arm around her waist. She loved that he was comfortable making such a public claim, and she was proud that he wanted her at his side.

As always, being in such a crowded place put her on alert, her protective instincts kicking in. Even with a weapon tucked against the small of her back—totally illegal here, not that she gave a shit—she was still a little on edge.

She was aware of exactly where the tables were positioned, which patrons might pose a possible threat, and where the entry and exit points were. That heightened awareness was a part of her and would take a long time to fade, if it ever did.

Not only did Rycroft stay, he wound up buying a round of beers for everyone. They did a group toast, enjoying mingled conversation and laughter. God, it felt incredible to laugh.

"So, where's everyone off to next with all the money we earned?" Chloe asked, popping a handful of nuts into her mouth. "I'm going back to meet Heath's relatives."

"And then do some rock climbing," Heath added, pulling her in close.

Eden looked up at Zack. "I want to meet Zack's dad and stepmom. Then I don't know what we'll do."

"We'll buy a place with a huge yard for your poison garden," Zack said, smiling down at her.

That was sweet, and fitting. Kiyomi turned to Trinity. "What about you?"

"Wedding planning. And then…" A smile tugged at the edges of her mouth. "We want to adopt."

Kiyomi's eyes widened. "That's amazing! Oh, you'll be *such* a good mom." What a lucky kid.

"Hope so." Trinity nodded toward the others down the bar. "Georgia and Bautista will go back to Miami, and Briar and Matt have a daughter waiting for them back home." She glanced at Amber and Megan. "What about you two?"

"We'll go to California," Amber said. "I want to find out exactly how Jane was involved in our parents' accident, and then we're going to pay our respects at their graves."

Kiyomi nodded, aching for them. They'd been through so much these past few days, probably more than any of them. Their own aunt had been behind everything, even killing her own sister and brother-in-law to get control of the girls. "And then?"

Amber and Megan looked first at Ty and Jesse, then each other. "I'm going to do some freelancing," Amber said. "Specializing in hunting down human traffickers."

Kiyomi chuckled. "Perfect. Megan?"

"Ohhh, I've got big plans. Like starting a horseback archery program for veterans. I think it would be great therapy for a lot of people. But wherever Ty and I wind up, I don't want it to be far from this one." She nudged her sister with her hip, earning a little smile from Amber.

"Eden?" Kiyomi asked.

"I'd like to write a book about poisonous plants and their uses—non-lethal uses," she clarified with a little grin. "And maybe do some botanical research of my own. Maybe find a cure for something."

"Cool. Chloe? Though I'm kind of afraid to know the answer."

Chloe snickered. "Well. There's no way I can just 'retire' quietly."

"None," Heath agreed with a sigh.

"I'd miss the action too much," Chloe continued. "Think I'll hang out a shingle, do some freelancing as a demolitions expert." Her eyes gleamed as she shrugged. "Could be fun."

"*So* fun," Heath deadpanned, and the others laughed.

"I'm just glad she'll have an expert combat medic with her," Kiyomi teased.

"And you?" Trinity asked, drawing Kiyomi's attention. "What do you want to do?"

Kiyomi glanced over at Marcus, who was now talking with Ty, Matt and Rycroft down the bar. Rycroft was on his third beer already. Looked like he'd be catching a later flight home. "I'm toying with the idea of setting up some kind of foundation for orphaned girls. To protect them from exploitation in a way we weren't."

"Totally fitting," Trinity said.

"But before I direct any energy into that, I think I'd like to go on a short holiday," Kiyomi added. An actual holiday, something she'd never been able to have before.

"Yeah? Where?" Megan asked.

"Japan. I want to meet my relatives there."

"Does Marcus know?" Amber asked.

Kiyomi leaned across the bar and called down it. "Marcus." He looked up at her, raised his eyebrows. He was so damn hot. And all hers. "Will you take me to Japan to meet my relatives?"

He looked surprised for a moment, then his face softened in a tender smile that turned her inside out. "I'll take you bloody anywhere you want to go, love."

"Awwww," Megan said, putting a hand to her heart as she gave Kiyomi a meaningful look. She knew Marcus better than anyone. "Kiyomi…"

Kiyomi smiled. "I know." He loved her. It seemed like a miracle. "And before you say it, yes, I'll take good care of him. And Karas and Rollo."

Megan smiled and raised her beer glass. "Thank you."

Kiyomi glanced at the others, and a sudden sense of bittersweet sadness crept in as the end of the evening loomed before them. Once they walked out of this pub, everyone was going their separate ways.

They'd all gone so long without each other during their time as operatives, Kiyomi couldn't bear to be separated from her sisters for good. Not after everything they'd been through, and what they meant to each other.

"Promise me," she said, looking from one sister to another, a hard lump forming in her throat. She was excited about her future with Marcus, but she would miss these women immensely. "No matter what happens after this, we all stay in touch. And if we ever need each other, we'll always be there to have each other's backs."

"Absolutely," Chloe said as the others nodded in agreement, and reached out to squeeze Kiyomi's hand. "Loyal Unto Death, Bitchilantes ride or die. *Forever.*"

"Forever," they all chorused together, and sealed the vow with another group hug.

Kiyomi closed her eyes and breathed it all in.

So this is what freedom feels like.

****

Marcus stood with Rycroft at the curb outside the

pub, waiting for a cab to take Rycroft to Heathrow. "What's your take on the threat level now?" he asked quietly. Kiyomi was talking with Amber and Megan a little ways down the sidewalk. Marcus wanted to take this opportunity to be crystal clear about any potential danger still facing Kiyomi and the others.

Rycroft shook his head. "It's over. All Jane's associates are either dead or under arrest. She operated strictly on a need-to-know basis, and her operatives had no family or close friends. No new threats have been identified."

"What about Rahman's people?"

"His group has splintered. The three people in the best position to take over his network are interested in power and money, not avenging Rahman. There's been no chatter about Kiyomi or any of the others."

Good. "Will you continue to monitor things?"

"Of course. I'm not anticipating any further threats—as long as they all stay out of trouble." His gaze shifted to Chloe, talking with Eden and Trinity. "Although that's gonna be harder for some than others."

Marcus chuckled and shook Rycroft's hand as the black cab pulled to the curb. "Thank you for everything."

"Thank *you*."

Marcus inclined his head. "I expect you'll be glad to get home after all this."

"Can't wait. But honestly?" Rycroft smiled fondly at the Valkyries. "I'm actually gonna miss them all. I've kind of become fond of their brand of crazy."

Marcus chuckled. "Me, I'm looking forward to a bit of quiet for a change." He couldn't bloody wait to get Kiyomi back to the manor and be alone. It would take a while for both of them to truly believe the threat was gone, but time alone was exactly what they needed.

Rycroft got into the cab. Marcus shut the door for him and watched the cab pull away.

"Hey."

He turned to find Megan walking toward him. He'd already said goodbye to everyone else and had been saving her 'til last. He had something long overdue to say to her.

"Ty's bringing our rental around," she said, and slid her hands into the pockets of her down vest.

"You headed to London?"

Megan nodded. "We're flying to California in the next day or two." She glanced at her shoes, then up at him. "So I guess this is goodbye for real this time."

"Not goodbye. Just see you later," he corrected. "And I should have said this ages ago, but… Thank you for what you did for me. I know I was an ungrateful bastard at the time, but I'm glad you pulled me out of that prison and made me live."

She smiled. "You're welcome. And now you've got someone to live for."

"Aye. Also thanks to you." Without her, none of this would have been possible.

Her smile turned a bit sad, her eyes growing damp. "I'm really going to miss you, you know."

"I'll miss you too, love." He drew her into a hug, squeezed her tight, ignoring the pain as his stitches pulled. "But it doesn't matter how far apart we wind up. I'll always be here for you. You know that, right?"

She sniffed, nodded. "Yeah. And same back." She hugged him hard, then stepped back, wiping her face. "You're happy?"

A smile spread across his face. "Aye."

"Good. Take good care of her for me."

"I will." Ty pulled up to the curb beside them. Marcus set a hand on her shoulder, jerked his head at the car. "Go. He's good for you."

"I know."

He ran his thumb across her cheek, wiping a stray tear away. "Be happy, lass."

She huffed out a laugh. "I plan to be."

He stood at the curb, waved when the car reached the corner and Megan looked back at him. She would always have a special place in his heart. But the rest of it…

He looked around as Kiyomi strode toward him. His brave, beautiful Valkyrie survivor, her wounded arm strapped to her chest. "Everyone gone now?"

"Yes." She wrapped her good arm around him, gave him a smile that set his heart thudding. "Take me home, Marcus."

Chapter Twenty-Eight

K iyomi paused with the little ceramic teacup partway to her lips when her great-aunt and great-uncle suddenly stopped talking, their gazes riveted
to something over Kiyomi's shoulder. She glanced back
to see a woman in her early-fifties standing there.

She covered her mouth with one hand, staring at Kiyomi as tears pooled in her eyes.

"Emiko, come in." Her great-aunt stood and beck-
oned to the woman to join them. When she did, her great-
aunt gave Kiyomi a wobbly smile. "This is Emiko. Your
mother's half-sister."

For a moment, Kiyomi couldn't breathe. She'd never
been so grateful for Marcus's presence. He'd flown her
here the day after her stitches had come out. Her shoulder
was sore and stiff, and her entire left arm ached like a bad
tooth. The swelling had gone down enough, however, that
she only had to wear the sling at night.

He sat beside her now, a silent anchor for her to lean
on as a rush of emotion made her chest tighten. "*Konichiwa*," she murmured.

Emiko stepped forward and wrapped her slender

arms around Kiyomi's ribs. "*Konichiwa, nie.*" Hello, niece.

It was awkward hugging a total stranger, but Kiyomi returned the embrace, patting the woman's back. She seemed overcome.

Several moments later, Emiko finally let her go and pulled back to beam up at her, the other woman's face wet with tears. "I am so glad to meet you," she said in slow, clear Japanese.

"She speaks our language well," Kiyomi's great-aunt said with a laugh, drawing Emiko to sit down on the cushion set before the low table where the tea service was laid out.

Emiko dabbed at her eyes with a tissue. "You look just like your mother."

Kiyomi leaned forward, overcome with curiosity. She only had vague memories of her mother, no clear pictures of her face. "I do?"

Her great-aunt and Emiko nodded, then her great-aunt's whole face lit up. "We have photographs." She struggled to her feet, grabbed her cane, and shuffled into the next room, returning with an album.

Setting it on the table, her great-aunt flipped through it, and stopped. "Here." She turned it toward Kiyomi. "Your mother and you when you were small. Maybe four or five."

Kiyomi stared down at the picture, that well-used vault inside her creaking open once more. She did resemble the woman in the picture. It was like staring at her own reflection.

Marcus slipped an arm around her and leaned closer to look. "Do you remember this?" he murmured.

She shook her head. It was taken at the beach. She was wearing a red swimsuit with white polka dots on it, and her mother was wearing a deep blue wrap dress that hugged her slim figure.

"I was there," her great-aunt said. "I took this picture."

"She was beautiful," Kiyomi whispered, voice rough.

"So are you," Emiko said with a fond smile.

The next two hours went way too fast. They told her the story of how her mother and Emiko had become separated. Kiyomi's grandmother had become pregnant out of wedlock for a second time, causing a major scandal. Her father had sent her away to await the birth of her second child, and Emiko was given up for adoption weeks later. She had only found out about her half-sister when she'd turned eighteen and become curious enough to do some digging.

No one knew anything about Kiyomi's father except that he had been a Japanese-American sailor stationed here temporarily and he was apparently the love of her mother's life. After she lost him while carrying his child—whether because he'd left Japan or because he'd died, no one was sure—she'd never been the same. Never recovered from it.

The sadness had been too great a burden for her to bear. And one day, when Kiyomi was still a girl, her mother had finally succumbed to the heartache and taken her life.

When it was time to go, her great-aunt gave her the photograph to take with her. Kiyomi slipped her shoes on at the door and turned to face her hosts, unsure what to say. Her great-aunt and great-uncle—and her mother's half-sister stood close together, gazing at her with a mix of fondness and sadness.

Putting her palms together, Kiyomi bowed at the waist slightly and thanked them for their hospitality. "*Omotenashi ni kansha shimasu.*" Her Japanese was far from perfect, but they seemed to appreciate her efforts.

They beamed and replied in Japanese. "It was our

honor to meet you."

She smiled, bowed slightly again, then backed out of the doorway. It had been a long time since she'd come to Japan, on an op that had only taken two days. She'd forgotten how polite everyone was here.

Marcus stepped back, bowed slightly and thanked them in Japanese. Her aunt and great-aunt giggled at his accent, but he merely smiled. They walked down the pathway leading to the front door, pausing at the end of it to wave. She'd promised to keep in contact, and she intended to honor that.

She sighed. Marcus arched a brow at her, his cane thudding lightly on the ancient stepping-stones leading around the side of the compact yard. Even in mid-November the garden was beautiful, full of lush green grass and artfully arranged beds of moss punctuated by Japanese maples turned fiery red for the fall.

"I thought the visit was brilliant," he said.

"It was." Better than she'd expected, really. "It must have been a shock for them when I reached out initially, out of the blue like that." *Hey, you don't know me, but I'm your long-lost relative. Wanna meet up so I can ask you about the past I know nothing about?*

"I liked watching you talk with them."

"I'm so rusty compared to what I used to be. I haven't worked in Japan since I was in my early twenties."

He grinned at her. "There's still so much about you I don't know."

"Well, I can't give you everything all at once, can I? Need to keep the mystery there, keep you interested."

He made a low sound and tugged her close, spinning her to face him. "No chance of me getting bored with you."

She melted, put a hand on his bearded face. "Thank you for bringing me here. For being there for me, and not just today."

Since Jane had died Kiyomi had done three more therapy sessions. Marcus had sat with her through them, her strong, steady rock. He'd even talked about doing some sessions on his own soon, to deal with everything he'd been through. They both wanted to move forward without the chains of the past to drag them down.

"It's my privilege. And they were wrong, you know." He searched her eyes. "You're even more beautiful than your mother was."

At that, she smiled. "I love you for saying that."

They walked through the village hand in hand, taking in the sights. All the homes here were old and built in the traditional style, something that was lacking in the bigger cities like Tokyo.

At the top of the hill, they paused in front of a Shinto shrine with its distinctive tiled roofline and exterior timbers painted a bright, vivid red. The cherry trees were nearly bare, but in the spring she could imagine how they would look bursting with clusters of fluffy pink blossoms.

She pulled in a deep breath, gazing around. "It's so peaceful here." Every day she felt more at peace. Her old life was over. She finally had answers to some of the questions that had always haunted her. And she had Marcus.

"Aye." Marcus stopped and bent down. She glanced at him, thinking something was wrong with his shoe.

But he was gazing up at her, on one knee as he set his cane aside and took her hand.

Her heart began to pound. He wasn't going to— She was just reading this wrong, he couldn't possibly be—

Marcus reached into his pocket and withdrew a little paper origami crane. "You know I love you."

She nodded, speechless, heart thudding in her ears.

His eyes were so full of warmth it made her heart clench. "You already own my heart. You may as well have the rest of me too." He held up the crane to her, nestled in the center of his palm. "Marry me, love, and be mine forever."

Hardly able to believe this was real, she took the crane. Inside it was a diamond solitaire ring with a thin, white gold band. Simple. Stunning. And perfect for her.

She opened her mouth to speak, but only a tiny sob came out.

Kiyomi dropped to her knees in front of him and flung her arms around his neck, burying her face in his throat. "Yes," she choked out, then laughed in pure joy. "A million freaking times, yes."

Epilogue

Christmas Eve

"How's it coming in here?"

Kiyomi looked up at Trinity standing in the bedroom doorway. "It's…I dunno." She switched to Japanese and spoke to her aunt and great-aunt, who were both muttering to each other as they fussed with the *obi* tied around Kiyomi's waist. "This sucker is a lot harder to put on than you might think," she said in English to Trinity.

"Oh, but the results are more than worth it." Trin beamed at her as she came forward in her plum-colored maid of honor gown. She stood behind them, meeting Kiyomi's gaze in the antique full-length mirror placed in the corner of the room. "You look so gorgeous."

"Thanks." She smiled at her reflection. Her hair was pinned up with little wisps escaping to frame her neck and face, and her makeup was subtle. "I wasn't sure about this design initially, but now I'm glad I went for it."

As a nod to her mother and Japanese heritage, her wedding dress was kimono-inspired. The head seamstress at the bridal shop in town had custom made it for her. The main part of the gown was an ivory satin, with wide kimono-style sleeves.

Kiyomi had commissioned her to make the *obi* out of the same plum-floral fabric of the robe she'd worn the first night she'd gone to Marcus. That night would always signify the moment when she'd fallen in love with him, and she'd wanted to incorporate it into their special day.

"Is everyone else ready?" she asked Trinity.

"Yep, all present and accounted for." She folded her arms and leaned against the wall, watching Kiyomi, her wedding band gleaming on her finger. She and Brody had tied the knot at his family's horse farm in the Shenandoah Valley two weeks earlier, with all the Valkyries and their partners in attendance. Now everyone had reunited once again here at Laidlaw Hall to celebrate another wedding. "You nervous?"

"Not even a little." She tugged at one layer of the *obi*, trying to line it up with the others, and got her hand smacked for her trouble. Her aunt reprimanded her in Japanese, now gathering the folds of the *obi* together to form the bow.

She grinned at Trinity in the mirror. Her Japanese family still had no inkling of what she was, or anything about her former life as an assassin. When she'd invited them, they'd jumped at the chance to fly here for the wedding, even before Kiyomi had insisted on paying for their trip. "Guess I'll just stand here and let them do their thing."

"I think that's a wise decision."

Finally, her aunt and great-aunt stood, turned her a few times to inspect everything, then smiled their approval and deemed her ready. Her aunt took her by the arms to give her a wobbly smile. "Your mother would have been so proud of you," she said in Japanese.

Kiyomi bowed slightly, touched. The picture of her

and her mother was sitting in a frame in the master bedroom up on the top floor. "Thank you, aunt." Both women kissed her cheek and left to go take their seats for the start of the ceremony.

Trinity walked up and put her chin on the top of Kiyomi's shoulder, looking into her eyes in the mirror. "Look at you."

"I know. Hard to believe, right? I've come a long way, baby."

Trin laughed. "I'll say." She wrapped her arms around Kiyomi's waist from behind. "How's the shoulder holding up?"

"Still attached." The swelling in her left arm and hand was finally gone. Everything was healing well but she had radial nerve damage that meant the back of her arm and hand ached constantly. Her range of motion was slowly improving, but it would never be one-hundred-percent.

A small price to pay for her freedom, and the chance to marry the man she loved.

They both turned when Eden appeared in the mirror, carrying two bouquets she'd made for the occasion. "Ready in the nick of time," she said, handing Kiyomi hers.

"Just gorgeous, thank you." Kiyomi raised the bouquet to her nose and inhaled. "Mmmm." She recognized the white flowers. "Gardenia?"

"Yes. They represent joy. The pink peonies represent a happy marriage. And irises, to symbolize faith, valor and wisdom. I thought that represented you the best."

Aww. "And there's something poisonous in here too, right? I'd be disappointed if there wasn't."

Eden grinned. She was a new bride herself, since she and Zack had eloped when they'd gone back to meet his dad and stepmom. "Well, maybe just a couple things."

"That's my girl." Kiyomi hooked an arm around her

neck and pulled her in for a hug. "It's gorgeous and I love it. Thank you for being here."

"Are you kidding? I wouldn't have missed it for anything."

Chatter came from the hallway as a group of people approached. Kiyomi picked out Chloe's voice long before she came into view.

The blonde stopped short in the doorway, staring at Kiyomi, her diamond engagement ring sparkling on her finger. Heath had proposed back in the States after he'd taken her rock climbing. "Holy shit. Now that's a wedding dress."

"You like?" Kiyomi did a slow circle as the other Valkyries spilled into the room amongst oohs and aahs.

"I brought the ring bearer," Megan said, grinning as Karas trotted past her. The dog came right up to Kiyomi and sat, ears cocked. She was still daddy's girl, but Karas was completely devoted to Kiyomi now as well. "She's got this down by heart, since it's her second time."

"Sweetheart, you look stunning," Kiyomi told Karas, reaching down to ruffle her ears. Eden had even put a mini bouquet in her collar with flowers to match Kiyomi's bouquet.

Trinity clapped her hands to get everyone's attention. "I'm still team leader, whether you bitches like it or not."

"Bitchilantes," Chloe corrected with a frown.

"So all of you march your butts down to the conservatory. Sync your watches, because this operation's starting exactly on time."

"Wait." Everyone stopped to look at Kiyomi. She'd sworn she wouldn't get all mushy and emotional, but having all her fellow Valkyries here to support her on this special day meant the world to her. She held out her arms. "Group hug?"

Chloe led the charge. In under three seconds flat she was engulfed by her sisters. One last hug, and it was time to go. Trinity herded everyone out of the room, went down to make sure the coast was clear, then came back up for her. "They're ready for you."

Kiyomi reached for her hand. She'd been thinking of what to say to her for weeks now. "I need to tell you... This wouldn't have been possible without you. I was...broken when I came here. You helped me put the pieces back together again. You've been there for me at every turn, good and bad, and I just want you to know I love you for it."

Trinity flushed a little and smiled. "I love you too, sweetie. But you put *yourself* back together. Because you're the strongest one of us all." She squeezed Kiyomi's hand, excitement brimming in her dark blue eyes. "Now let's get you down to your sexy husband."

Marcus was about to become her *husband*. What an incredible thought.

It felt like she was dreaming as she followed Trinity down the stairs to the main floor. As it was Christmas Eve the manor was done up in all its holiday splendor, the air smelling of evergreen boughs.

Her heart started to beat faster as they passed the library where the largest of the Christmas trees stood, glittering with lights and ornaments in front of the tall windows.

Trinity led the way out the back door to the conservatory. She paused at the door to look back at Kiyomi. "Ready?"

"Yes." There were no nerves. No little whispers of doubt or fear in the back of her mind, that she was making a mistake, that he would be in continual danger because of her.

She was ready to claim her man once and for all in front of everyone she cared about.

Trin winked. "See you on the other side." She swept into the conservatory and walked up the aisle.

Kiyomi waited until the music changed. No one was escorting her up the aisle. She was giving herself away, and that was as deliberate as the flowers Eden had chosen for her bouquet.

Everyone turned to face her as she stepped over the threshold. She didn't even notice any of the others, her gaze finding and locking on Marcus. He stood waiting for her at the same spot where Megan and Ty had married a few short months ago, stunningly handsome in his tux, and—

He shaved off his beard.

Showing her that he no longer felt the need to hide his scars from her or anyone else. She was so damn proud of him.

A wide smile spread across his face as he locked gazes with her. She smiled back, her heart aflutter as she walked toward him.

She'd never imagined loving anyone this much. Hadn't realized herself even capable of it until him. Now everything had come full circle for her and the family gathered in this room.

It was because of Marcus that they had been brought together here initially. Laidlaw Hall had started out as their headquarters, and become her refuge.

But the man waiting at the end of the aisle for her would always be her home.

—The End—

MARCUS'S YORKSHIRE PUDDINGS
(Makes 6 large puddings, or 12 small ones)

INGREDIENTS:
1 cup flour, sifted
1 teaspoon salt
1 cup cold milk
½ cup cold water
4 eggs
2 tablespoons vegetable oil or roast drippings for the batter, plus a small, additional amount for the bottom of each muffin tin

METHOD:
-Either by hand or in a blender, beat eggs and oil, water and milk

-Add flour and salt and blend/beat until smooth and frothy

-Let the batter sit in the fridge for at least 1 hour or more (tip: store in a measuring cup for ease of pouring into tins later)

-Preheat oven to 500 degrees

-Put a small amount of oil or drippings into the bottom of each section of your muffin tin (12 for a regular muffin tin, or 6 for a large one), then heat the tin in the hot oven for 1 minute

-Stir batter one last time, pull tin out of oven and immediately pour batter evenly into tins

-Bake until puffed and beginning to brown (depending on what size you are making, it could take anywhere from 8-20 minutes), then turn oven down to 400 degrees WITHOUT OPENING OVEN, and continue to bake until golden brown and crisp

-Do NOT open oven door while the puddings are baking, or they will collapse

-Serve with lots of gravy!

Dear reader,

Thank you for reading ***Beautiful Vengeance***. I hope you enjoyed the finale to this series. If you'd like to stay in touch with me and be the first to learn about new releases you can:

• Join my newsletter at:
http://kayleacross.com/v2/newsletter/
• Find me on Facebook: https://www.facebook.com/KayleaCrossAuthor/
• Follow me on Twitter: https://twitter.com/kayleacross
• Follow me on Instagram: https://www.instagram.com/kaylea_cross_author/

Also, please consider leaving a review at your favorite online book retailer. It helps other readers discover new books.

Happy reading,
Kaylea

Excerpt from

Broken Bonds

Crimson Point Series
By Kaylea Cross
Copyright © 2020 Kaylea Cross

Chapter One

Aidan shut the bedroom door behind him quietly and headed for the kitchen. Ella looked up from where she was sitting at the island in the fading afternoon light, devouring her allotted amount of leftover Halloween candy for the afternoon. "Don't spoil your supper."

"I won't." She shoved a miniature chocolate bar into her mouth, then frowned. "Mom's sleeping again?"

"Aye. Thought I'd let her sleep a little longer while I make her tea."

"I'll do it." She slid off the stool and took the kettle to the sink to fill it.

Aidan smiled to himself as he watched her. This past year had been the best of his life. He'd married Tiana in Edinburgh in July, and gained a daughter in the process. Ella still wore the ring he'd given her last Hogmanay, never took it off.

"When are we going to Mr. Beckett and Miss Sierra's house?" she asked, setting the kettle on the stove to heat.

"We're meant to be there for five." He was looking forward to it, because it was Friday night, and it had been a *week*.

Things had been challenging at work lately. He, Beckett and Jase had all been running themselves ragged while scrambling to finish up several projects for the company, and sending out bids for several more. The staff problems they'd had lately had made things tough for everyone.

Due to various issues like unreliability, substance abuse, and mental health reasons, Beckett had been forced to let three employees go over the last month or so. They'd been so busy he hadn't yet had the time to hire replacements for them, so Aidan and Jase had been helping pick up the slack.

Aidan had been there yesterday when Beckett had a run-in with one former employee, angry at being let go and threatening to sue. They hired veterans whenever possible, and most of their staff were great employees. This one... He had severe mental health issues that needed to be addressed by medical professionals.

Beckett had tried to get him help, but now it was up to the lad to help himself. The whole thing was hardest on Beckett and Jase, because it hit far too close to home after what happened with Carter.

"Perfect, that's Walter's dinnertime," Ella said. She looked over her shoulder at him, frowned as she swept her blond hair out of her face. "Are we gonna tell everyone tonight?"

"Maybe. We'll see."

"I think we should tell them."

He waited until she reached into the cupboard for Tiana's favorite mug before sneaking one of his favorite chocolate bars from her stash. She caught him just after he'd popped it into his mouth, and her blue eyes narrowed. "Saw that," she accused. "Next time just ask. It's not like I won't share with you."

Aidan chuckled. The lass was so much like her mother. Feisty. No man would ever push her around, and for that he was grateful. The thought of her becoming a teenager in a few years and then the boys coming to sniff around was enough to double his blood pressure. "Thank you."

"Can you get the tea bag for me? I can't reach."

"Sure." He crossed to the cupboard and took out a bag of peppermint tea, then resisted the urge to help as Ella poured the boiling water into the mug. She wanted to prove her independence so badly. After the events of the previous summer, letting her have some freedom while trying to make her feel safe and secure proved a constant balancing act for him and Tiana. "Want me to take it to her?"

"No, I can do it." She walked slowly from the kitchen, concentrating on not spilling the mug. He opened the door for her.

Lying on her side in their bed, Tiana opened her eyes and smiled. "Is that for me?" she said in a sleepy voice.

"Yes. But we need to go soon, so don't go back to sleep after."

Tiana grinned. "Wow, so bossy. But thank you, sweetheart." She sat up, kissed Ella, and took the mug. Smiling past her daughter at him, Aidan felt that familiar tug at his heart. These two lasses were his whole world, and there was nothing he wouldn't do for either of them.

After Tiana showered and changed, they walked up the hill to the old Victorian house together through the chilly but clear November air. Beckett's family had lived in the house at the top of Salt Spray Lane for generations. It was a bonny place with a spectacular view of the sea below the cliff.

Partway up the lane, the sound of a lawnmower reached them. Ella gasped and took off at a run. "I bet he's driving Walter!"

"We're lucky she let us get away with just a cat," Aidan said to Tiana as Ella raced up the hill.

"I know. If it was up to her, we'd live on an animal sanctuary."

"Aye." Aidan smiled at Ella as she raced away, her ponytail bobbing. "I love her big heart."

"I do too." Tiana squeezed his hand, her cheeks turning pink from the cold and her red hair blowing in the breeze.

"You just keep getting more beautiful."

Her cheeks flushed darker. "Whatever. Flatterer."

"It's true." God, he loved her. He was the luckiest man alive.

When they reached the edge of Beckett's property, Aidan chuckled when Beckett came into view on the ride-on mower. "And to think this is the man who said he never wanted a dog."

Beckett raised a hand in greeting as he drove toward them, his old rescue basset-cavalier mix Walter riding shotgun on the seat beside him. No one would ever guess it to look at him, but old Walter was an adrenaline junkie.

They'd found out quite by accident that his most favorite thing in the world was riding in the back of a dune buggy with his doggles on and his long, furry ears flapping in the wind. Then he howled like a maniac and begged to go faster.

Standing on the grass, Ella laughed and clapped her hands, hopping up and down in excitement. "Can I ride too, Mr. Beckett?" she called out.

Beckett's hard features softened in a lopsided grin as he stopped the mower in front of her. "Sure, come on up." He waited while Ella clambered in and hauled Walter into her lap, then started up the mower and carried on.

"This is definitely going on our Christmas card." Aidan pulled out his phone and started taking both video and pictures. It was too priceless.

"Come on," Tiana said with a laugh, and tugged him toward the house.

Everyone else was already there and greeted them

with hugs and handshakes. Beckett's wife Sierra was bustling around the kitchen with Poppy. Poppy's fiancée Noah, the town sheriff, Sierra's brother and Beckett's best friend since childhood, was setting the table. Jase, a former Green Beret who'd served with Beckett, was busy with his wife Molly corralling their eighteen-month-old daughter, Savannah.

Savannah squealed in delight when she saw Tiana, and toddled over. Tiana scooped the little one up and gave her smacking kisses on the side of her neck that made Savannah belly laugh.

The entire scene filled Aidan with warmth. "What can I do to help?" he asked Sierra.

She shoved two platters of chicken breasts at him. "Anywhere on the table. We're just about ready to eat."

Ella traipsed in a few minutes later, pink-cheeked and grinning from ear to ear. Walter hobbled after her, looking decidedly less cheerful now, the tips of his ears dragging on the old hardwood boards and his red-rimmed eyes staring up at everyone mournfully.

"We finished the lawn," Ella announced. "Mr. Beckett said the grass didn't need mowing, it's just easier to clean up all the mess the cedar and fir trees leave that way. We should borrow it, Mac. That way we won't have to rake anymore."

"Aye, brilliant." He ruffled her hair. "Now go wash your hands, it's time to eat."

Everyone gathered around the long rectangular table. Normally Walter liked to lie beneath it in case something should fall accidentally—or on purpose, in Ella's case—during the meal, but with Savannah around he chose to hide in his crate beside the fireplace instead, safely out of reach from little hands.

From his seat at the head of the long, rectangular farmhouse table, Beckett raised his glass of beer. "Thanks for coming." One side of his mouth lifted in a rueful grin as he glanced from Aidan to Jase. "It's been a helluva week. Couldn't have done it without you both."

"You're right about that," Aidan agreed, earning grins around the table before he turned his attention to the food. "Looks amazing as always, ladies," he said to Sierra and Poppy.

"Did you make pancakes, Miss Poppy?" Ella asked.

Poppy owned a local café/bookshop in town called the Whale's Tale. She paused in the act of scooping up a spoonful of scalloped potatoes, a chagrined look on her face. "I didn't, sweetheart, sorry. But next time you come for a sleepover I'll make you whatever kind of pancakes you want, okay?"

"Okay. Chocolate chips with strawberries, and lots of whipped cream. And that chocolate sauce you make."

Poppy smiled. "Dark chocolate ganache."

"*Yum*," Ella declared, her expression becoming decidedly less enthusiastic as Tiana began putting salad and vegetables onto her plate for her.

The meal was louder and more boisterous than usual with Savannah adding her shrieks and little noises to the conversation. Jase and Molly took turns wrestling her on their laps, stealing a few bites before passing her over.

"Would've brought her high chair, but she hates it," Molly said, quickly shoving a bite of asparagus into her mouth while Savannah yelled in protest and reached a chubby hand out for the food.

"I'll take her for a bit." Ella hopped down from her chair and carefully gathered Savannah up under Molly's supervision.

"Watch her like a hawk," Molly told her with a gentle smile. "She's fast and into everything."

"I will. Come on, Savannah. We'll go for a walk."

Aidan smiled as he watched Ella hold Savannah's little hands and carefully guide her clumsy steps around the living room.

"She's a natural little mother already," Jase said.

"Aye." He caught Tiana's eye. And wasn't that a blessing.

Sierra grabbed her camera to capture shots of the two girls as they made their way around the living room. After the meal was over the adults visited for a while, and Savannah began to start fussing. Ella steered her back to Molly and handed her over with an exhausted sigh that made everyone chuckle. "Man, babies are a lot of work."

"Aye, they are, and you didn't even need to change her nappy."

"She's just hungry and tired," Molly said, handing Savannah to Jase while she got out some cut-up fruit for her they'd brought.

"I'm gonna go hang out with Walter for a while now, if that's okay." Ella looked at Beckett and Sierra.

"Sure, he'd like that," Sierra said. "In fact, he'd love it if you took him for a short walk."

"Okay!"

Beside him, Tiana tensed and opened her mouth to argue, but Aidan squeezed her hand in gentle reprimand and she caught herself before saying anything.

Ella zoomed across the room to get the dog, still hiding in his crate. "Come on, Walter. We're going for a walkies."

"Just up the lane," Tiana told her, anxiety in her eyes. "And take a flashlight with you."

It took some coaxing, but Ella finally managed to lure the old lad out with a biscuit. Walter waddled through the living room, giving Savannah a wide berth.

"Here, take this with you," Jase said, taking his grandfather's WWII leather bomber jacket from the back of his chair and handing it to her. "It's cold out."

Ella shrugged it on, the coat swallowing her little frame as Jase did up the zipper for her. She got the leash on Walter, took the flashlight Beckett offered her and opened the door to the porch, then stopped and looked back at her mother and Aidan. "Wait, are we gonna…" She looked pointedly at the others and back to them, raising her eyebrows.

Aidan glanced at Tiana and raised his eyebrows as well. *Are we?*

Tiana laughed and shook her head. "You're both so impatient. But all right." She leaned back in her chair and smiled. "So, we have—"

"I'll do it! I wanna tell them!" Ella cried, abandoning Walter at the door and rushing to the table. Aidan draped an arm across her shoulders as she squeezed her way in between him and Tiana.

Everyone watched Ella expectantly as they waited for her to speak. She was lapping up the attention, a proud smile on her face as she patted his and Tiana's shoulders. "We're havin' a wee bairn."

End Excerpt

About the Author

NY Times and USA Today Bestselling author Kaylea Cross writes edge-of-your-seat military romantic suspense. Her work has won many awards, including the Daphne du Maurier Award of Excellence, and has been nominated multiple times for the National Readers' Choice Awards. A Registered Massage Therapist by trade, Kaylea is also an avid gardener, artist, Civil War buff, Special Ops aficionado, belly dance enthusiast and former nationally-carded softball pitcher. She lives in Vancouver, BC with her husband and family.

You can visit Kaylea at www.kayleacross.com. If you would like to be notified of future releases, please join her newsletter: http://kayleacross.com/v2/newsletter/

Complete Booklist

ROMANTIC SUSPENSE

Vengeance Series
Stealing Vengeance
Covert Vengeance
Explosive Vengeance
Toxic Vengeance
Beautiful Vengeance

Crimson Point Series
Fractured Honor
Buried Lies
Shattered Vows
Rocky Ground
Broken Bonds

DEA FAST Series
Falling Fast
Fast Kill
Stand Fast
Strike Fast
Fast Fury
Fast Justice
Fast Vengeance

Colebrook Siblings Trilogy
Brody's Vow
Wyatt's Stand
Easton's Claim

Hostage Rescue Team Series
Marked
Targeted
Hunted

Disavowed
Avenged
Exposed
Seized
Wanted
Betrayed
Reclaimed
Shattered
Guarded

Titanium Security Series
Ignited
Singed
Burned
Extinguished
Rekindled
Blindsided: A Titanium Christmas novella

Bagram Special Ops Series
Deadly Descent
Tactical Strike
Lethal Pursuit
Danger Close
Collateral Damage
Never Surrender (a MacKenzie Family novella)

Suspense Series
Out of Her League
Cover of Darkness
No Turning Back
Relentless
Absolution

PARANORMAL ROMANCE
Empowered Series
Darkest Caress

HISTORICAL ROMANCE
The Vacant Chair

EROTIC ROMANCE (writing as *Callie Croix*)
Deacon's Touch
Dillon's Claim
No Holds Barred
Touch Me
Let Me In
Covert Seduction

Manufactured by Amazon.ca
Bolton, ON